VENTURA + ZELZAH

J.G. BRYAN

SANTA
MONICA
PRESS
TE/N

Published by: Santa Monica Press LLC
P.O. Box 850
Solana Beach, CA 92075
1-800-784-9553
www.santamonicapress.com
books@santamonicapress.com

SANTA
MONICA
PRESS
TEEN

Printed in the United States

ISBN-13 978-1-59580-100-5 (print)
ISBN-13 978-1-59580-781-6 (ebook)

Publisher's Cataloging-in-Publication data

Names: Bryan, J.G., author.
Title: Ventura and Zelzah / by J.G. Bryan.
Description: Solana Beach, CA: Santa Monica Press, 2022.
Identifiers: ISBN: 978-1-59580-100-5 (print) | 978-1-59580-781-6 (ebook)
Subjects: LCSH Los Angeles (Calif.)--History--20th century--Fiction.
| Los Angeles (Calif.)--Social life and customs--Fiction. | San Fernando
Valley (Calif.)--Fiction. | Teenagers--California--Fiction. | Friendship-
-Fiction. | Bildungsroman. | BISAC YOUNG ADULT FICTION / Social
Themes / Friendship | YOUNG ADULT FICTION / Boys & Men |
YOUNG ADULT FICTION / Lifestyles / City & Town Life | YOUNG
ADULT FICTION / Social Themes / Drugs, Alcohol, Substance Abuse |
YOUNG ADULT FICTION / Coming of Age | YOUNG ADULT FICTION /
Historical / United States / 20th Century
Classification: LCC PS3602.R935 V46 2022 | DDC 813.6--dc23

Cover and interior design and production by Future Studio
Cover photo: iStock.com/trekandshoot

For Rich

"Memory believes before knowing remembers.
Believes longer than recollects,
longer than knowing even wonders."
—William Faulkner

Chapter One

Douglas! Lassie needs to go for a walk before you go to bed. Douglas? Did you hear me?"

"Yeah, Mom, I heard you," I moaned.

"Do it now, please," my mom implored.

"Okay, okay," I said as I looked down at Lassie lying on the floor next to my bed, her eyes begging me to get a move on.

Lassie. What a stupid name. I pleaded with my mom not to pick something so obvious. And our Lassie wasn't even a Collie, she was a Sheltie. Don't get me wrong, I loved my dog, I just refused to call her Lassie. I just called her "L" for short. It's much cooler than Lassie, and when my friends at school ask me what "L" stands for, I just tell them it doesn't stand for anything. Her name is just "L." Sometimes the kids think it's a lame name, but other kids think it's cool. It certainly beats Lassie by a country mile.

"Come on, girl," I said to L as I tied the laces of my Adidas Superstars and pulled on my Lakers sweatshirt. Even though it was spring, the Valley still got pretty chilly at night. After I put L's leash on her, I grabbed my Dodgers mini-baseball bat and shoved it up my sleeve just in case Mr. Asshole, who lived in the apartment building next door, was out there defending his parkway with his seriously threatening German Shepherd, Prince, by his side.

For some reason, this jerk thought that the grassy area right next to the curb—which belonged to the city, by the way—was his turf, owned by the apartment building he lived in, and that no dogs from the neighborhood were allowed to pee or poop on it. My mom's boyfriend talked to someone down at the city, and they said that parkways are fair game as long as we cleaned up the pile of dog shit. Unfortunately, if there was ever a fight, L wouldn't stand a chance against Prince, which was why I was carrying my trusty Dodgers bat hidden up the sleeve of my sweatshirt; when Mr. A got a look at my defense to his offense, he'd hightail it back behind the safety of the oversized glass doors that led into his apartment complex quicker than Davey Lopes stealing second base.

As I made my way out the front of our building—a mix of condominiums and townhouses like ours that had been bestowed with the *very* grandiose-sounding name of "The Encino Royale"—it was pleasant outside. The cherry trees were in full bloom, and traffic was light on Lindley Avenue on this Sunday night. "Come on, girl," I encouraged L. "Go pee-pee."

I continued to walk L down the street, past Mr. Asshole's apartment building, and all seemed quiet on the Western front. Even with all of the lights shining throughout the Valley, the stars were out in full force on the moonless night. The air was cool and crisp, and I breathed in deeply, inhaling the smells of orange blossoms and sage. As I turned around and made my way back toward our complex, I stopped and let L sniff the base of a huge Ficus tree. The Ficus' roots had grown so large that they had torn up the sidewalk next to the tree, creating a major tripping hazard. I'd seen some of the old folks try to get around the undulating sidewalk while using their walkers and it wasn't a pretty sight. While pondering the tree and the sidewalk, I missed the fact that Mr. Asshole had appeared in front of his building and was now guarding his measly patch of parkway grass with his already snarling German Shepard.

I began to walk toward Mr. Asshole and Prince, and I felt my pulse quicken and my heart begin to race; my palms started to sweat. As I got closer to the edge of Mr. A's property, I allowed L to start sniffing the grass on the parkway. Mr. A immediately made his move toward me. "Hey! What did I tell you about letting your dog on our grass?" Mr. Asshole was tall and thin, probably in his early sixties, and he favored baseball caps he had obviously gotten for free from local establishments to cover his balding head. Tonight it was a particularly ugly orange and blue cap from the local Union 76 gas station.

"And what did I tell you about the parkway being public property?" My voice cracked, briefly erupting into a high pitch as I attempted to yell back with all the false bravado I could muster at age thirteen. Undeterred, Mr. A and Prince continued to move threateningly toward us. When they got about fifteen feet away, Prince began barking at L, who barked and snarled in kind, which only resulted in smirks appearing on both Mr. A's face as well as Prince's menacing snout.

In defense of my sweet, harmless dog, I wiped the sweat from the palms of my hands on my pants, took a deep breath to steel myself, and then allowed the bat to slowly make its way down my arm and out of my sleeve, but as it began to slide into my still sweaty hand, L lunged at Prince, my hand got caught up in the leash, and the bat slipped through my fingers and landed on the sidewalk with a loud clunk.

Everyone immediately froze: L, Prince, Mr. A., and me—all locked in position staring down at my miniature Dodgers bat rolling harmlessly off of the sidewalk and onto the parkway grass.

"What the hell is that?" Mr. A looked up at me with anger in his eyes. "Were you going to threaten me? Were you going to hit my dog with that bat?"

"Well, I-I was just trying to protect my dog," I stammered, pulling on L's leash and taking a few steps back to further distance ourselves from our two adversaries.

"Listen, kid," Mr. A warned, pointing a long, thin finger straight at me. His face was gray and unshaven, and he scratched his dimpled chin with a clearly dirty fingernail and then took off his hat and ran his fingers through what was left of his balding head of gray hair. "Just keep your dog off of my lawn."

"But my mom's boyfriend called—"

"I don't care who your mom's boyfriend called. Pick up your bat and get away from my property before I call the police," he ordered. I began to get the sense that he was a bit drunk, and when he let Prince lunge at us one more time, I took the hint, bent down to get my bat, and walked L clear out into the street to go around Mr. A and his evil dog, who weren't about to move an inch to let us by.

My encounter with Mr. A and Prince had definitely not gone as planned, and my revenge fantasy had fallen woefully short. After finding a couple of bushes that were to L's liking, as well as a quick pit stop at a fire hydrant up the street, I headed back into our townhouse, looking a little worse for wear.

"What happened to you?" my mom asked as soon as I walked in the door. She was sitting on the sofa in the living room reading *Tinker, Tailor, Soldier, Spy* and, being my mom, could immediately see the disappointment on my face.

"Mr. A and Prince were outside guarding their turf."

"And . . . ?"

"Let's just say I lost this round."

"Well, don't worry, Douglas. I'm sure you'll get the upper hand next time." She returned to her book, obviously engrossed in the story.

"Yeah, I guess so," I replied, though I knew the battle was probably lost forever. Oh well, I'd just have to walk L down to the corner lot—unless Mr. A was nowhere in sight, in which case I'd encourage L to shit all over his lawn and I *wouldn't* clean it up. "I'm going to go to bed. Goodnight, Mom."

"Goodnight, honey," my mom said, glancing up quickly as she turned the page and blowing me a kiss. "I love you."

"Love you, too," I murmured as I began to walk up the stairs, L trailing behind me, ever loyal in spite of my failure to defend her outside. That night, she'd cuddle up next to me in bed, and the two of us fell asleep, and subsequently spent the night dreaming of various ways we would dominate Mr. A and Prince. At one point, L's dreams were so violent she started twitching wildly and even barked a few times, awakening me from a deep sleep. I pet her tummy, and she calmed down, and we both drifted back into dreamland.

The next day, a Saturday, was normally ripe for sleeping in, but today was no ordinary Saturday. Why? Because at precisely 2:00 P.M., I would be sitting down at Theeeeee Movies of Tarzana with Natalia, a girl I'd been hanging out with since the beginning of the year after we spent the afternoon together at a New Year's Day party her parents hosted and invited our family to attend. Natalia, who lived in the same condominium complex as us, was truly beautiful, with soft, incredibly clear olive-colored skin, sultry green eyes, jet black hair, and very large breasts for someone her age. She moved here with her parents from Argentina only a few years ago, so there was definitely something a bit exotic about her.

The movie we were going to see was The Who's *Tommy*, which was just hitting the theaters. I have two older brothers, and Natalia has an older sister, so we were both hip to The Who and couldn't wait to see this flick. At 1:00 P.M. I knocked on Natalia's door; she greeted me with a megawatt smile and a tight, white blouse whose buttons seemed to be bursting at the seams. It was hard not to stare.

"Hey, Natalia. You ready?"

"Yeah, just give me a second to get my purse. You want to come in?"

Before I could answer, Natalia's dad, a big, loutish guy with a pleasant enough face but a bark that would do Prince justice, piped up from the couch in their living room where he had been reading the newspaper. "Douglas, please come in!"

Crap. I was hoping to avoid having to talk to him. He was super strict and was always ready with the third degree for anyone who dared to date either of his daughters.

"Hello, Mr. Guinzburg," I said nervously as I came through the door. I always mangled their last name, pronouncing it like "Ginsberg," when it was really something altogether different.

"Where are you kids off to?" he asked, his voice thick with an Argentinian accent.

"I told you, Daddy, we're going to the movies," Natalia answered for me.

"What movie?" he demanded.

"*Tommy.*"

"Tommy? Who is this Tommy?"

"It's a movie by The Who, sir," I interjected.

"The Who? What is The Who?"

"They're a rock and roll band, Daddy."

"What is this movie rated? Is it R rated?" Mr. Guinzburg was ready to shut down this whole production.

"No, sir, it's PG," I assured him.

"Hmmm . . . okay, well you two have a good time."

"Thank you, Mr. Guinzburg." Phew.

"*Tienes mango?*" Mr. Guinzburg asked Natalia.

"*Si, Papi. Chau!*" she responded.

"*Chau,*" he said curtly, returning to his *L.A. Times*.

Having survived the interrogation from Natalia's dad, we turned and headed out the door.

"Boy, your dad is tough," I said, breathing a sigh of relief.

"I know. I'm sorry. But don't worry, he's actually really sweet, and he likes you a lot."

"He does? He told you that?"

"Yes, he said 'That Douglas is a very nice boy. And I like his parents, too.'"

I was happy to hear that Natalia's dad approved of me, and even though he was referring to my mom and her boyfriend, Art, as my parents, I was glad he liked them as well. Most people just assumed my mom and Art were married, and they rarely disabused anyone of this notion, because the truth of the matter was that they would be married if it weren't for the child support payments my dad made to my mom every month. If she and Art were to get married, she wouldn't be able to collect these any longer, so they figured they might as well just shack up for the next five years or so until I turned eighteen, at which point the child support would end. It made sense to me, even though it pissed the hell out of my dad.

"Well, I'm glad he likes me, and I know my parents like your parents, too," I said as we stepped down the condominium's wide, brick entrance stairs. My mom and Art had actually socialized with Natalia's parents, having gone out to dinner a couple of times and attended some parties together, and while my mom and Art seemed to genuinely like them as well, they did complain about how much Natalia's mom talked.

"She talks so much I hardly spoke the whole night," my mom whined after one dinner out with them. Art found Mr. Guinzburg's lone topic of conversation—his life as a pharmacist—to be beyond boring. But still, they were "good people" in Art's words, and that was good enough for him.

"I'm really looking forward to seeing this movie," Natalia said as we made our way up Lindley Avenue. "I just LOVE Roger Daltrey. He's such a FOX!"

Hmmmm . . . maybe *Tommy* wasn't the best choice. There was no way in hell I could compete with Daltrey. Then again, maybe Daltrey would get Natalia so worked up that I'd get to make out with her during the movie.

After some idle chit-chat about Daltrey, The Who, and other bands we liked—she was a huge Elton John fan while my taste ran more toward the Neil Youngs and

Jackson Brownes of the world—we boarded the RTD and headed down Ventura Boulevard to the theater. The bus was relatively empty for a Saturday, just a couple of young Mexican guys with hairnets on their head and aprons in their laps, catching forty winks while either coming from or going to their job at a restaurant, as well as a smattering of older folks who were probably just out running their Saturday errands.

"Yeah, I've been listening to The Beatles since I was five years old," I said, continuing the music conversation as we took a seat together.

"Really? That's amazing!"

"I used to borrow my sister's copy of *Meet the Beatles* and put it on my little toy record player—which actually worked pretty well!"

"No way!" she said, hanging on my every word.

"And I'd get up and dance and sing along. I knew the lyrics to every song!"

"That's incredible," Natalia said, laughing and smiling that stunning smile of hers.

"I think I still know all the words," I bragged. "They're etched into my memory. 'I Want to Hold Your Hand,' 'I Saw Her Standing There,' 'All My Loving' . . . I know them all."

"Maybe you can sing them to me sometime." Natalia leaned her body into me, and I liked it.

"Maybe," I mused, enjoying the moment before she straightened up and moved away.

It was lucky we were a bit early to the theater, as a line had already started to form, and by the time we got to the ticket booth, the line was all the way up the street and around the corner on Yolanda. No way was everybody getting in.

"Why don't I get the popcorn while you go grab a seat?" I suggested.

"Sounds good," Natalia replied with a smile.

"Butter?"

"Sure."

"What do you want to drink?"

"How about a Tab?" And with that, Natalia gave me a little peck on the cheek and smiled a devilish smile at me. "I'll try to find a seat toward the back," she said with a wink.

Was I the luckiest guy in the world, or what?

See me, feeeeelll me, touch me. . . .

The movie was one of the craziest things I had ever seen—and was definitely not "make out" material—but by the time Ann-Margret was slithering around in a sea of beans, Natalia and I had our tongues in each other's mouths, and my hands were rubbing her breasts and nipples. But when I tried to take Natalia's hand and place it on my very erect penis, an obvious line in the sand had been crossed.

"Douglas!" Natalia whispered as she pulled her hand and her mouth away from me. "I'm not that kind of girl!"

"Oh, okay, sorry," I said.

"Hey, you two! Pipe down!" someone grunted from a couple of rows behind us.

"Sorry," I apologized over my shoulder. Natalia slunk down in her seat; I could see her face redden in the light from the screen.

We pretty much just held hands during the remainder of the flick, and the bus ride on the way home and the walk back to our complex was relatively quiet.

"What did you think of the movie?" I asked in an

attempt to break the silence.

"Pretty good," she replied.

"That Keith Moon character was crazy. I don't know what that was about," I said, shaking my head.

"I know!" she agreed. "He's so funny, though."

"Leave it to Keith Moon to pull off something weird like Uncle Ernie!"

And with that we both smiled, the ice broken.

I took Natalia's hand gently into mine and looked at her sweetly in her fabulous green eyes. "Hey, I'm sorry if I got a bit frisky in there."

"That's okay. Maybe one day, you know?"

Seizing the opportunity, I stopped her on the sidewalk about a block from the Royale, turned her face toward mine, and gave her the deepest, most sensuous kiss I had in my thirteen-year-old repertoire.

"That was nice," she said, looking deeply into my eyes. "I really like you, Douglas."

"I like you, too," I said. "Want to do it again?" I asked with perhaps a bit too much enthusiasm.

She smiled, seemingly appreciative of my zeal. "We better not. I'd be in big trouble if my dad drove by and saw us out here."

"Okay," I said. But I did continue to hold her hand, and I held it until we reached her front door, where we said goodbye, smiling at each other the way that young lovers do.

Walking back to my townhouse, I looked up at the pink and purple sky, the fading sunset bringing with it a cascade of colors, and breathed in the clean, damp, early-spring, Valley air. Neil Young's "Sugar Mountain," popped into my head, and I couldn't help but softly sing a few words: "Oh, to live on . . . Sugar Mountain."

As I opened the pint-sized wrought-iron gate that led into the similarly pint-sized patio outside of our unit, my reverie was broken by unusual yelling coming from inside the house. This immediately struck me as odd as we were normally a fairly calm, mellow family.

"You don't pay a dime in rent!" I heard my mom screaming.

"But Mom . . ." my older brother David pleaded.

"You don't do your own laundry. You don't do any chores whatsoever around the house. You don't even make your bed!"

As I walked in the front door, David was seated on the first flight of half-stairs leading from the living room up to the dining room and kitchen on the second floor. My mom was standing at the top of the landing looking down at him. They didn't even acknowledge my presence, and my mom's screaming continued unabated.

"And you have the goddamn nerve to tell me to get off my ass and get a job! Who the hell do you think you are?"

"I'm sorry, Mom, I just meant that maybe, if, you know . . ." David was toast, and he knew it. If he had seriously told Mom to get off her butt and get a job, she'd never forgive him.

I already knew what this was all about. Ever since my mom and my dad got divorced, money had been tight. My mom never worked outside the home. Oh sure, she did some stuff out in the community while they were married, but she never held a paying job. I know that shortly after I was born she was the president of the local chapter of B'nai Brith. And I think she was the team mom a couple of times for my brother's baseball team. But mostly she raised her three kids—my sister Julie, the oldest at twenty-one; my brother David, the problem middle child at nineteen; and then me, "the happy surprise," or "the oops baby," or even "the mistake," depending on who you chose to believe.

Anyway, after the divorce a couple of years ago, my mom picked up a job here and there. My brother and sister were pretty self-sufficient by that point, so I was the only one who required anything of her, but during the day, when I was in school, she was pretty much free to work. She became a travel agent, even got her real estate license, but all in all our lifestyle had taken a bit of a haircut compared to when my mom and dad were still together.

Plus, the fact that my brother was nineteen and still living at home and not doing much with his life was pissing my mom off big-time, so she decided to put some pressure on him and start charging him rent. It was a fairly minimal amount—a hundred bucks a month or something like that—but my brother took it as a personal attack, felt like his own mother was tossing him out on the street, was refusing to do her duty as a mother to take care of her child. Every insecurity resulting from the fact that he was a middle child came bursting through the surface.

Of course, I knew where this was ultimately leading: He would take it out on me, like he always did, because I represented everything that was wrong in his life. As far as David was concerned, there is life before Douglas, and life after Douglas. Life as the golden child, the baby of the family, and life as the forgotten middle child who has suffered from a lack of attention ever since the day Douglas was born.

My mom had by now calmed down and was speaking

in a low, controlled voice. Now both my brother and I knew she was seriously serious. "I'm withdrawing my offer for you to pay rent to live here. I'm giving you thirty-day notice. I want you out of here by April fifteenth."

"What? That's absurd!" My brother was incredulous.

My mom continued in that same low, measured tone. "I don't care if you have to go live with your father and that twenty-six-year-old bimbo he married. Or get an apartment. Or rent a room. Or move into a commune in Chatsworth. I just want you out of here by the fifteenth."

And with that Mom stormed upstairs, leaving my usually tough, brash, nineteen-year-old brother sitting on the stairs, broken, a few tears rolling down his cheeks.

"Sorry, dude," I said. "Maybe she'll change her mind."

"No fucking way," he sobbed.

"Well, maybe Dad will help you."

"You think?"

"A bit, anyway. Don't you know anyone you can move in with?"

David thought for a second. "I guess Sam would let me stay with him. He's got a couch anyway."

"Are you guys talking again?" The last I had heard, David and Sam—friends since elementary school—weren't even speaking to each other after Sam accused David of burning his couch with a joint and insisted that he pay for the repair to the cushion. David refused, Sam told him he wouldn't talk to him until it was fixed, and that was that. Apparently somebody gave in, and I can guarantee it wasn't David.

"No. But if I fix the cushion, I'm sure he'll be cool with everything."

David's willingness to yield to Sam's demands was a

shocker and totally unlike him. Well, I guess desperate times called for desperate measures.

"How'd your date with Natalia go?"

Was this a sudden maturation I was witnessing? My brother didn't usually give a rat's ass about my life.

"Incredible," I said with a big smile.

"Wow. By the look on your face it must've gone *really* well. Did she blow you or something?"

I felt the air leave my entire body. My beautiful angel, blowing me in a movie theater? Who was I? Roger Daltrey? "Of course not!" I shot back. Then, after once again returning to the reverie of the day, I smiled a sly smile and said, "But I did get to second base." Sure, it was stretching the truth a little bit since Natalia still had her blouse and bra on when I felt her breasts, but I figured that was just a small technicality.

"You old dog, you! Way to go, Douglas!" Why stuff like this was so important to David I'll never quite understand. It wasn't like he was living vicariously through me—he was quite the ladies' man and had had *a lot* of experience with girls. I mean, he practically lived at the Red Onion, where he'd hook up with older single women, usually divorced, and after a few drinks—or a half-dozen anyway— go back to their place for a night of screwing. Needless to say, these always took the form of one-night stands, and David was always eager to share the lurid details with me.

Anyway, I was delighted to get his approval on my date with Natalia and bounded up the stairs to go check on my mom. David's spirits also seemed to lift as he got up from the stairs and walked into the kitchen to make himself a salami sandwich.

I found Mom sitting alone on the edge of her bed,

crying softly. Art didn't seem to be around; perhaps he had run out to grab a pizza or something for dinner. At least I hoped that was where he had gone; I was starving.

"Mom, you okay?"

"I'm just so sick of his crap. I love him, but I'm sick of it. I can't take it anymore."

I walked over to her, sat down on the bed next to her, and put my arm around her shoulders, pulling her into me. "It's okay, Mom. It'll be better this way. He *should* be on his own by now."

"Will he hate me forever?"

"He doesn't hate you. And he'll probably be thanking you in a couple of years."

"What did I ever do to deserve you?" Mom said, stroking my cheek. "You're my sweet angel."

I smiled and felt my cheeks going a bit flush.

"Hey—" my mom said excitedly, pulling away from me and looking at me directly in my eyes, "how'd your date go? How's Natalia? How was the movie?"

"It was great," I said standing up and heading off to my room. "We had a lot of fun," I added over my shoulder.

"That's it? That's all I get?"

"Yep," I smiled as I walked out the door.

"Oh, pooh on you!" I heard her yell after me in jest.

That night, after dinner—I was right: Art showed up with a ton of Chinese food from Ho Toy's way over on Van Nuys Boulevard—I headed out to The Encino Royale's clubhouse to see if anybody was around. Since it was Saturday night, I figured some of the guys from the complex would be in there shooting pool and generally messing around.

The clubhouse was a one-room hang-out with a pool

table, a Foosball game, and some tables and chairs; it was located at the back of the grounds, next to the pool. People would often come in day or night and play cards or backgammon or mahjong. On the weekends in the late afternoon there was a regular group who'd gather for cocktails and appetizers. Just outside the pool and the clubhouse was a Jacuzzi that saw all kinds of crazy action. From late-night sex—yes, I've seen it with my own eyes—to raging, margarita-soaked, Jacuzzi bacchanals.

When I reached the clubhouse, there was nobody around. I walked in just to make sure and from the smell in the air, I immediately knew where everybody was. Connected to the clubhouse, and in back of the Jacuzzi, was a sauna, where Ronnie and the other guys would occasionally go to smoke pot, especially when they were too lazy to venture out to the alley behind the complex. Sure enough, as I went through the side door of the clubhouse and stood outside the sauna, the skunk smell got stronger, and I could hear lots of giggling going on inside. I grabbed the handle of the door to the sauna, and in my best adult, authoritative voice, I yelled as I flung it wide open, "Alright, you guys, what's going on here?"

Hank and Weddy both screamed, scared they'd just been busted, but Ronnie sat there unperturbed, glancing at me askew, the orange glow of the joint hanging nonchalantly from his lips, making him look like Humphrey Bogart or some other detective from an old, black-and-white movie. "Want a hit, Douglas?" he said, cool as a cucumber.

"One of these days, Ronnie," I said. "One of these days I'll figure out a way to get to you."

"Never, Douglas. I'm unflappable. Want a hit?" Ronnie took the joint out of his mouth and held it toward me.

"No thanks, I'm good."

"Pussy," Ronnie said in his typical fashion.

I just rolled my eyes like I had done a thousand times before. I had been offered pot ever since I was in the fourth grade when the older brother one of my friends from my old neighborhood took us up into his treehouse and lit a joint. He was my current age at the time, maybe even a year or two younger. My brother and sister had been smoking grass for years—hell, they told me they'd even smoked with Mom a few times—and they grew a couple of plants in our backyard after Dad left, so it wasn't like pot wasn't a part of my life in one way or another. But because it was just a normal thing, it didn't have that cachet for me of being something forbidden that it had for so many other kids. Hank and Weddy's parents would absolutely murder them if they ever found out. Ronnie got his stash from his dad, so he'd obviously be down with it, and while I'm not sure about Ronnie's mom, she was pretty much oblivious to most of what goes on in life, so she probably wouldn't have cared one way or the other. And my mom would probably just raise her eyebrows, shake her head, and go back to reading *TV Guide* if I ever started smoking. Hell, when I was all of nine years old, she and Dad left me alone with my brother and sister when they went off to Vegas for the weekend. David and Julie threw a huge party that got so out of hand they had to call the police on themselves. They locked the door to keep people out, but kids from all over the Valley came to the house and just started climbing over the backyard fence to get into the yard. Let's see, on that one night alone, as I wandered around the party, I watched the older kids smoke pot, drink alcohol, eat mushrooms, and drop acid. It was quite an education for a nine year old!

"What are you guys doing tonight?"

Ronnie, Weddy, and Hank just stared back at me with dull eyes.

"You're looking at it," Weddy finally piped up, a big smile spreading across his face. His eyes were like two slits, peeking out from beneath his red bangs, and the freckles on his face seemed particularly pronounced tonight. We called him Weddy because his last name was Wedderspoon, but that seemed like a chore to say every time, so we just shortened it to Weddy. He hated to be called Greg. No one knew why, though we once heard it was a name all the men in his family were given, though this didn't make much sense to us either since his dad went by Gus, well, when he wasn't being called Dr. Wedderspoon, that is. Weddy was damn smart. His dad and older brother were both doctors, and even though his mom and dad were divorced, and he didn't get to see his dad all that much since Dr. Wedderspoon had moved to Arizona, medical school and a career as some type of doctor was definitely in Weddy's future, no matter how much pot he smoked, mushrooms he ate, or acid he dropped.

"Hey, Douglas," Hank said through a thick haze of smoke, "how'd your date with Natalia go?" Leave it to Hank to be thoughtful, even when he was stoned. He wasn't nearly as big of a stoner as Ronnie and Weddy, and he and I had grown to be pretty close friends over this past school year.

"Oh, it was great. We went and saw *Tommy*."

"Cool."

"You get any action?" Weddy asked, his eyes suddenly coming to life.

"Shut up, Weddy!" Ronnie cried out. "What the fuck do you know about action? Of course he got action, didn't you, buddy?"

"Yeah, yeah, we kissed and stuff."

Ronnie reached out and pinched my nipples. Hard. "With those tits I hope you at least got to second base!"

"What the fuck, dude? That hurt!"

"Aw, I'm sorry, you wimp."

"Go fuck yourself." I was pissed off. Not only at the pain Ronnie had just inflicted, but at how he could talk so crudely about my future girlfriend.

"Come on, Douglas, he's just messing around," Hank said.

"I think Ronnie's just jealous cause he ain't getting any," Weddy challenged.

"Oh, don't you worry about me, boys," Ronnie proclaimed with his typical bluster. "I get plenty of action."

"Yeah, right. Who was the last girl you kissed?" I knew he hadn't kissed a girl since the time he practically forced himself on Pam McDonald behind the gym after school one day last year.

"I'm not the kiss-and-tell type. Girls don't dig that stuff," Ronnie said defiantly.

"Okay, Ronnie, whatever you say. That's a very convenient excuse." I looked over at Weddy for confirmation, but he just sat there, staring into space.

"No excuse," Ronnie said while taking a big hit off the joint he had just re-lit. "Just the truth, and nothing but the truth, so help me God."

"What do you know about God?" Hank smirked.

"Well, obviously, I'm no bar mitzvah boy like you, but I've got my own special relationship going on." Ronnie smiled in his devilish way. Hank, whose bar mitzvah was several months ago, simply rolled his eyes.

"Hey! Anyone want to go skinny dipping?"

"Shut up, Weddy, you faggot. Why would I want to go skinny dipping with you?" Ronnie could be brutal when he wanted to be, could just cut right through you with an insult.

"I—I just thought it would be fun," Weddy said sheepishly.

"It's okay, Weddy," I said, "Ronnie just doesn't want to do it because he knows we'll all laugh at the size of his tiny prick."

"Fuck off, Douglas. You know I'm packing a good ten inches in here," Ronnie said pointing with both index fingers toward his crotch.

With that, Weddy, Hank, and I started rolling around on the wooden benches inside the sauna, laughing hysterically at Ronnie's absurd claim.

"Yeah," I finally said once the laughter began to subside, "you're a regular Johnny Wadd."

"You know it!" Ronnie said confidently. "Oh, fuck you guys." And with that, Ronnie stormed out of the sauna, taking the joint with him.

"Hey! Ronnie Wadd! Where you going with that? There's still some good hits left on that thing." Weddy was the first one to follow Ronnie out the door. By the time Hank and I moseyed outside, they were gone, presumably finishing the joint without Hank in the alley behind the complex.

"You want to go find them?" I asked Hank.

"Nah, I'm good. Let's just sit here for awhile." We each took a lounge chair by the pool and laid down, looking up at the stars in the sky. The Valley lights had long ago extinguished much of the ability to make out constellations, but sometimes, on dark, nearly moonless nights like this one, when the air was brushed clean by the cool, springtime weather, you could make out the Big Dipper or even find Orion's Belt. I closed my eyes for a minute, then put my hands up around them to shield my pupils from the light of the pool, and began to search the sky. Hank quickly joined me.

"I see the North Star!" Hank was good, but I also knew my constellations from the astronomy class I had taken the previous summer. That and all the trips to the Griffith Observatory I had taken with my dad when I was a little kid, sitting in the same seats where Hank, Ronnie, Weddy, and I sat listening to Pink Floyd and Led Zeppelin during Laserium, after we somehow convinced Ronnie's older sister and her friends to take us along with them one Saturday night during our most recent Christmas break.

"And there's the Big Dipper pointing right at it," I added.

"Hey! Check it out—is that Venus right there?"

"Where?" I asked.

"Over there, out west, low in the sky."

"Maybe," I said.

"It is," Hank demanded. "I'm sure it is."

"Okay, I'll give it to you."

Several quiet minutes went by, just me and Hank, lying on our backs, looking up at the nighttime sky.

"Douglas?"

"Yeah?"

"Do you think Ronnie really has a ten-inch cock?"

"No way, dude," I replied with a straight face. "I've

seen it in the locker room, and I bet he doesn't even reach three inches when hard."

And with that we started laughing, laughing so loud it began ricocheting off the walls of the condos surrounding the pool, laughing so loud some of the people who lived next to the pool began yelling out of their windows for us to shut up. But Hank was stoned, and so he couldn't contain himself, and his laughter was so contagious that I couldn't stop it, either. Finally, we got up and retreated to Hank's townhouse, where we continued laughing in his bedroom until deep into the night while we played APBA baseball—I let Hank take the Dodgers while I took the Mets—and I kicked his ass nine to nothing, behind two homeruns from Dave Kingman and a sparkling pitching performance by Tom Seaver.

Chapter Two

On Monday morning, my friends and I all gathered at our usual meeting spot behind the cafeteria at 7:30 A.M. We always got to school early to give us plenty of time to gamble and harass one another. During football season, on Tuesdays, Andrew Kagen would bring the odds that were printed in the *L.A. Times* that morning for the games that would be played that upcoming Sunday. Andrew was definitely the ringleader, a kid who was already addicted to gambling. The week before school let out last December had been particularly heated.

"I'm willing to take the Bears plus seven," I said to no one in particular, hoping a Rams fan would take the bait.

"That's ridiculous!" Andrew shouted. "The line is only four and a half."

"Well, there's a premium for all of those Rams fans among us," I countered.

"It's a stupid bet," Andrew reiterated, looking at the guys around me for some confirmation.

"Sorry, Douglas," Hank said, "I'm with Andrew on this one."

"Me, too," Weddy agreed. I looked at a couple of other guys who generally joined our betting group, but neither Moose or Sven or Clark would take the bait.

"I'll take the Rams and give you six," Ronnie announced.

"Done!" I said, happy to take the Bears and their defense against my beloved Rams, especially in Chicago, where a freezing snow was forecast for the weekend. This would be one of those Sundays where I'd be able to root for my favorite team, but only to win by, say, three or four points.

"You're an idiot, Ronnie!" Andrew snapped.

"Shut up, Andrew, before I stuff you in that trashcan over there." It was true, Ronnie had been known to grow so disturbed by Andrew—who was generally considered to be the most annoying kid at school—that he would pick him up and deposit him in the nearest trashcan, where Andrew would whine and cry and try desperately to get out of the garbage, pleading for help that was always *extremely* slow to come. We'd often leave him there until just before the bell, finally extracting him so that we could all race to class and get in our seats before school started. If Andrew were ever to get a tardy, his parents would kill him; Andrew's dad was an attorney, and Andrew was expected to follow him into law, so school was taken *very* seriously in the Kagen household.

"Anyone want to give me the Falcons and thirteen against the Steelers?" Andrew wiped a bead of snot from his nose—his nose was always running—and looked around the group as if he had just made us the most generous offer in the world. "Come on, guys!" he implored. "That's a lot of points! And Bradshaw's supposed to be banged up, to boot!"

"Give me fifteen, and you've got a deal," Weddy said.

"Fuck you, Weddy," Andrew shot back. "Fuckin' deadbeat." This was also true. Weddy was not known for paying off his bets on time. "Are there any *serious* gamblers out there? Come on, guys!" Andrew implored again.

"Okay, just because you're such an asshole," Ronnie said, "I'll take the Falcons and fourteen."

"Thirteen and a half," Andrew bargained.

"No way." Ronnie stood his ground.

"Fine, no bet then. Anyone else?"

"Well," Hank began.

"Okay, okay, I'll take the thirteen and a half," Ronnie agreed. "Anything to beat your ass. And I heard Bradshaw has already been declared out for the game."

"Done!" Andrew said. "And by the way, the news this morning said he's gonna play, and I bet the odds go up well over two touchdowns by the time Sunday rolls around! Sucker!" he taunted.

"That does it, asshole!" With that, Ronnie picked the rather small and thin Andrew up, threw him over his shoulders and promptly deposited him into the nearest trashcan headfirst. No matter how many times this happened during the school year, we always broke into hysterics; Weddy even spewed his morning chocolate milk all over the place that day, the dark liquid running through his mouth and out his nostrils.

With football season long over—the Steelers capping off their incredible year with a Super Bowl championship—and nobody that interested in betting on baseball or basketball until the playoffs rolled around, we turned our attention to pitching pennies, although, by this point in our lives, being the big-shot gamblers that we were, pennies had given way to nickels and dimes and even the occasional quarter.

"Okay, Hank, baby needs a new pair of shoes. Let's see you take this thing," I said, encouraging my teammate. Because we were always pressed for time in the morning, we often paired off in teams of two, with each player alternating taking a toss each round. This morning, it was me and Hank versus Andrew and Ronnie, and Weddy and Moose. Hank, who was the best athlete in the group, was a natural, and everyone always fought to be his teammate, but he usually chose me. Sure enough, Hank tossed a dime in the air and it landed several inches closer than the next-best toss, thrown by Moose.

"Ohhhhh," Moose groaned. As his name implied, Moose was a big kid who sort of looked like a large side of beef. "Hey! Wait! You were over the line!" Here we go again. Moose hated to lose and was always looking for a way out, even if it meant cheating. I couldn't stand playing against him in any sport, because he was always calling cheap fouls, or claiming a ball was out of bounds when it was clearly nowhere near the line.

"Give me a break," Hank calmly replied as he went to pick up the coins.

"Did anyone else see it?" Moose yelled, looking around wild-eyed.

"Nope. Sorry, didn't see it," Weddy replied. Moose looked toward Ronnie for validation.

"I ain't bailing you out!" There was no love lost between Ronnie and Moose ever since Moose had messed up a science experiment earlier in the year that Ronnie had been partnered with him on.

"His toe was awfully close to the line," Andrew said, always looking to sow division and discord.

"You see!" Moose turned toward me and Hank.

"He said his foot was close to the line, not that it went over," I entreated.

"Well, I say it went over!" Moose took a couple of

menacing steps toward me. While he was nearly twice my size, I stood my ground. I had been threatened by Moose out on the sports fields and courts many, many times over the past year or so, and knew he was all bark and no bite.

"Hey! I thought I told you kids to stop gambling!" Mr. Forest appeared from out of nowhere, hustling toward us with the goofy run-walk that was his hallmark. He was a history teacher and was universally despised and ridiculed across the campus, by both kids and teachers alike. This was a guy known for showing movies to the class narrated in French—the films were really meant for the kids taking French—just so he could point out a five-second glimpse of a bridge he once crossed on a long-ago visit to Paris. He was also infamous for grading papers solely based on the number of pages in the report, which led to kids filling their assignments with blank paper, or pornographic drawings, or just pure gibberish—we all knew he never looked at what we had written—and had all watched time and time again as he simply held the report in the palm of his hand as if weighing it, checking the last page for the number, and then assigning a random grade.

Come report card day, there would always be an angry mob of kids outside his door immediately after the last bell had rung, while he hid behind the chalkboard, sobbing loud enough for all to hear. And it seemed like a week didn't go by without some kid chasing Forest through the campus, angry about some idiotic thing the teacher had done, and we'd watch as Forest tore through the cafeteria, seeking refuge in the teachers' lunchroom. Some days, class would be delayed while a maintenance worker would be called over to pry a penny that had been superglued over the keyhole on the door handle to Forest's classroom. Even today, I had noticed as I passed the teachers' parking lot on the way into school that someone had let the air out of all of the tires on his car. Once again, like so many times before, Forest would be calling AAA at some point during the day.

As usual, we just ignored Forest, finishing up our last few tosses, gathering up our coins, and not saying a word to the creep. He stood there, arms folded, scolding us for disrespecting him. "You know, I could've taken a job teaching history at UCLA, but sacrificed, SACRIFICED, to teach you little monsters," he rambled on. "I'm tired of all of you—all of you! Do you hear me?" We rolled our eyes, continued to pay him no attention whatsoever, and broke off in different directions, heading to our individual classes. "I'm going to report you to Principal Huffington!" I could hear him shouting as Hank and I made our way to Power Reading, the class we shared as our first of the day.

It was nice starting off each morning with a simple elective, as it allowed us to sort of ease into the day. Both Hank and I loved to read, and this class had actually increased our reading speed tremendously. Power Reading was taught by Mr. Lincoln, a former jockey with a limp who believed that reading quickly, with strong comprehension, would lead kids down the path toward a brilliant and fulfilling career. At least, that's what he would tell us whenever any of us would show signs of slacking off in his class. Most of us just liked the class because it was easy, and it gave us the skills to read our English and History assignments much faster than kids who didn't take the class. Lincoln used a pretty clever system where he'd flash a line on the screen for a split second, and you'd be forced to try and read what he had just shown you. Some-how, this technique worked like magic, and most of us who had actually followed his directions had doubled or even tripled our reading speeds without any loss of com-prehension. In fact, many of us had increased our speed *and* our comprehension as we got deeper and deeper into the class.

"Hi, Douglas!" I heard Natalia call my name from across the senior quad. I wanted to run over to see her, but stepping onto that lawn as an eighth grader was for-bidden; only ninth graders could walk across it, and if a seventh or eighth grader even dared to set foot upon the green grass, even so much as cut a corner, a group of self-assigned enforcers—mostly kids who would go on to play football the following year at Pershing or Wood-row Wilson High—was sure to greet you off campus after school for an ass-whipping.

"Hi, Natalia!" I waved and smiled back.

"You two seem to be getting pretty serious," Hank nudged me with an elbow to the ribs.

"She's a pretty special girl," I smiled.

"It's okay. We'll all forgive you when you stop hanging out with us to spend more time with her," Hank kidded.

"Never happen," I said calmly. "There's no way I'd dump my friends for a girl."

"We'll see about that, dude," Hank said, opening the door to Mr. Lincoln's classroom. "We'll see about that."

Little did I know that my loyalty would be put to the test just a couple of hours later during our "nutrition" break. As I approached the cafeteria, I saw my friends huddled in a group in our usual spot across from the win-dows where kids would wait in lines to order all manner of crappy food, from warm, spongy bagels to soggy French fries to scrambled eggs that had not only been overcooked in the first place, but that had now been sitting for God knows how long, turning them into a cold, hard, encrusted pile of grossness.

"Douglas!" I heard Natalia call my name just as I approached Hank, Weddy, Ronnie, and the rest of the guys.

"Hey, Natalia!" I smiled and waved.

"Come here and wait in line with me!" she pleaded.

As I turned back to my friends, I could see that Ronnie had been watching the whole exchange.

"Go on, Douglas. Go run to her like the little bitch you are!" The rest of the group laughed along with Ronnie.

I rolled my eyes and made my way over to Natalia. "How's your morning going?" she asked.

"Okay, I guess. We got our math quiz back, and I got a ninety-six, so I'm pretty happy about that."

"Great! Congratulations!" Natalia enthused. "You want anything to eat?"

"Yeah," I said, "I was thinking about getting a cinnamon roll."

"I'll order for you," Natalia offered, and I handed her thirty-five cents. After getting our food we found an open spot at a table and sat down next to a group of kids we didn't really know. We mostly ate in silence, exchanging bits of small talk here and there. I could clearly see my friends over her shoulder, and they seemed to be enjoying gossiping about me, cracking jokes to each other and making lewd gestures behind Natalia's back. At one point, she caught me looking at them.

"Is everything alright?" she asked, glancing back over her shoulder, but not seeing anything untoward.

"Yeah, yeah, fine. The guys are just goofing around."

"Oh, are they giving you a hard time for sitting with me?"

"No, no," I lied. "I think they're just teasing Andrew as usual."

"If you want to go back to your friends, I won't mind. I know you like to hang out with them at nutrition." Wow. Was Natalia a great girl or what?

"It's okay. I see them enough. I like sitting here with you." I smiled, and she smiled back, and for the next few minutes we mostly sat silent, occasionally looking into each other's eyes and sometimes even giggling. When the bell rang, we stood up, collected our trash, and made our way to the trashcan.

"Well," she said, tossing away her napkin, "I have to go to English class. Where are you headed?"

"I have PE now," I said. "With everyone's favorite—Mr. Vineland."

"Oh, God!" Natalia exclaimed in horror. "I hear all the boys hate him. Isn't he the guy who used to be a Marine?" The girls all had female PE teachers, so they didn't really have much interaction with the boys' PE teachers.

"Yeah, and he treats us all like idiots, even likes to refer to us as 'Private.'"

"Private?"

"Yeah, I guess it's the lowest level you can be as a Marine. Anyway, I better get going because if you aren't in place *before* the bell rings, he'll mark you as tardy and make you run a bunch of laps."

"Jeez, sounds like he needs to get a life," Natalia laughed.

"Tell me about it!"

"It was nice spending nutrition with you, Douglas." Natalia looked at me with her gorgeous green eyes, and I felt my heart skip a beat.

"Yeah, we should do this more often," I smiled.

"See you later," Natalia smiled back at me before turning and walking away.

"Bye, Natalia," I said, watching her leave. She took one more glance over her shoulder, and once again I could've sworn my heart broke its normal rhythm.

"Hey! Loverboy!" I heard Ronnie yell as loud as he possibly could so that even Natalia, who was now walking out of the cafeteria area, could easily hear him. "You going to PE or what? Remember, we're running cross-country today. Vineland's gonna kick your ass if you're late!"

"I'm coming, I'm coming," I said, turning toward Ronnie, who was walking with Hank and Weddy to the locker room. It was pretty cool that the four of us were in PE together this year. That hardly ever happens, but somehow the scheduling Gods got it right and put us together for our favorite class of the day. Now, not only did we get to play sports at lunch and after school in BAC—that's the acronym everyone uses in place of the incredibly lame "Boys Afterschool Club" that some teacher probably came up with twenty years ago—we also had PE where we got to go at one another on a daily basis. We all loved playing both with *and* against each other. Sometimes, it's actually more fun to battle and beat your friend than to win with him. Funny how that works.

Only today, there'd be no battling. Hank would undoubtedly jump out to the front, and within about a minute or so, it would become a two-man race between Hank and Tommy. They were by far the best track athletes in our grade, with Hank holding the advantage in the sprints and medium distance races—basically anything under eight-hundred yards—while Tommy was stronger in the longer runs. The cross-country was essentially our marathon; nearly two miles around the track, the playing fields, and then around the outside of the school, running on an ankle-spraining mixture of grass, dirt, and weeds.

I hated it.

In fact, I hated any exercise that didn't involve a ball and some form of competition. Basketball, baseball, football, tennis, hell, even soccer and handball—all good. But make me do pull-ups, sit-ups, lift weights? Forget it. And running? What was the point if there was no ball involved?

So as we took off, with Hank and Tommy predictably up front, and Ronnie—who, because of his solid build was tough in any sport—in the top quarter of the runners, Weddy and I hung in the back tenth of the crowd, running just hard enough to make sure that we would finish ahead of our arch-nemisis: Moose. Nobody wanted to lose to Moose, who was a highly competitive athlete, but who was so big that he just couldn't handle the long-distance runs. Put Moose as your goalie in soccer and there was no way the other team would get more than one goal, and that would only be via some fluke. Moose was just too big, took up too much of the space at the net to be able to get the ball by him cleanly.

In football, the last guy you wanted to face if you were the quarterback was Moose on the other side of the line of scrimmage. Moose would dominate the game just with his pass-rushing skills, swiping away the offensive lineman with an effortless swat of one of his big paws. He wasn't great in basketball, but his sheer size made him a formidable opponent on both offense and defense, in the key and around the rim. And baseball? He held the record for the longest home run in the history of the local Pony League—a blast that the coach guessed was approximately three hundred seventy-five feet, which was incredible for a fourteen year old. Moose also fancied himself as a pitcher, but he was so wild that he once threw a no-hitter while giving up nine runs in the process because he kept loading the bases with walks and hit batters. Kids shivered with fear every time they had to step up to the plate and face him and his wickedly wild, turbo-charged fast ball. Likewise, his curveball only broke about a third of the time, so sometimes it'd break across the plate, but most often it just came straight at your head and never changed course, forcing you to hit the dirt or take a knock on your helmet.

Weddy could easily be up there running with Ronnie, and depending on how he was feeling he might still end up there even as we passed the one-mile mark. I huffed and puffed and lifted my large legs up and down as best I could. I swear, I'll run all day on a basketball court and never get tired, but running just for the sake of running? After a few hundred yards I was usually done. In fact, I looked around and, spotting Moose safely in the back of the pack, battling with Dale Erlund, a kid in the Special Ed program who sometimes did PE with us, for last place, and seeing that Mr. Vineland was up at the front with Hank and Tommy, I decided it might be time to catch my breath and walk for a bit.

"Weddy," I said, breathing hard, "why don't you make your move and head up toward Ronnie?"

"Nah, not today," Weddy said.

"Why not?"

"Just don't feel like it."

"Well," I said, "I need a break, so I'm gonna walk for a bit."

"Okay," Weddy said, slowing down. "I'll join you."

We began walking, catching our breath, and keeping our eye on Moose as runners here and there slowly made their way past us.

"Hey, Weddy," I asked, "how come you don't run up at the front with Ronnie? I know you can do it."

"Yeah, but my dad isn't a big fan of running."

"Really? Why not?"

"Says it's too hard on the bones, especially for kids who are still growing. He prefers calisthenics." Weddy's dad, since he was a doctor and all, was always on top of the latest diet and exercise trends. If he thought running was bad for you, who was I to argue? And it was true, Weddy had earned his gold trunks in the Presidential Fitness Test because he was so great at push-ups and pull-ups and the broad jump, and when it came to running, he could pull it together and finish high enough to get just the right amount of points to qualify for the trunks. Me? I was pathetic. The only reason I was even able to earn two stars was because they had a softball throw—it essentially replaced the shot-put, which they felt was too dangerous for a bunch of hyper junior high school kids—and, again, give me a ball and I could compete with the best of them. But pull-ups and push-ups? Forget it. I was average in the broad jump because of my strong legs, and could actually finish in the upper part of the pack in the fifty-yard dash because I was fairly quick and didn't mind short bursts of running, but the six hundred-yard dash was just plain inhumane.

In fact, when I first came to Cabrillo they made me take the Presidential Fitness Test, and it was the most humiliating experience of my life. Here I was, a good athlete when it came to basketball, baseball, and football, but I had never even done more than a handful of push-ups, sit-ups, or pull-ups, had never done any sort of running whatsoever, had never even heard of the Presidential Fitness Test, and on my second day of school, a drizzly January morning—I had transferred in the middle of seventh grade, immediately after Christmas break—the sadistic Mr. Vineland made me take the test, without even giving me any advance warning.

"But it's raining outside!" I protested, tearing up. In those days, I was so miserable with our family's move and having to go to a new school that I cried at the drop of a hat.

Vineland glanced out the window of his office and smirked, "That? Barely a mist. Go change."

"But I haven't gotten my PE clothes yet."

"Not my problem," Vineland said. "You should've already had them in your possession before school started up again." Vineland had a huge handle-bar mustache that he kept finely waxed and in impeccable condition, and he twisted the ends with his fingers as he looked me in the eye. What a bastard.

"But my mom didn't—"

"Not my problem," he cut me off. "You can take the test in your street clothes. Now get out there and get stretched, Private." Vineland looked at me and smiled his twisted smile.

So that's what I did. Dressed in heavy jeans and an oversized jacket that I refused to remove because all I had underneath was a Hang Ten T-shirt, and I feared I would freeze in the drizzling, fifty-something degree weather without it. I did zero pull-ups and five push-ups.

"Seriously!" Vineland barked as he stood there, watching me hanging from the pull-up bar, my arms completely extended, not able to curl up even an inch. "Not one?"

I choked back the tears and remained silent, hanging there from the bar, too terrified to even try to do a pull-up again. A few kids had gathered around to watch, and I saw the knowing smirks on their faces.

"All right. Get down, Private," Vineland instructed. I let go of the bar and landed awkwardly on my feet.

"Can you do anything with a ball?" Vineland sneered.

"Yes, sir," I said with as much confidence as I could muster.

We made our way over to the softball field and, once there, I took off my jacket. I knew I could throw a ball, but it'd be impossible to do it wearing a heavy coat. After my toss, an effective throw of over one-hundred-fifty feet, I finally got a compliment out of Vineland: "Okay, so you can throw a ball. But it won't do you much good if you've got no strength or stamina."

Just wait until you see me out on the basketball court, I thought to myself.

After the broad jump, in which I did okay, it was time for the six hundred. "Okay," Vineland instructed, for this you're going line up here," he said, tapping a white line on the track that was painted onto the asphalt of the playground, "and run around the track four times."

"Four times?" I complained.

"Yes, Private, and it's supposed to be a dash, so you're going to need to run as fast as you can the whole time. I'd suggest you take off your jacket for this exercise."

The drizzle had by now turned into a steady light rain, so I sullenly refused to take it off.

"Have it your way, Private." He held his stopwatch, which hung from a thin rope around his neck—a rope I imagined strangling him with—in his hand, finger placed atop the silver knob, and shouted, "On your mark! Get set!" but he suddenly dropped the watch and got right in my face. "Is that the best you can do?" he screamed.

I hadn't moved an inch, and stood there casually, as if I were standing in line at the movies. As PE was about to end—I was even hoping I'd somehow be saved by the bell— the group of kids watching my pathetic test had grown by the dozens and they all laughed at "the new kid."

"When I say 'on your mark,' you're supposed to get on your mark, and when I say 'get set,' you're supposed to get set!" he ordered.

I placed my toes on the line and faced forward.

"Okay, better. On your mark!" he resumed, continuing to shout so that the whole playground had now turned to watch. "Get set!" I didn't move, but at least I was facing in the right direction. Vineland just sighed and said, quietly, having given up the fight, "Go!"

I took off, not exactly at breakneck speed, but I was running, trying to get as far away from Vineland and the kids who were watching as possible. Unfortunately, as I rounded the turn and came to the other side of the track across from them, I felt a sense of dread as the reality that I would have to come around and pass them several more times set in and my pace slowed down dramatically. As I approached the starting/finish line the first time, the kids were laughing as Vineland sat there, counting out my time for all to hear; I would find out later that my six hundred-yard dash time was one of the slowest in the history of the school. I had to repeat this humiliation for three more laps, each of which got progressively slower and slower, the laughter from the kids growing louder and louder, and Vineland's "encouragement" becoming more and more berating with each lap. By the time I walked across the finish line, tears were streaming down my face. It was, shall we say, an inauspicious debut in front of what felt like my whole school.

"What the hell are you two clowns doing?"

Speak of the devil.

Weddy and I had been so focused on making sure we stayed ahead of Moose that we didn't see that Vineland had made his way to the back of the pack. We immediately picked up the pace and started jogging again.

"I'd expect this from you," Vineland sneered as he stared me down; he had always hated me ever since the day of that first fitness test, and refused to acknowledge my prowess on the basketball court, a sport he felt was "for sissies," but we all knew he hated it because so many Black guys played it professionally and it was no secret he hated Blacks. We didn't have that many Black kids at the school—just a busload or two from neighborhoods out in the city somewhere—but the ones who did go here seemed all right. We played basketball against several of the Black guys, and while we weren't really friends with them—they hung out with kids who lived near them and we hung out with kids who lived around here—everyone got along for the most part, and we respected one another's skills on the court.

"But," Vineland continued, "I'm very disappointed in you, Wedderspoon." And with that Vineland poked

Weddy hard in the chest with his index finger. "Now get your sorry ass up there," he ordered Weddy, who immediately picked up his pace and began passing runners right and left. Vineland didn't even pay me a glance as he turned and followed Weddy, practically nipping at his heels in his own cruel way of forcing my friend's pace.

I continued to plod along, even falling back just far enough to let Moose get within striking distance, and as soon as I saw him put it into second gear and try to catch me, I picked up my pace and lengthened my lead. "You're such an asshole, Douglas!" I heard Moose yell from behind.

"Psyche!" I yelled back.

"I'm gonna kick your fuckin' ass this afternoon in BAC, you sonofabitch!" Aside from being the largest kid at the school, Moose also had the filthiest mouth. Well, next to Ronnie, anyway.

We had a big game coming up after school today. The Blue team, with me, Hank, Weddy, and Ronnie, was tied for first with the Red team, which featured Moose and his best friend Clark—another big kid who had an incredibly strong inside and mid-range game—and a couple of other good players. Playing each other today would be for sole possession of first place, and a great deal of pride was on the line. The key to the game was actually going to be Ronnie, as we would need every ounce of his size and grit to battle the twin towers of Moose and Clark, who we also called "The Big Lefty" because, well, he was tall and a southpaw to boot.

The barking about the afterschool battle of the titans became more heated once the cross-country run was over and we were back in the locker room showering. "Hey,

Clark," Moose shouted across the rows of lockers as he struggled to tie his shoes, his wet hair dripping down his shirtless and meaty body. "Tell these fuckers how we're going to destroy them today!"

"Hey! Watch the language!" we heard Coach Dufrense, a former Division One gymnast who was short but very stout, yell. "Who the hell was that?" The whole locker room burst out laughing at the coach's use of a curse word, and by the time everyone had calmed down, Coach Dufrense had left the room.

"We're gonna kill 'em inside," Clark challenged. "They're gonna get one shot on offense, and we'll get multiple chances to score every time we get the ball."

It was true: If Ronnie didn't keep one or both of them off of the boards, we'd be one and done every time down, and they'd kill us on the offensive boards, getting several chances to score on every possession.

"With me and Hank filling it up, one shot is all we'll need, boys!" I shot back, trying my best to undermine their superiority in rebounding the ball.

"Shut up, Douglas! You're just a God damn pesky parasite, riding on Hank's coattails. You're so streaky you're more likely to go zero for ten than anything else. You don't scare us." Moose was right, I was a classic streak shooter, but when I got hot, I got *really* hot. I also lived and died by the shooter's mantra: No matter how many I've already missed, I just knew the next one was going to go in.

"It's all about the boards, my friends," Clark said. "And we will dominate."

"I beg to differ!" I heard Ronnie's voice rise above the on-going murmur of the locker room. "Remember, you're gonna have to go through me to get those rebounds."

"Fuck you, Ronnie!" Moose shouted. "You don't scare us!"

"Hey, Moose, you fat fuck!" Ronnie came right back at him. "You're gonna have a heart attack trying to keep up with me."

"What did I say about the language!" Mr. Dufrense was back. "Come on, guys, cut it out." Unlike Mr. Vineland, nobody really feared Mr. Dufrense—he was too kind and had a sort of sad way about him—so he was usually forced to plead with kids in order to get them to do what he was asking.

"See you on the court, suckers!" Moose said as he walked out the door of the locker room, continuing to try and pull his tight Hang Ten shirt over his still-wet body, struggling to get the cotton fabric over his girth. The Big Lefty followed closely on his heels.

"Blue by six!" Ronnie shouted out. He loved making predictions, often likening himself to Ali telling everyone in what round he was going to knock out his opponent. And I gotta say, Ronnie was usually pretty accurate. Hank appeared just as I was closing my locker. As usual, he had stayed out of the barking match, always preferring to let his extraordinary game do the talking.

"You ready?" Hank and I always walked over to English together after PE.

"Yeah. Did you catch all that?" I asked him.

"Some of it," Hank said casually. "Those guys don't worry me. Besides, I have a big game on Saturday against a really good team, and I'm much more concerned about that." Hank played in a top-notch youth league that was a couple of levels above all of us mere mortals. In fact, he didn't even start on that team, named The Knights, though he ran the point for the second unit. There were plenty of kids who were shoo-ins for starting on their high school varsity squads as freshmen next year. Hank would definitely play varsity at Woodrow Wilson when we got there, but it was doubtful he'd start. A lot depended on how he progressed over the summer and during ninth grade.

It turned out that Hank was right, and Ronnie was wrong: We won by thirteen points, not six. Not only did Hank thoroughly dominate the game—he was just too damn quick for Clark and Moose and the rest of their team, grabbing the outlet from Ronnie and weaving his way down the court for an easy lay-up or a pull-up fifteen-foot jumper again and again and again—but I had a solid outing as well, going five for eight on set shots from the outside, including several twenty-footers. Ronnie more than held his own on the inside, battling for every defensive rebound, and coming up with most of them. Andrew—who was generally not a very good athlete—had also played well, often leaving his man to double-team either Clark or Moose. As I predicted, Hank and I were so hot that there weren't many offensive boards on our end to be had. Even Weddy chipped in with a few buckets, and he played stellar D on their point guard, whose normally pinpoint passes to The Big Lefty and Moose would set them up for easy baskets down low, but who today seemed off his game, committing several turnovers, mostly due to Weddy's solid defense. This also allowed us to put Hank on Sven, their best outside shooter, and Hank totally shut him down.

"What do you have to say now, big mouth?" Ronnie got into Moose's face after one of the coaches blew his whistle, ending our game, and we were walking off the court.

He and Moose had battled each other all game, throwing elbows, and grabbing, holding, and pushing each other while the coaches tried not to call too many fouls.

Moose took exception and shoved Ronnie, hard, in the chest. "Get the fuck out of my face, you moron!" Moose growled.

"I ain't scared of you!" Ronnie didn't budge. Like I said, Moose was the biggest kid in the school, but Ronnie was the toughest. "I'll kick your ass just like I kicked your ass on the court!"

"Fuck you, Ronnie," and with that Moose threw a punch that missed Ronnie by a good foot and a half. Moose stumbled forward and Ronnie kicked him in the ass, sending Moose to the ground. Now he was really pissed, and as everyone began to form a circle, Moose got up awkwardly to his feet. Ronnie had by now crouched down, fists out in front of him, in a classic boxer pose. His dad was once an amateur boxer and had taught him how to fight.

"You want a piece of me, bitch?" Ronnie snarled.

"All right, ladies, break it up!" Mr. Vineland stormed through the circle and stepped between the two gladiators. "Everyone get out of here and go home. As for you two knuckleheads," he said angrily, pointing at Moose and Ronnie, "you want to put on the boxing gloves and step into the gym?" The truly sadistic Vineland loved nothing more than to put together boxing matches between two kids who were fighting and watch them pound each other with what were essentially oversized pillows on their hands. It was tough to do much damage with those gloves, but you could put a kid down on the floor if you got enough punches to land and sort of pushed him over.

Neither Ronnie or Moose wanted anything to do with

Vineland and his little guilty pleasure, so they declined, shook hands with each other at Vineland's insistence, and we all walked away from one another—Moose, Clark, Sven, and their teammates in one group, and Ronnie, Hank, Weddy, Andrew, and me in another.

"Vineland's a creep," Ronnie said as we walked toward the locker room.

"I hear he's got this huge collection of Bert and Ernie dolls and memorabilia," Weddy said. We all burst out laughing, bumping into one another and slapping Weddy on his back.

"Actually, I always thought of him as more of a Pet Rock guy," Andrew joked.

"Well, he's definitely got stones for balls," Ronnie said. "Prick."

I could see my mom waiting in her powder-blue Buick Riviera on the side of the school next to the softball field. "Anybody need a ride?" I offered.

"I do!" Ronnie raised his hand.

"My dad's picking me up 'cause I have practice," Hank said. Even after playing our BAC game, he still had plenty of juice left to go and practice with The Knights, whose coach was known to run his kids ragged during practice so that they'd be the best conditioned team in the league.

"My mom's picking me up and taking me to look at paint colors for my room," Weddy said with a groan. "But thanks anyway."

"I'm good, thanks," Andrew added.

We all collected our books and stuff out of our lockers and, still in our sweaty PE clothes, headed our separate ways, Ronnie and I walking toward my mom.

"You played great, today, Ronnie," I said. "You really

kept those guys off the boards."

"Thanks. Must've been the Lucky Charms this morning!"

"The Breakfast of Champions!" I said, throwing my arm around him. We shared a laugh and hopped in the car, feeling giddy that we had kicked Moose and Clark's butts and now held sole possession of first place in BAC.

Chapter Three

My mom was being totally chill about the upcoming summer: "Take it easy. Enjoy yourself. You've been working really hard this year and are getting excellent grades. You deserve a break," she said as we drove home from school one beautiful spring afternoon, a Friday with the endless possibilities of the weekend lying ahead.

It was true. I had worked my ass off this past year. I was a pretty good student, with a mix of As and Bs, but unlike, say, Weddy, who was so smart he just coasted through school, stoned half the time, and *always* got straight As, I had to claw my way to As in classes I liked, and scramble to get Bs in classes I didn't care that much about.

But while my mom had no problem with me just sort of hanging out with my friends all summer, my dad was definitely not down with that plan. In fact, I was sort of dreading my Sunday with him the day after tomorrow, because I knew he was going to broach the subject and push me to work for him. Just what I wanted, a summer spent sweating in the warehouse of my dad's printing business, helping to haul rolls of paper from where they were stored over to one of the printing presses. And it's not like I'd get to actually drive the forklift or anything. How exciting.

When Sunday did finally roll around, I sat on pins and needles throughout our breakfast together at Art's Deli, just waiting for my dad to drop the summer job bomb, while we made small talk about school, and sports, and his printing business—especially the soaring cost of paper, which he said was killing him—but once we were back in his car on our way to the car wash, I believe it took exactly twelve seconds for him to begin "the job talk."

"So, Son, what are your plans for the summer?"

"I'm not sure, Dad."

"You know, there are plenty of jobs you can be doing in the warehouse. You're old enough and strong enough now."

"Maybe," I said, feigning interest.

"It'd be nice for you to earn some real money to build up your savings account. It's great that you've done odd jobs over the years. It builds character. But it's really just chump change."

"Gee, thanks."

"Son, come on . . ."

"I worked hard at those jobs," I glared. "Let's see you clean up the dog shit from two Great Danes every day for two months."

"Hey, I did some pretty nasty jobs when I was a kid."

"Whatever. The Krahns paid me five dollars a week, which was a lot of money for a nine-year-old."

"I'm not trying to belittle your jobs. That car washing business that you and Nick Einhorn put together was very impressive."

Dad was obviously now trying to butter me up. He was keeping his eyes on the road, enjoying his beloved Jaguar XKE convertible that he had bought after divorcing my mom— who always claimed it was his "mid-life crisis car"—and smoothing things over between us all at the same time. He was the master of doing fifty tasks at once. His employees dreaded one-on-one meetings with him. He'd sit there, listening to you but not listening to you, maybe fidgeting with the reports you'd brought to him in advance of the meeting, or maybe just filing his nails or doing something both meaningless and annoying, and just when you thought you'd successfully slipped the one thing you *didn't* want to tell him—BANG. "Hang on a second. Go back. What did you just say about the receivables for March?" And you were toast. Both for your fuck up of the numbers on the reports you gave him earlier in the week *and* for trying to slip that fact by him nonchalantly.

"Next time you come in here with something hanging over your head, *start* with it," my dad would demand in no uncertain terms.

"Yes, sir," the employee would stammer before slinking out of my dad's office.

Yep, my dad could be fucking tough. But he was also fair. His employees genuinely loved him and for the most part were very loyal; some of them had been working for him for over twenty years.

"Anyway," my dad said as he turned into Encino Car Wash, "think about it. At two-fifty an hour, you could make fifteen, twenty bucks a day depending on how many hours you worked."

"Okay, I'll let you know, Dad. But Mom said I could at least take some time off after all of the hard work I put into school this past year."

"Of course she did," he said disdainfully as he put the car in park, opened the door and handed the keys to his Jag to the car wash attendant.

"Give me the standard plus," he said to the Mexican guy dressed in a white jumpsuit and holding a small pad of paper.

"Standard plus? No tire dressing?" he asked.

"Not today, thanks."

"Okay. Please take inside to cashier. Gracias."

"Gracias," my dad said, taking the paper with the number three written on it.

These days, I was seeing my dad on Sunday mornings and afternoons, and for dinner with both him and Cindy on Wednesday nights, when we'd either eat at their house or go out for a fancy dinner at Monty's. Unless we had tickets to a game, our Sundays were typically spent just like today: having a late, leisurely breakfast at either Art's Deli in Studio City or Brent's up in Northridge if we were tired of Art's, followed by a trip to the car wash. By the time we were done with the car wash it was usually somewhere around two o'clock, which didn't leave a lot of time to do anything too ambitious, so I'd simply accompany him on some type of errand—to the tennis shop to get his racket re-strung, or to the stereo store to check out the latest equipment, or maybe we'd go to Sy Devore to pick out a new suit for a business trip he was taking. Today, after the car wash, we were going to over to Rudnick's to pick out a new suit for me to wear to Lee Schwartzman's bar mitzvah next Saturday.

I enjoyed running errands with my dad, but I wasn't crazy about the car wash. Perhaps it was because of all those summers back in Northridge when my parents were still married and Nick Einhorn and I would wash cars for people who lived in our neighborhood. August would get so fucking hot the water from the hose would never cool down, which meant that we'd get no relief from the water we were using. Let's just say that it was far from refreshing to be working in one hundred eight degree weather while getting drenched with warm water as we scrubbed down a dirty car.

But in spite of the fact that my dad swore for years that he'd "never buy anything other than American," he was in love with his silver XKE, with the black interior that would absolutely bake in the Valley summer heat, and he insisted on getting it washed once a week, and he never, ever went more than two weeks without washing it, even during the Valley rainy spells of February, March, and April.

Every time we went to the car wash it was the same drill: My dad would order the Standard Plus. The guy would try to upsell him to the Standard Premium, which included putting Armor All on the tires. My dad would politely say no, the guy would write the number three on the piece of paper, and we'd head inside. From there it was simply a long hallway leading to the cashier. One side, of course, was a wall of glass where you would follow your car as it went through the various stations: Get wet, add soap, scrub, rinse, and dry. Very exciting when you're five years old, not so much by the time you're thirteen and had seen it a zillion times.

Fortunately, the other side of the hallway contained alcoves with stuff you could buy. Snacks and greeting cards made up the first alcove, and the last alcove contained various automotive products and gadgets—everything from scented air-freshener figures you'd hang from your rearview mirror (Jesus, flowers, flags, etc.) to bean-bag-bottomed ash trays to lighted mirrors you'd attach to your visor—but the middle alcove was where the books were, and that's where I'd spend my car wash time.

Most importantly, they carried tons of *Mad Libs* titles. I loved *Mad Libs*. Hell, what kid didn't? I had also noticed one day, while kicking back on the couch watching *Get Smart* re-runs with David, that one of the creators of the show was a guy named Leonard Stern, and I knew that the *Mad Libs* books were published by Price, Stern, Sloan.

In Mrs. Clapton's English class, we had an assignment to write a research paper about anything related to books that wasn't a book report, so I decided to write about the publisher of *Mad Libs* in order to find out if there was any connection to *Get Smart*, and lo and behold, I discovered that there was. I ended up writing a really interesting essay about Price, Stern, Sloan that not only earned me an "A" from Mrs. Clapton, but I learned all about these amazing three guys who published *Mad Libs*.

I found out that not only did Leonard Stern help create both *Mad Libs* and *Get Smart*—two of the most entertaining and funny things on Earth—but his partner on *Mad Libs*, Roger Price, created *Droodles* and was an early contributor to another one of my absolute favorite things to read, *Mad* magazine. David and I were huge fans of *Mad*, and shared magazines and paperback books all the time, even re-creating jokes and bits at the dinner table from the twisted minds of Don Martin, Mort Drucker, and the other amazing writers and artists at *Mad*, much to my mom's consternation, though Art would usually laugh right along with us.

The other amazing thing about Price, Stern, Sloan that I uncovered during my research was that both Roger Price and Leonard Stern were writers for one of the funniest TV shows of all-time, *The Steve Allen Show*. How great is that? I used to watch the re-runs, as well as the later incarnation of the program, with my dad, who was a huge fan of Steve Allen, as were David and I.

Larry Sloan, the third guy, was a brilliant publisher, not only of *Mad Libs*, but of some of the most popular joke books ever published, many of which I owned. He was the first one who said, "Hey, why are we only allowed to sell our books in bookstores? Why not a hospital gift shop? Why not a car wash?" My dad, when I told him about this, had an all-new appreciation and admiration for both Sloan and *Mad Libs*.

So thanks to Price, Stern, Sloan, and *Mad Libs*, my Sundays at the car wash were a hell of a lot less mundane and, best of all, my dad invariably bought a *Mad Libs* for me if there was something new that came in that I really wanted, as well as the occasional joke book from Price, Stern, Sloan, like *The World's Worst Knock-Knock Jokes* or *The World's Worst Moron Jokes*. This didn't happen every time we went, but it occurred often enough that it was sort of like panning for gold: Some weeks I'd come up empty handed, but other weeks there'd be a bright, shiny nugget waiting there for me on one of those tall, revolving wire racks.

It always took a bit longer to get out of the car wash than everyone else. My dad would always approach the poor guy who was drying off the car, spraying the windows, and wiping down the dashboard, several minutes before he was done, for "the inspection." My dad would invariably point out drips and streaks and specks of dirt or maybe the stubborn drop of tree sap that refused to come free during the wash, and the car wash attendant would have to follow him around the car, dabbing and spraying and drying all over again. Eventually, my dad would end up making the guy go grab a couple of clean towels and he'd give the car a once-over, especially on the inside, where my dad wouldn't even bother asking the guy to wipe this or that, he'd just go over the whole dashboard a second time himself. Still, he was always generous with his tips, usually giving the guy a dollar or two, which always made them smile and instantly forget whatever level of humiliation had just been laid upon them; it was a lot more than the quarter or fifty cents that most customers tipped.

We pulled out of the car wash and headed over to Rudnick's, which had long served as the go-to place for any young or teenaged boy who needed a suit for a bar mitzvah, wedding, or graduation. Of course, I was not a big fan of the process of putting on polyester suit after polyester suit until we found one that fit well enough so that it could be altered by the in-house tailor in order to look decent on me. But I wanted to look good for Natalia and the rest of my friends at the bar mitzvah, so I pretended to enthusiastically agree with the opinions of the salesman and, most importantly, my dad, since I knew that he would ultimately decide which suit would look the best on me.

My dad stepped closer to me, his light green eyes hyper-focused on the knot he was tying in the tie he had picked out. It wasn't enough to just lay the tie next to the shirt, vest, and jacket; he insisted that I had to put everything on in the proper order to truly get a sense of whether the outfit looked good on me. I could make out every pore on his handsome face as he stood just inches from me.

"The suit maketh the man, Son," my dad said, stepping back and observing his creation. As expected, he had chosen every piece of clothing, overruling the salesman, a slim guy in a perfect-fitting black suit with a matching perfect smile that revealed two impressive rows of perfectly straight, white teeth.

"You're absolutely right," the salesman said, nodding his head vigorously when my dad changed out the tie the salesman had picked out with the one my dad had confidently plucked from the large assortment of ties laid out on a wooden oval table.

Browns and tans were the popular color of the day, so that's what we went with, pairing the matching beige jacket, button-up vest, and pants with a crisp white shirt and a wide tie that featured alternating white and chocolate brown stripes. The pants flared out at the bottom, not quite as much as bell-bottoms, but enough that I thought it added a hip touch to the outfit as a whole . . . well, as hip as a three-piece suit can be anyway. We topped everything off with a brand new pair of brown patent leather loafers with two leather tassels on top that, while not exactly comfortable—they pinched my toes together a bit too much for my liking—were an ideal match for the suit. Plus, their fairly substantial wooden heels made me look taller, which was always a good thing in my mind.

"You look like a real mensch, Son!" my dad said proudly. I turned around and studied myself in the mirrors, three tall sheets of glass bordered with a gold frame and arranged in a manner that allowed you to easily see all sides of your body as you turned around. I had to agree with my dad; the suit was a good match for my skin tone and the color of my hair. I was confident I'd be looking sharp at Lee's bar mitzvah.

"Fantastic!" The salesman smiled and clapped his hands together a little too enthusiastically. "Let me get the tailor!"

After enduring the tailoring process, standing as still as possible while a guy who only spoke Russian and a smidgen of broken English tugged and pulled and pinned and marked up seemingly every inch of the jacket and pants with piece of chalk until he was satisfied, I gingerly made my way back into the dressing room for my least favorite part of the whole suit-shopping experience: Trying to get out of the new suit without disturbing any of the tailor's pins or marks. It was an excruciating task, carefully removing the jacket and placing it in on a hanger and then attempting to take off the pants without losing a pin where he was to hem them at the bottom. You couldn't just yank them off, you couldn't use one foot to step on the other pant leg and pull your leg up, you literally had to stand on one foot while trying to raise the other leg high enough to then reach down and very methodically and gently tug the hemmed pant over your foot and letting the rest of the leg follow. This was a tough balancing act, even for an athletic guy like me, but I somehow managed to do it without disturbing the tailor's work, saving me from his wrath. That's right, the tailor was not shy about cursing at you in Russian if you came out of the dressing room having made a mess of his measurements; it had happened to me in the past.

"Thanks for buying me the suit, Dad," I said as we walked out of the store.

"My pleasure, Son. You're growing up to be a fine young man."

I smiled, reveling in his compliment, which he didn't hand out easily, instead saving them for when he really meant what he said. The car ride back to my house was rather quiet, the Dodgers were playing the Reds in Cincinnati, so we listened to Vinny call the game, and marveled at the power of the "Big Red Machine," though my

dad still insisted that Roy Campanella was a better catch-
er than Johnny Bench.

The week flew by rather unremarkably, and suddenly
it was the weekend again, highlighted by Lee Schwartzman's bar mitzvah. Lee was the youngest kid in our class—
his birthday was just a few weeks after mine, making me
the second-youngest—but his Torah studies hadn't gone
all that well and they had to postpone the bar mitzvah a
couple of times until the rabbi felt he was ready to successfully read from the Torah.

Lee didn't really have many friends at school, and I
barely knew him myself; the most contact we had ever had
was when we were both sick one day last year and found
ourselves waiting in the nurse's office for our parents to
pick us up from school. But the tradition at Cabrillo was
for anyone having a bar mitzvah or bat mitzvah (though
there were far fewer of those as it was seemingly more
important in the Jewish community for some reason for
a boy to go through the ceremony than a girl) to invite as
many kids as possible, even those with whom you had the
remotest of connections.

My family wasn't religious at all; well, we were when
my parents were still together and my brother and sister
were young—David even got bar mitzvahed. But as the
years went by we became less and less religious. My parents tried to get me to go to Hebrew school, but I hated
it. Who in their right mind wants to come home from a
full day of regular school, only to have to leave in an hour
to attend Hebrew school for another two or three hours?
Not this hombre. I wanted to go play in the neighborhood
with my friends.

By the time my parents were going through a divorce,

they were tired of fighting me on this issue, and the straw that broke the camel's back was when I said to them, "Most kids, myself included, only want to get bar mitzvahed because of all of the money they get from everyone, and I don't think that's a legitimate, even moral, reason to get bar mitzvahed." Well, what could they possibly say? They knew I was right, and so they folded. Stopped making me go to Hebrew school and gave up on the idea that I'd ever be bar mitzvahed. Hell, my dad eventually married Cindy, who was raised by an itinerant preacher under what was his own convoluted interpretation of the Baptist faith. And Art was a definite atheist. When he was younger he worked in a lab and had a pretty deep interest in science, so his feelings were understandable. All in all, religion played virtually no role in my life by this point, with the exception, of course, of the circuit of bar and bat mitzvahs I was obligated to attend.

So, after picking up my new suit at Rudnick's after school on Friday, I found myself showered and dressed and walking out the door at 3:45 P.M. on a beautiful, warm Saturday afternoon. It was the kind of spring day that lets you know summer will be here soon, when I could've— and by all rights should've—been playing basketball with my buddies, but was instead rushing to make the service, which started at 4:00 P.M. Fortunately, Lee was getting bar mitzvahed at Temple Judea, which was practically across the street from where we lived. Even better, Judea was a Reform temple, which meant that there would only be one ceremony, relatively short and sweet, followed by a party. The bar mitzvahs we all dreaded were the ones held at Valley Beth Shalom, a conservative synagogue that made its thirteen year olds complete two long ceremonies—one in the morning and one in the afternoon—which was just pure agony for us kids who had to sit through them, and I'm positive more than a few adults felt the same way.

As I walked outside, I immediately saw Natalia waiting in the courtyard. "There you are!" she said, smiling. She looked absolutely beautiful, her hair and make-up done up to perfection and wearing a very pretty dress with pink and yellow flowers.

"Sorry," I said, knowing full well I was running late. "I had trouble with my tie." It was true; I couldn't tie a tie for the life of me. Art finally had to take it, put it around his own neck, tie it, and then loosen it up, slide it off of his own head, and put it around mine where he then adjusted the knot as best he could.

"You look great!" Natalia beamed. "I like the color of your suit."

"Thanks," I said, beaming. "There were other shades of brown," I pointed out confidently, "but I liked this one the best."

I gave Natalia the full-on once over; God, she was beautiful. "You look absolutely stunning," I marveled as I approached her, but when I leaned in for a kiss, Natalia pulled away.

"Hi, kids!" I heard her mom say from behind.

"Later," Natalia whispered and then winked. She had obviously seen her mom coming from over my shoulder. "Hi, Mom. What are you doing out here?"

"You two look so cute together. I wanted a picture."

"But we're late, Mom."

"*Tomalo con sod.* It'll only take a second. Come on now, get closer."

I put my arm around Natalia and drew her in, the

scent of lemons reaching my nose. We smiled as naturally as we could as Mrs. Guinzburg took picture after picture on her Kodak Pocket Instamatic.

"Okay, Mom. I think that's plenty."

"Just one more," she said, clicking off several additional shots.

"Okay, Mom, we're leaving now." Natalia took my hand and led me toward the front gate.

"Goodbye, Mrs. Guinzburg!" I called out.

"Have fun, kids! You both look great! I like your tie, Douglas!"

"Thank you!" I happily replied over my shoulder.

"Chau, mi tesoro!"

"Chau, Mami!"

As we crossed Lindley and made our way toward the temple, I was already feeling hot and uncomfortable; polyester was always murder on a warm day, but I don't think Rudnick's even carried suits made out of anything else. My hand was starting to sweat and, feeling a bit self-conscious, I released it from Natalia's and wiped it on the leg of my pants. "Sorry," I apologized, "I'm so hot in this damn suit my hand is sweating."

"That's okay. I don't mind," Natalia said sweetly, reaching out for my hand and taking it once again into hers.

"Hey, lovebirds!" I heard Ronnie call out. He was standing near the entrance to the synagogue with Weddy, Hank, and Andrew Kagen. I glanced at Natalia to see if she was embarrassed, but there wasn't a trace of redness on her perfectly pale cheeks, though she did seem to grasp my hand a bit more tightly.

"Hey, guys," she said calmly. "How's everyone doing?"

"Fine, Natalia," Hank said. "You look very pretty today."

"Don't be making any moves on our boy's girlfriend, Hank," Ronnie warned mockingly.

"Don't be an ass, Ronnie," Weddy snapped.

"Thank you, Hank. You look nice as well." With that, Natalia caught sight of a group of her friends, including her best friend, Vicki. "Douglas, I'm going to go say hi to Vicki and the girls. I'll see you at the party?"

"Sure," I said. The boys always seemed to sit with the other boys and the girls with the girls at these bar mitzvahs. Only later, at the party, out on the dance floor or in the shelter of the shadows, would the two mix.

"See you later," she said to the group.

"Bye, Natalia," we said in unison.

"Looks like things are getting pretty serious between you two," Ronnie said, poking me in the ribs as Natalia walked away.

"It's good right now," I concurred.

"Hey, Ronnie!" I heard the unmistakable voice of Moose coming up behind me. "I see there's a hoop out there in the back of the parking lot. Maybe after the ceremony I can kick your ass in a little one on one." I turned around to see Moose and Clark approaching us.

"Fuck you, Moose. I'll take you *and* your girlfriend there on, spot you three buckets and still destroy you."

"What did you say, asswipe?" The Big Lefty was pissed at being called Moose's girlfriend, and I didn't blame him.

"Hey, guys," Weddy, being his usual diplomatic self, stepped in. "Come on, now. You're all acting like assholes. Don't ruin Lee's bar mitzvah for him. You're his guests for Christ's sake."

"Uh, Weddy, I don't think saying that other lord's name is allowed on temple grounds," I joked. Everyone laughed and the tension seemed to break, though Moose and Clark simply turned and walked away without saying anything, continuing to glare at Ronnie until they were out of sight.

"Goodbye, ladies," Ronnie called out after them, though they either didn't hear him or pretended not to hear him.

"Ronnie! Seriously?" Weddy asked.

"Sorry, buddy. I just can't help myself sometimes," the always straight-shooting Ronnie replied honestly.

"Hey. Anybody want to pitch some pennies?" Andrew asked, obviously trying to change the mood and the subject.

"Here?" Hank asked incredulously.

"We'll be struck down by the hand of God," I agreed.

"Or at least by the hand of Rabbi Jacobs," Weddy added, laughing.

"Besides, it's hot out here," Ronnie said. "Let's go inside."

"Pussies," Andrew muttered as he followed the rest of the group into the sanctuary.

"Anyone want to get high before we go in?" Weddy asked.

"We don't have time," Ronnie was quick to point out, displaying a rare showing of self-control and common sense. "Besides, we can run over to the alley in between the ceremony and the party."

Leave it to Ronnie to have it all planned out. He and Weddy loved a particular spot just off the alley behind our complex, because it offered a fair amount of seclusion, tucked as it was between the garages of two buildings

across the way. The only problem was that Hank's kitch-
en window looked right over it, so if his mom was standing at the sink, she had a direct view of them getting high.
"Those two hoodlums were smoking grass in the alley
again today," she'd tell me and Hank. "Are you sure you
don't know those boys?"

"No ma'am," I'd lie again and again. If she ever knew
Hank was hanging out with Ronnie and Weddy, she'd kill
him.

"Sounds like a plan, Sam." Weddy gave Ronnie a slap
on the back. You couldn't have picked two more mis-
matched characters to be friends than Weddy and Ronnie, yet I guess that shows the powerful ability of pot to
create bonds between people, turning even the unlikeliest
of kids into friends.

The ceremony was a typically boring affair. Hank and
I fidgeted in our seats and played "Rock, Paper, Scissors,"
and even a bit of "Paper Football" on the pews in the space
between us, very gently flicking the triangular piece of paper Hank had fashioned from a page torn out of the bar
mitzvah program on what was, out of necessity, an extremely short field. Ronnie and Weddy, after seeing what
we were up to, followed suit.

Lee, the bar mitzvah boy, seemed to do fine, though I
wouldn't really know if he screwed up. But at least there
weren't any groans from the audience. I heard a kid from
Cabrillo a couple of years ago actually got booed for his
poor Torah-reading performance. I guess everyone figured he deserved it for not taking it seriously enough—
it was well known that he had rarely attended Hebrew
school—and wasting their time. Needless to say, the party was a huge drag of an affair, and the kid's father was

seen smacking him on the head on numerous occasions throughout the evening.

Natalia was sitting next to Vicki a few rows up from us, on the other side of the aisle. She would turn and look over her left shoulder and smile and wink so many times during the ceremony, that Ronnie decided he should give me a pop in the ribs with his elbow every time she did it; I ended up with a couple of nice bruises as a result. Likewise, I noticed Vicki giggling and whispering to Natalia every time we exchanged glances.

It was becoming painfully obvious that I was going to be expected to dance with Natalia during the party and, as Hank was quick to point out, it undoubtedly meant that he would have to do the same with Vicki since the four of us would probably be hanging out together at some point. Hank didn't mind though; he and Vicki had known each other since grade school, and their older sisters were friends.

I, on the other hand, was not crazy about dancing, unless top-notch rock and roll was playing, and we would definitely not be hearing much top-notch rock and roll tonight. The band, as was de rigueur at all Encino and Tarzana bar mitzvahs and weddings, was the Allen Horn Band. Allen was the cousin of my dad's business partner, a talented horn player and band leader. His son Richard was the drummer, and his grandson was being groomed to take over keyboards one day. All in all, there were about a dozen players in the band, which primarily played the songs of the Big Band era—Glen Miller, Benny Goodman, Tommy Dorsey, and the like—and played them relatively well. It was stuff that Art listened to at home, some of which I actually enjoyed, though I wouldn't want to dance to it.

However, in a misguided attempt to be "groovy," the Allen Horn Band also did really bad covers of contemporary pop and rock, incredibly schmaltzy versions of everything from "Bad Bad Leroy Brown," to "Jungle Boogie," to a particularly horrible attempt at "Rikki Don't Lose That Number," which was the one song Allen allowed Richard to choose for the set. Like I said, I had seen these guys at least a dozen times, and was not particularly looking forward to dancing to their lame attempts at coolness. There was truly nothing at all inspiring about watching Allen Horn "get down" during the guitarist's solo on the Steely Dan number.

As soon as the Torah was paraded around the room and returned to the ark, the ceremony wrapped up quickly—gotta love the Reform Jews; they know how to keep things relatively short and sweet—and everyone made a hasty retreat for the doors.

"Well, that wasn't so bad," Ronnie said, seeming in a particularly good mood today. Someone had mentioned that his dad had gotten a good deal on an old Camaro and he was thinking about fixing it up and giving it to Ronnie when he got his driving permit next year. Ronnie was the oldest of all us, having been held back when the schools adjusted from the "A" and "B" format when we were little kids. I, on the other hand, skipped up during that transition, and I was young for my grade to begin with, so I wouldn't be driving until nearly this time in my *junior* year of high school. This meant that I would be relying on Ronnie, Weddy, and Hank to get around from the second semester of tenth grade all the way nearly through the end of eleventh grade. I was going to owe them big time by the time I would finally be able to drive.

"Yeah," Hank agreed, "gotta love the Reform Jews. They keep it short and sweet."

"That's what I was just thinking!" I shouted, perhaps a bit too excitedly, before executing the Soul Brother #2 handshake with Hank. There were seven Soul Brother handshakes in all, something only Hank and I shared. Number two featured the traditional hand clasp and fist bump opening but was finished off with each of us executing a finger gun, pointing our index fingers at one another while cocking our thumbs.

"You clowns want to join us in the alley?" asked Ronnie as he and Weddy began heading for the exit.

"Nah, I'm going to pass for now. Maybe later during the party," Hank answered.

"Okay, we'll see you guys in a bit," Weddy said as he and Ronnie turned and walked away.

"Want to check out our table?" I asked Hank. The party was in a large multi-purpose hall at the back of the temple. Besides hosting parties and events, they could even play basketball games in there; I heard the cantor had a sweet jump shot.

"Sure," Hank said. "I hope they sit the four of us together with some of our other friends."

Normally, all of the kids sat together, and all of the adults sat together. But everyone knew to sit me, Hank, Ronnie, and Weddy together, so that meant there was always two to four empty spaces at our table. Usually, they'd just put some other kids with us, whether we knew them or not, which was cool, but if we were down on the priority list, like today where we didn't really know the bar mitzvah boy all that well, we'd get the remainder table in the corner of the room where they just threw together whoever was left on the guestlist, meaning we could end up having a table like the one we had at Tammy Sanders' bat mitzvah, where we were sat next to Tammy's mom's distant cousin from Philadelphia who seemed oddly proud of the fact that he was a gynecologist, along with his second wife, who also happened to be his nurse, and his two glum-looking twin daughters, who had no idea why they'd been dragged across the country to the bat mitzvah of some relative they'd only met once or twice in their lives, and they had to do it with their bimbo of a stepmother in tow to boot.

Fortunately, when we found our table, we were happy to discover four of our classmates sitting there, at what was actually a pretty decent location. Evidently we were higher up on Lee's list than I had realized.

"Hi, Douglas!" I heard Natalia call out from behind. I turned to find her and Vicki sitting at the table directly in back of us.

"Hey, Natalia. Hey, Vicki."

"Hi, girls," Hank added.

"Want to join us?" Vicki asked. Hank and I both knew Vicki had wanted Hank to ask her out for a long time, but Hank just wasn't into her that way for some reason. It wasn't that he didn't like her—he did—but only as a friend, which was always tough for the person on the other end who wanted something more than that.

There was an empty seat on either side of the girls, so Hank and I moseyed over and sat down. We made small talk, mostly about the ceremony and the party, but eventually the conversation turned to sordid gossip about some of the kids we spotted in the room. "I heard that she went all the way with an eleventh grader over Christmas break," Vicki said about a girl in our grade I didn't really know.

"Oh my God," Natalia suddenly said, grabbing my arm. "I can't believe Lee invited Johnny Darling."

I looked over to see none other than Johnny Darling, dressed, as always, in a leather jacket, though he did have a matching leather tie for the special occasion. He was a tough kid who was already riding motorcycles even though he didn't have his permit yet. He was the second oldest kid in our class, right behind Ronnie.

"I thought Johnny beat Lee up last year," Vicki added.

"He did," Hank said. "But I think they made up once the school put them in AV together." It was true. Though neither of them wanted to do it, as a sort of penalty for their fight, which Lee had actually started in retaliation for all of the teasing Johnny had been torturing him with all year, the school arranged for them to both be in Audio Visual for the second semester, and now they had to work together, bringing projectors and films to various class-rooms and fixing and maintaining the equipment under the guidance of Mr. O'Leary, the brusque Irish AV teacher who was always yelling at his AV students to "quit acting the maggot!" In the course of all of this, Lee and Johnny had evidently become friends.

The party proceeded along standard lines: There was the candle-lighting ceremony, along with the obligatory playing of "Sunrise, Sunset" from *Fiddler on the Roof*; the proud speeches by the parents, siblings, and a couple of uncles and aunts; and, of course, the "Hava Nagila," com-plete with the hoisting of Lee up in the air while seated on a chair. This was always a blast unless you were the poor sap sitting in the chair terrified that a bunch of drunk adults and inattentive teenagers were going to drop you to your death.

Somewhere between the rubbery chicken and the Mexican flan that I always called "phlegm" because of their similar consistencies, Ronnie and Weddy reappeared, having spent half of the party in the alleyway. "What's up, fellas?" Weddy said through particularly squinty eyes, even for him.

"Yeah," Ronnie added, "what'd we miss?"

"Aside from Lee's drunken uncle getting tossed from the stage by Allen Horn when he tried to take over the microphone during a particularly sunny version of, well, 'Sunny,' not much," I answered.

"Yeah, that and the fact that Johnny Darling is here," Hank added.

"Johnny's here?" Ronnie said in disbelief. "Where is he? I love that guy."

We pointed out Johnny's whereabouts and Ronnie took off, in search of his similarly aged soulmate. Johnny had made it clear to everyone that he didn't really care much for Ronnie, but Ronnie wasn't one to let a small detail like that stop him. He thought Johnny was the height of coolness and hoped to ride motorcycles with him one day, so he continued to pursue his friendship no matter how many times Johnny rebuffed his efforts.

Weddy looked down at his food with the hunger of an underfed hyena and enthusiastically began diving into the chicken that had been sitting at his seat for a good forty-five minutes. He obviously had the munchies something awful and was in the process of chowing down his meal in about thirty seconds flat. Hank and I stared in silent amazement.

"Jesus, Weddy," Hank said. "Aren't they feeding you at home?"

"What?" Weddy said, glancing up from his plate while chewing a particularly large bite of white meat, tiny bits of chicken dropping from his lips.

"Slow down, dude. You're going to choke."

"Oh," Weddy said, waving his hand at Hank and putting down his fork and knife momentarily to grab a drink of water. "Sorry. Didn't eat lunch, and Ronnie's dope always gives me the munchies." He then took about three more large bites and was finished. "Ummm, ummm, good," he said, rubbing his belly.

"You're a freak, Weddy," I said. "But we love you for it." Weddy just smiled and scanned the room with a glazed look in his eyes.

"You boys ready to dance?" I looked up to see Natalia and Vicki standing behind Hank. The band had broken into a particularly peppy version of "Love Will Keep Us Together," the new Captain and Tennille song that was currently climbing the charts and seemed destined to dominate the radio for the foreseeable future. Hank and I rose from our seats and began to escort our ladies to the dance floor, which was filling up quickly, much to the delight of Allen Horn, who was singing the tune with a great deal of enthusiasm, even for him.

"Weddy," Vicki turned as we left the table, "Karen is sitting alone over there. Why don't you ask her to dance?"

I turned to see Vicki's friend looking directly at us, certainly keyed into what Vicki had just said, so Weddy really had no choice but to get up and go over and ask her to join him on the dance floor. Karen was pretty cute and everything, but her dad was a cop, working in the narcotics unit, so for a stoner like Weddy, she wasn't someone he'd normally hang out with. After spending half the party in the alley with Ronnie, Weddy undoubtedly reeked of pot, so it'd be interesting to see how Karen would react to him especially if we were on the dance floor and Allen Horn decided to slow things down with a ballad, requiring everyone to dance cheek-to-cheek.

Fortunately, the band kept things on the up-tempo side for the next half-hour or forty-five minutes, running through chart-topping hit after chart-topping hit, and we all had a great time dancing together. Natalia looked beautiful and was playful and sexy and extremely kind when it came to complimenting my, shall we say, "creative" dance moves. Hank, on the other hand, was a stud, as his incredible athleticism translated easily on the dance floor, where he looked like a *Soul Train* dancer, often breaking into moves and short routines to songs like "Kung Fu Fighting" and "Rock the Boat" that could leave you breathless. During the band's cover of "I Want You Back," people all around us literally stopped dancing to watch Hank do his Michael Jackson thing, and broke into spontaneous applause when the song was finished, not for the band, but for Hank and his fluid dancing.

"You're amazing!" Vicki cried out joyfully.

"Thanks," Hank said casually. Just another day at the office for my talented, athletic friend.

Predictably, the dancing portion of the set came to an end with the introduction of a string of syrupy ballads, beginning with "The Way We Were," and continuing through "Seasons in the Sun" and "Killing Me Softly with His Song." Evidently, Lee or his parents had requested that Allen play more contemporary stuff and less of the big band tunes. The evening would wind down in a slow haze, the lights dimmed as the party gradually began to peter out, Natalia and I wrapped in each other's arms, her fingers gently playing with the back of my long hair while I slowly stroked her cheek and looked into her emerald-green eyes. We kissed, several times, and held each other tightly, feeling our hearts beating together as one. Life was good.

Even Hank seemed to be enjoying himself, holding Vicki close and swaying to the music. Weddy had been able to escape Karen as soon as the music slowed down, having been rescued by Ronnie who had presented some excuse to Karen for having to leave with his friend, and once off the dance floor the two of them immediately high-tailed it out of there, undoubtedly heading straight to the alley to enjoy a doobie nightcap.

When the evening was over, Hank walked Vicki outside to go find her parents' car, while Natalia and I walked back home together, hand-in-hand, enjoying the moonlight and the balmy evening; summer was definitely around the corner, along with all of the endless possibilities it brought with it. "Are you going to be around much this summer?" I asked her.

"Yeah, when I'm not working in my dad's store," she answered with a frown.

"I know. I'm trying to avoid having to work in my dad's warehouse."

"Do you think you'll have to?"

"Tough to say. He'll definitely want me to, but my mom might stick up for me and say I don't have to. And now that they're divorced . . ." My voice trailed off. "Anyway, I hope we can spend a lot of time together this summer," I said after a few uncomfortable moments, the combination of the dancing, the springtime air, and the powerful vibe between us making me feel brave and bold.

"I'd like that," she replied, looking me in the eyes as I held the iron gate to our complex open for her. She kissed me lightly on the lips and I felt my heart skip a beat.

"I'll definitely have weekends free," she said. "And I'll be home every day by four or five. My dad doesn't make me work until closing. My mom usually picks me up in the mid-to-late afternoon."

"Cool," I said. We approached her unit and stood outside the gate to her patio.

"I had a really nice time tonight, Douglas," Natalia said softly while brushing my bangs out of my eyes.

"Me, too," I replied. "It was a lot of fun dancing with you." I pulled her tight and felt my penis start to get hard against her body.

"Now, now," she smiled. "Don't get too fresh, little boy." We kissed, our tongues twisting around and around for what seemed like eternity until she broke off and pulled away. She glanced up at her parents' window on the second story overlooking us. The lights were dark, but you never knew if Mr. Guinzburg was lurking in the shadows. "I better go," she said, her cheeks most definitely flushed. "I'll call you tomorrow."

"Goodnight, Natalia," I said as she turned to unlock the door. I almost said the "I love you" words, but thought better of it. "Talk to you tomorrow" was all I could manage. Natalia smiled, batted her eyes, and shut the door. I walked back to our unit and realized for the first time this spring that the Jacarandas were in bloom, their incredible indigo flowers bursting from every tree in sight. Some people hated the smell of the flowers, but others, like me, loved these trees, and legend had it that if you were lucky enough to have a flower fall from a tree and land on your head, a particularly long run of good luck was coming your way. As I approached the gate to our patio, I reached up and, lo and behold, plucked a fresh Jacaranda flower from my shoulder. Did that count?

As soon as I walked in the door, my mom, whose alarm never failed to amaze me—no matter how quietly I came into the house, she always heard me—called out, "Hi, honey! How was it? Did you have a good time?"

"Hi, Mom. Yeah, it was fun."

"Come in here and talk to us," she said. She and Art were in the small TV room off of the kitchen. I made my way up the stairs to the second level where I saw L coming out of the TV room, wagging her tail.

"Hey girl," I said, bending down and giving her a kiss on her forehead. She had a beautiful coat, and while most people wouldn't necessarily consider her to be a "sweet" dog—she'd always had a bit of a nervous edge to her and living cooped up in a townhouse with no yard hadn't helped her disposition—we all loved her anyway.

"Hi, Mom. Hi, Art," I said as I entered the TV room. They both immediately burst into howls of laughter. I turned toward the screen to see Tim Conway as an incompetent dentist on the *Carol Burnett Show*, unintentionally stabbing himself in his arm and then in his leg with a needle filled with Novocain. As usual, Harvey Korman, Conway's "patient," unsuccessfully tried to stifle his laughter while Conway hilariously limped about the room with a dead arm and a dead leg. The three of us howled with laughter right through to the end of the scene, when the show took a break for a commercial.

"Those guys always crack me up," Art said. He was lying there in his favorite recliner, dressed in a light blue, one-piece jumpsuit, the zipper pulled halfway down the front, revealing his tan, muscular chest and the gold chain he wore around his neck. A small, golden horn of some sort hung from the chain. Art, who religiously golfed with his buddies twice a week, on Tuesdays and Saturdays, was perpetually tan; he loved being out in the sun, whether it was on the golf course, at the beach in Malibu where he used to live, or just around the pool at the back of our complex.

While Art was a pretty good golfer, shooting in the low eighties on a regular basis, he was an even better pool and ping-pong player. And I never saw anyone throw a Frisbee better than Art. He was left-handed, and when he tossed a Frisbee he had a unique motion, more of a flip than a throw, but man was he accurate, and he could make that thing fly a mile. He claimed Ryan O'Neal taught him the technique when the two of them used to hang out on the beach in Malibu on occasion. This was during Art's "wild days" as my mom called them, though she had since tamed his swinging early-seventies behavior, and he was now the picture of the perfectly domesticated husband— or live-in boyfriend, anyway.

All in all, David, Julie, and I liked Art okay enough; he was certainly better than the small parade of boyfriends my mom had had in the wake of her marriage, none being worse than Mike, who actually lived with us for a short time. From the get-go, David, Julie, and I pegged Mike for a pathological liar; it was so obvious to us, but my mom, blinded by the passion of a post-divorce affair, just wouldn't believe us.

Whether it was his stories of running guns for the Black Panthers in the sixties, or having made a million dollars as an early investor in Mr. Coffee—he also claimed to personally know Joe DiMaggio, and even promised to introduce us to him, but of course that never happened, though he did give me an "autographed" poster of good ole Joe holding up a cup of coffee freshly made in his Mr. Coffee machine—Mike was always full of tall tales or flat-out lies. Just for kicks, David and I took the DiMaggio poster over to the baseball card shop in Tarzana where they confirmed the signature was a fake, obviously forged by Mike himself. My mom finally saw the light when a friend of a friend told my mom about how Mike was aggressively hitting on her at a real estate seminar.

A year or so before the seminar, when they were first starting to date, Mike had told my mom that his future fortune was to be made as a real estate baron. He had originally claimed that he was planning to buy "well-kept" foreclosures in "up-and-coming neighborhoods," but my mom had recently discovered through another friend who was married to a realtor that, in reality, Mike had bought a couple of filthy, rundown homes he had picked up on the cheap in foreclosure down on the steps of the courthouse in San Fernando, and which he was now renting out to poor Mexican families. The coup de grace came on a Sunday in early May, when Mike, his son Jimmy, David, me, and my mom drove out into the wilds of Tujunga, where Mike had found a home in a non-descript suburban neighborhood set right up against the Angeles National Forest, a tinderbox of hundreds of thousands of acres of government wildland. Homeowners in this area couldn't even buy fire insurance because no company in their right mind would insure anything within miles of here.

We took Mike's convertible Cadillac, an older model with a lot of miles and cracked white leather seats, but which suited Mike to a T. Jimmy sat up front, of course, as he was a big kid. Only a couple of years older than me, and younger by about as much than David, Jimmy stood well over six feet, maybe even six-one or six-two; it was tough to tell for sure because Jimmy was also overweight, definitely in the neighborhood of two-fifty, or at least knockin' on the door. He had been an offensive lineman in high school as a freshman, but a knee injury and, honestly, a lack of athleticism, put an early end to his football playing dreams. He was pretty much an irritable asshole most of the time, just like his dad.

Apparently, Mike had only recently bought this house, but he already had to evict the first tenants he had rented the house to after only a few months for failing to pay their rent. They were supposed to have moved a couple of days ago, and Mike didn't really have any reason to believe they hadn't moved out, but just in case he had insisted that Jimmy, David, my mom, and I accompany him out there to check up on the place. If there were any issue, Mike knew there was strength in numbers, even if that meant recruiting his girlfriend and his girlfriend's kids, especially David, who was pretty good with his fists.

We pulled up to the house—a crappy post-war job built on the quick and set on top of a postage-sized lot—and I'm sure there were plenty of raised eyebrows among the neighbors as five white people crawled out of a convertible Caddy. As we approached the front door and saw the empty walls and rooms through the windows, it was obvious that the tenants had moved out as promised. However, ferocious, maniacal barking roared at us from behind the walls, stopping us dead in our tracks halfway up the cracked and uneven used brick walkway. Two enormous black Dobermans appeared at the living room window, their paws pounding on the glass so hard it was a wonder it didn't break into a million pieces.

The tenants had moved out all right, but they had left their dogs behind.

"Jesus Christ!" Mike moaned.

"Those poor animals!" my mom cried out.

We walked around the house, the dogs going crazy the whole time, and through the dirty windows, we could see a few puddles of piss and some piles of poop dotting the worn-down parquet wood floors in the living room.

"What is wrong with people!" Mike complained.

"Hey! Come back here!" Jimmy shouted from the other side of the house. "You gotta see this!"

We all made our way around to the back door, which led directly into the kitchen. As we squeezed our heads together and peered in through the glass door, which was divided into a dozen or so panes separated by wood mullions with peeling pale green paint, we were stunned to see mounds and mounds of dog kibble covering the entire kitchen floor. Evidently, the people who left the dogs were "kind enough" to pour bags and bags of dog food onto the kitchen floor. There was enough kibble to easily sustain these two beasts for weeks.

"I wonder if they left them any water," my mom asked, concerned.

"Maybe they filled up the bathtubs," I suggested.

"You're probably right," David agreed.

"Well, I ain't going in there. Let's go home," Mike insisted.

"But what about the dogs?" I asked, alarmed. "After all, it's not their fault these people were assholes."

"Hey, watch your mouth." Mike hated cussing, but he had hooked up with the wrong family, as curse words were just words to us.

"All right, calm down, everyone," Mom said, ever the peacemaker. "We obviously can't go in there—those dogs will tear us apart. So let's go back home, and we'll call a shelter or the SPCA or even the dogcatcher if we have to."

"Sounds like a good plan to me," Mike said, starting to walk back to his Caddy.

"Don't you think you should leave a key?" my mom shouted to him. "Otherwise, you'll have to come all the way back out here to meet whoever we get to round up the dogs."

Mike turned around and started walking back toward my mom, a look of arrogant disgust on his face. "Are you crazy? Leave a key in a neighborhood like this? They'll strip the house clean. Every fixture and copper wire and copper pipe will be gone by tomorrow morning."

"First of all," my mom began to instruct, "I don't think there's one speck of copper in this piece of shit. It's definitely all PVC." One thing about my mom: Give her attitude, and she would throw it right back in spades. "Secondly, who in their right mind is going to break into a house with two nasty Dobermans on the other side of the door, you nitwit? Now go stick the key under a rock or something near the back door and let's get out of here." With that my mom stormed off toward the Caddy, leaving Mike slack jawed and silent. With hunched shoulders and the look of a hound dog who's just been scolded, he walked over to the kitchen door, found a rock in some half-dead bushes planted along the side of the house next to the door, and slid the key beneath it.

When we got home, my mom immediately confronted Mike about the girl she'd heard he'd been hitting on at the real estate seminar, and despite his denials she knew her friend was a reliable source, and so she threw him out of the house the next day, much to David's, Julie's, and my utter delight. Along with the obvious fact that he would always be a philanderer, my mom had lost all respect for him after seeing the rental house debacle up close and personal; she knew she could never be in a relationship with a slumlord.

She met Art not long after Mike left, and it was a relief to have someone who at least seemed honest and forthright and who treated my mom and all of us extremely well. Not that there weren't a few bumps in the road along the way. For instance, Art seemed to feel threatened by my dad's successful printing business, and while Art's automobile parts business was solid, he only had a couple of people working for him while my dad had dozens. So Art used to try and impress us with his money, like the time he handed me a hundred-dollar bill and asked me if I'd ever seen one before. I had, actually, though only once or twice before, and when I nonchalantly said "yes" and passed it back to him, he was obviously more than a little embarrassed. Later, my mom had to talk to him about not worrying about competing with my dad and to just be himself. Things were a lot better between all of us after that, at least until the Great Snoring Incident.

You see, Art had the habit of falling asleep in his

recliner in front of the TV at some point nearly every evening, before snoring so loudly that we couldn't even hear the TV no matter how loud we turned it up. The double Scotch he drank over the rocks at five o'clock every day when he got home from work undoubtedly contributed to his early evening sleepiness, but he worked hard for his money and looked forward to his daily, late-afternoon cocktail. One night his snoring was so bad that we started giggling, and when the giggling started to get more pronounced, Art woke up from his little catnap only to discover us laughing at him and he stormed out of the room, grabbed his keys, and rushed out the door. Nobody knew where he went, but he came back the next morning, obviously chastened by his overreaction, and apologized and even laughed about the event.

"Hey, Douglas, we have some exciting news!" my mom turned her head away from the TV and tried to get my attention. "Douglas?"

"Yeah, what's that?" I asked distractedly. My eyes were glued to an ad for Charlie perfume featuring a gorgeous blonde in a flouncy dress driving up to a nightclub in a convertible Rolls Royce, where she gets out and makes her way into the club, saying a knowing hello to every man who she passes by, before settling in with the guy who was apparently her lucky date for the evening. Damn she was hot.

"Hello?" my mom said again, annoyed that I wouldn't turn my eyes away from the commercial, which had now ended.

"Yeah, I'm listening," I said, finally turning my gaze toward her.

"David has found an apartment and is going to be

moving next week."

"Oh yeah?" I said. "Where is it?"

"On Balboa up near Sherman Way. It's a two-bedroom, and he's going to be sharing it with Sam."

"Cool," I said.

"And so," my mom continued, glancing over at Art with excitement, "Art and I have been talking and we think it'd be fun if we converted David's room into a sort of game room. We thought we'd get a pool table and maybe another TV for up there."

"Sounds like fun," I said.

"You could invite your buddies over for a game of pool," Art added. "I think we can probably hang a dart board on the wall as well."

"And Art can teach you how to play pool," my mom said.

"I already know how to play pool, Mom. My friends and I play in the clubhouse every now and then."

"Well, there're still a few tricks I can teach you." Art winked.

"I'm sure there are," I smiled wearily.

"I thought you'd be a little more excited," my mom groaned.

"I am, I am," I insisted. "I think I'm just a little tired from the bar mitzvah and everything. It's been a long day."

"Okay, honey. Why don't you get ready for bed and get a good night's sleep? You can tell me all about the party in the morning."

"Okay," I yawned. "Goodnight, Mom." I leaned over and gave her a kiss on the cheek, which she returned in kind. "Goodnight, Art. And I'm excited to play pool with you."

Art smiled. I knew that would make him feel good. Ditto for my mom. "Goodnight, kid," Art said warmly.

"I love you," my mom added.

"Love you, too," I softly said as I walked out the door and headed upstairs to my bedroom. It had been a really fun day, and I felt like things were going extremely well with Natalia. It would be cool to have a pool table; I could invite my friends over and impress them with my skills—once I got some practice under my belt, of course. Because while I did play with Hank every now and then in the clubhouse, I wasn't very good, and I knew that Art could probably help me up my game. Hank, as with everything sports-related he tried, was an excellent player, but I was confident that with Art's training, and some practice, I could probably become as good as he was one day.

I wasn't sure how I felt about David moving out, but I guess if he was cool about it, everything was all good. My relationship with him could probably best be described as a love-hate brotherly bond. Because my dad was so busy building his printing business by the time I came along, David became my de facto dad when it came to teaching me about all sorts of things. Sports, of course, was the biggest; it was David who taught me how to throw, bat, shoot... ..He introduced me to all kinds of amazing music, gave me the honest skinny on sex—he even taught me how to cheat at poker. We loved to listen to comedy albums together, from Bill Cosby to George Carlin to Cheech and Chong, and we had the same taste in TV shows as well, watching anything from *The Three Stooges* to *The Rifleman* to *Get Smart* to *The Beatles* Saturday morning cartoon show together on a regular basis. He even introduced me to many classic movies, from anything by Woody Allen—*Take the*

Money and Run was our personal favorite—to more so-
phisticated R-rated films like *A Clockwork Orange* or *The
Godfather*, parts one *and* two.

But the flip side of the coin was a bit darker. Again, David held quite a bit of jealousy toward me, and any shrink
worth his weight in salt would point to my "stealing" of
the title of "baby of the family" away from him, along with
the classic middle-child syndrome as the cause for his anger toward me. Most of it was stupid, passive-aggressive
stuff, like changing the channel on the TV when I was in
the middle of watching something, or stealing food off of
my dinner plate when I wasn't looking, or cheating me at
Monopoly so that I could never beat him.

Sometimes, though, the harassment got a little bit
more aggressive, like the time he was mad at me for some
unjustified reason and he threw me into the footwell behind the front passenger seat of my mom's Buick and,
while standing outside the car with the door open, proceeded to flip the switch that automatically moved the seat
backward while simultaneously holding me down with his
size twelve sneaker. I screamed and screamed as David's
newfangled torture device crushed me into a little ball.

Another time, David and Sam were going to their high
school baseball practice, and I really wanted to tag along.
I was only nine or ten at the time and thought it was cool
to watch the older guys play baseball. They really didn't
want me there, but my mom made them take me along.
However, after David backed the Buick out of the garage,
he told me that they had to pick up four other teammates
along the way and since there wasn't enough room for everyone, I'd have to ride in the trunk.

So into the trunk I climbed, and they slammed the lid

down. Every few minutes or so, the car would come to a stop, and I'd hear a car door open and some muffled voices. This happened on four different occasions, and I assumed there was a car full of baseball players on the other side of the wall separating me from the back seat. It was pretty hot and stuffy, and I started to sweat a little bit after we had picked up the last passenger, but I figured I had no choice but to deal with it as there was no way you could fit seven people in the car unless I sat on someone's lap, and there was no way that was going to happen. But upon reaching the baseball field, when David and Sam popped open the trunk, I climbed out and discovered it was all a gag; there was nobody else in the car, and David and Sam were falling all over themselves with laughter. In hindsight it *was* a pretty funny stunt, but David almost suffocated me to death in pulling it off.

David threatened me with real murder if I ever breathed a word of this to Mom or Dad, so I dutifully and fearfully kept my mouth shut. Of course, when I caught David and Sam climbing down the big olive tree in our backyard that reached up to the roof of our house, smelling like a skunk and giggling uncontrollably, I told Mom and Dad, and in the end David and Sam got in big-time trouble for smoking and *growing* pot on our roof. My mom told David that a nosy neighbor from across the street had seen the pair of boys on the roof and reported it to my parents, and to this day David had no idea that I was the fink.

Still, all in all, I was going to miss having David around. In some ways he was my best friend *and* my worst enemy, but doesn't a guy need both of those individuals in his life in order to become a man one day?

Chapter Four

By Memorial Day weekend, we were all itching for summer to get here, so we decided to brave the crowds and go to Magic Mountain. The trick was going to be how to convince someone's mom or dad or older brother or sister to take us there. Fortunately, my mom decided it was safer for her to take us than anyone else's parents, because she was probably the only parent who would actually spend the day inside the park, out of sight, but close by just in case we needed her.

From the day it opened, Magic Mountain had attracted a much rougher crowd than, say, Disneyland. Whereas Disneyland had this squeaky clean image with plenty of undercover security to keep everyone in line—there was even a rumor that they had guys with binoculars trained at all times on the Skyway, looking for people smoking joints as they sailed above Sleeping Beauty's castle (of course, that didn't stop any serious head from lighting up, and it was definitely the most popular place to get high in all of The Happiest Place on Earth)—it was pretty common to see long hairs in the parking lot chugging beers at nine in the morning at Magic Mountain. But at least that was better than when the park first opened and served alcohol inside the grounds. At that point, motorcycle gangs from Southern and Central California would practically take over the place, getting wasted, fighting, and throwing up in the bushes after going on the roller coasters drunk.

Stopping the alcohol sales put the kibosh on that action, and things were a lot more mellow now. The whole park had a much more relaxed vibe, and the focus was on the rides, which offered way more thrills than the tame attractions at Disneyland (Matterhorn excluded, of course). So, a plan was hatched for Hank, Weddy, and Ronnie to meet up on Saturday at 8:00 A.M. in the alley behind my garage.

Everyone loved my mom's car. With its boattail flowing across the trunk, the Riviera—part of the deal when my mom and dad got divorced—took on some of the look of a Corvette Stingray. It was pretty luxurious inside, and the guys had plenty of room in the back seat.

The morning was nice and warm, a perfect late-spring day for Magic Mountain, and we drove the whole way up there with the windows rolled down and the radio blasting. My mom was always a joy to drive with; she loved nothing better than the freedom of an open road, the stereo cranking any kind of music—from Streisand and Sinatra to the Stones and Wayne Shorter, she enjoyed it all—and every window rolled all the way down. Her love of music and the open road came from her youth, when she used to travel back and forth across the country with her mom and dad, a music-loving traveling salesman who hawked everything from Fuller Brushes to watches displayed from his wrist to his elbow, sold after striking up casual conversations with easy marks at gas stations. He'd approach guys minding their own business, just filling up their car with gas, show them the watches, gesture to his "hungry" family in his car, and would make the sucker a deal he couldn't refuse. By the time the chump would discover the watch was a piece of junk, a cheap knockoff of an expensive Timex that definitely couldn't take a licking and keep on ticking, he'd be down the highway, long out of town, the whole family singing songs like "Happy Days Are Here Again" at the top of their lungs.

"Let the sunshine in!" my mom sang along with the radio cranked all the way up, her flaming red hair blowing in the wind streaming through the open windows. I sat on my knees, facing the back of the car so that I could talk to my friends and, as usual, we argued about sports. Ronnie, whose parents were originally from New York, had inherited his dad's passion for the Yankees, the Jets, and the Knicks. Hank, Weddy, and I were L.A. all the way.

"I'll take Frazier over West any day!" Ronnie yelled over the roar of the air rushing into the car, which pretty much drowned out the radio in the backseat, forcing my mom to sing solo up front.

"Give me a break," Hank said calmly. "West was the best. They even designed the NBA logo after him."

"Oh, that's bullshit. It's not him!" Ronnie yelled.

My mom, who had been enduring this for a good thirty minutes, cranked up the radio even louder to better hear Linda Rondstadt, one of her absolute favorites, storm through "You're No Good," a huge hit these past couple of months.

We were far north of the Valley by now, and I knew the area well. Back when I lived in Northridge, I used to go to the swap meet at the Saugus Speedway with Nick Einhorn and his grandfather. Nick was a grade ahead of me, but he lived across the street, so we were close friends. His grandfather loved to go to the swap meet, and at least once a month he'd pick us up at 6:00 A.M. on a Sunday, and offer us fresh donuts that he had bought on the way over from the Helms Bakery truck. Nick and I would chow down warm maple bars and cinnamon rolls while his grandfather would tell jokes and make the car "dance" as we drove down the street, turning it in crazy directions all over the asphalt in time to whatever song was playing on the radio.

Once, Nick and I bought some mice at the swap meet to take home as pets, but they had simply given us the critters in a brown paper bag. We were scared that his grandfather would be mad at us for bringing them in the car, so we tried to hide them. But on the way home, the mice escaped from the bag and were crawling all over the back of the car where we were sitting. Nick and I were in hysterics, laughing our heads off as we tried to clandestinely catch the four mice—we had each bought two—and get them back in the bag. Meanwhile, his grandfather was looking at us in the rearview mirror, knowing something was up and getting agitated. "What is going on back there?" he began shouting. Nick's grandfather always had a cigar in his mouth, sometimes lit, sometimes not. Right now he was simply chewing on a stub. "What are you kids up to?" We were finally able to corral the mice, and Nick's grandfather was none the wiser.

Sure enough, upon pulling into Magic Mountain's parking lot, there were scattered tailgate parties going on. "What the heck are these people thinking?" my mom asked incredulously. "It's barely nine in the morning and they're already getting drunk." She just shook her head and looked for a spot away from any partiers, though it was impossible to escape the sounds of *Physical Graffiti* blasting throughout the parking lot. I found it funny that all these Zeppelin freaks were here on a day when the Monkees would be playing the Magic Mountain outdoor theater. Well, it wasn't *technically* the Monkees, but Davy Jones would be singing Monkees' songs, and one other guy from the band—Micky Dolenz—would be playing, along with a couple of other dudes they had picked up to fill in for Peter Tork and Mike Nesmith, who apparently had better things to do than tour as an oldies act. We had all grown up watching *The Monkees* TV show, and while their music was a bit poppy for my tastes, we were all looking forward to seeing the concert tonight.

As expected, we had a blast that day. We took advantage of getting there early and went on the most popular rides in the morning, figuring we'd save the less popular attractions and the carnival games for later in the day so that we wouldn't have to carry all of our winnings around with us; Hank alone was sure to take home a couple of the largest of the stuffed animals at the basketball booth, and Ronnie was a dead-eye shot at the BB gun competition, shooting out the red star on the piece of paper hanging at the back of the booth faster than anyone who dared to take him on. He even beat a cop once.

We must've gone on the Gold Rusher and the Log Jammer four or five times each, and even managed to get a couple of rides on the newer, and more crowded, Mountain Express a few times.

"I heard they're building a new roller coaster that's going to have a three-hundred-sixty-degree loop," Weddy said as we were waiting in the longish line for the Express.

"No fucking way," Ronnie snapped. "How would that even be possible? What? You're literally going to go around in a circle? You're full of shit!" he said, disbelieving.

"I'm telling you, I read an article about it in *The Times*," Weddy insisted.

"That's absurd! You'd fall on your head!" Ronnie waved Weddy off with his hand.

"Sounds cool to me," I said. "Sign me up."

"Sign me up," Ronnie mocked. "You're an idiot if you believe him."

We passed by an older guy as we were weaving back and forth through the line, and he had evidently heard us talking. "It's true," he said. "It's going to be called 'Revolution' and it should be ready by next summer." The man continued down the line, moving away from us.

"Told you," Weddy said to Ronnie.

"Oh, go fuck yourself. How would that old guy know?"

'Why don't you ask him yourself the next time we pass him?" Hank chimed in. But, of course, Ronnie remained silent and never said a word to the guy whenever we passed him in the serpentine line.

A couple of cute girls were a few pairs of riders behind the old guy, and every time they passed us they'd giggle and whisper to each other.

"Why don't you say something to them, Ronnie?" I suggested.

"Who? Those two girls? What, are you crazy? They're probably not even ten years old."

"Never stopped you before," Hank laughed.

"Fuck off, Hank," Ronnie said.

"I bet they're at least twelve," Weddy chimed in.

"No way," Ronnie insisted.

I honestly wasn't sure. I thought they might even be thirteen, but it was hard to tell these days, as even young girls were wearing skimpier and skimpier clothing and this pair was no exception, outfitted in matching bright yellow tube tops and very tight jeans shorts with plenty of holes and loose fringe at the bottoms. The next time we passed them in line, I decided to be bold.

"Excuse me, girls," I said, much to everyone's surprise. "My friend and I were having a little disagreement." I pointed over to Ronnie.

"I'm not involved in this!" Ronnie said, throwing up his hands.

"As I was saying," I continued, "we were trying to figure out how old you two girls were."

"We're eleven," they said, giggling once again and moving forward to fill in the gap that had formed in front of them.

We did the same, and as we moved away from them, Ronnie said, "Told you so!"

"I thought you said you weren't involved in this!" I teased. Needless to say, the next four or five times we passed the girls, Ronnie made inappropriate remarks about "jail bait," to which the girls simply giggled and blushed, whispering to one another as they moved in the opposite direction, only to meet again in a minute or two, until they boarded the ride ahead of us. We never saw them again for the rest of the day.

By the time early afternoon rolled around, we were starving, so we stopped off at one of the little snack bars they had set up around the park. We each ordered cheeseburgers and fries, and as we were making our way to an open table, I felt something squish under my foot.

"Oh, shit, man."

I looked in front of me and slightly to my left, and sitting at a small, square, red plastic table with four short benches—one on each side—were four Chicano lowriders, several years older than us, all dressed identically in bright white T-shirts and blue jeans. Except there was something different about one guy's shirt: It was splattered with red dots or paint or . . . the Mexican dudes were all looking right at me and I followed their eyes down to my foot where I discovered a ketchup packet peeking out from beneath my shoe. Evidently, the squish I had felt was the crush of the packet of ketchup under my foot, which I had inadvertently stepped on, causing the packet to explode and shooting ketchup spray directly at this one fellow, simply obliterating his crisp, white T-shirt with an onslaught of Heinz.

I immediately felt a huge lump in my throat and my heart sank like a stone. "I'm so sorry," I stammered. "I didn't mean to—let me get you some napkins." The Chicano guys just glared at me, not saying a word. As I sat my tray down on an empty table nearby, my friends were dumbfounded and stunned into silence. None of us could believe what had just happened. We had a group of lowriders at school, and while they were generally cool, they were also known to be fairly badass; you definitely didn't want to piss them off.

"I'll help you," Hank offered.

"Better not," I whispered. "If they're mad, better it's all on me." I went over to the counter of the snack bar and grabbed a huge pile of napkins. Walking back toward the ketchup splattered lowrider, I handed him the pile of napkins. "I'm really, really sorry," I repeated. "I didn't see the ketchup on the ground. I wish whoever dropped it would've picked it up."

Señor Heinz took the pile of napkins from me without saying a word; his friends just continued to glare. He slowly began to wipe the ketchup, but the napkins were of little help; his shirt was ruined.

"Is there anything else I can do? Do you want me to see if they have anything inside the snack bar they can clean it with?" He stopped wiping his shirt and slowly raised his eyebrows, not saying a word. He then turned away and started speaking Spanish to his friends. Growing up in the Valley, I knew bits and pieces of Spanish, especially the swear words, and I could make out several of them coming from his mouth. Finally, I simply turned and walked away, heading back to my friends, not knowing what was going to happen next.

"Fucking *pendejo*," I heard one of them say.

Ronnie suddenly stood up and threw his hands in the air, "Hey, come on now, *mis hermanos*. We're cool."

I turned and saw that all four of the guys were also now standing, and it looked like they meant business. Ronnie pointed to the guy next to Señor Heinz, a tall lanky dude wearing a Dodgers cap. "Hey, don't I know you from Phil's Garage? Your dad has that fifty-seven Chevy, right? The one with the Duntov cam?"

The Chicano dude was confused, couldn't figure out where this young white kid was coming from, what his game was, what he was trying to pull. But it was true: Ronnie's dad was a respected mechanic in the Valley, and a lot of the lowriders took their cars to him for repairs. He could fix anything, especially old Chevys, which were popular among the lowrider crowd who'd cruise Van Nuys boulevard every Wednesday night. In fact, Ronnie's dad regularly bought parts from Art, and Ronnie and I first met at an antique car show at the Hollywood Bowl that Art took me to and that Ronnie's dad took him to as well. Ronnie's dad and Art ran into each other and said hello, and then Ronnie and I recognized each other from school. We didn't really know each other all that well, but we spent some time that day looking at the cool cars together while our dads talked shop, and we discovered we lived a couple of blocks away from each other and just sort of became friends from that day forward. Ronnie is also how I actually met Weddy as they were friends before I knew either of them, though they became friends with Hank through me.

"I'm Phil's son, Ronnie. I met you one time when your dad came in to get a new timing chain. I think we were listening to the Dodgers game on the radio together when they beat the Pirates in the championship series."

A light went on inside the lowrider's head, and his mood changed in an instant. "Oh yeah!" he said smiling and tugging at his Dodgers cap. "That was such a great fucking game! Hey man," he said, stroking his chin which had the barest beginnings of a goatee growing, and becoming more serious, "your Pops is one badass mechanic." He looked at each of his friends, especially Señor Heinz. "My dad won't take his car to no one else, homies."

Ronnie now turned his attention to the guy whose shirt I had destroyed. "Again, my friend here is so sorry for the accident," he said, gesturing to me. I responded with the best puppy eyes I could muster.

"Let me make it up to you," Ronnie offered. "The next time your friend here comes into the garage, I'll give him a few free shirts with my dad's logo on them to give to you. To, you know, replace the one my friend here accidentally ruined. Cool?"

"Yeah, I guess so," the guy said, still obviously not thrilled, but at least he didn't seem like he was going to kick my ass any longer.

"What size are you? Medium? Large? You're a pretty tall dude, I'd say a large, right?"

"Yeah, a large is good."

"Alright, my friend," Ronnie said smiling. "We all good here? *Estamos bien*?"

The four Chicano dudes looked at each other and then nodded in unison.

"I'll see you soon at the garage," Ronnie finished, pointing back over to his dad's customer.

"Okay, *amigo*," the Dodgers cap guy said as the four of them slowly walked past us toward the exit, Señor Heinz continuing to dab at his shirt with the pile of napkins I had given him, but avoiding any eye contact with me.

"You're fucking lucky, dude," Ronnie said after they were gone. "I thought for sure they were gonna kick your ass."

"Jesus, I know," I said, still shaken by the whole incident. "I owe you one, Ronnie. Thanks, friend."

"Aw, don't mention it," Ronnie said, sitting back down to his lunch as if this were all in a day's work. He was cool as a cucumber, but my hands were trembling as I tried to pick up my cheeseburger. "And, anyway," he added in an attempt to reassure me, "I always got your back."

"What? You were gonna take on those guys?" Weddy asked.

"Why not?" Ronnie said with his typical bravado. "I ain't afraid of a bunch of lowriders. The three of us just shook our heads. Ronnie was certainly one of a kind.

After lunch, Hank suggested we go on some of the new spinning rides that had recently debuted at the park. None of us had considered, of course, that spinning rides right after lunch might not be the best idea, and sure enough after we walked off of Spin Out for the second time in a row, Weddy lost his cheeseburger and fries in the bushes just after we exited the round room where we had been stuck to the walls while everything spun around and around and around. Seeing Weddy lose it almost caused me and Hank to follow suit, but we managed to hold our cookies. Ronnie, of course, was unperturbed. "You guys are pussies," was all he said, walking away from three guys with a definite green tinge to their faces.

We went on a few of the minor rides, but got bored quickly and so decided to kill a couple of hours before The Monkees concert at the carnival-style game booths, and as expected Hank won two of the largest stuffed animals they gave away—the most they'd allow any one person to win—in basketball, and Ronnie kicked everyone's ass in the BB gun shootout, winning two prizes of his own, so for the rest of the day we each had to carry a stuffed animal around with us as they were so big that Ronnie and Hank couldn't possibly carry two of them by themselves. Fortunately, all we really had left to do was sit and watch the show, so it wasn't that big of a deal to carry them around and, besides, it was a great way to meet girls.

"Wow!" A beautiful blonde came up to Hank. "How'd you win that?"

"Basketball," Hank said proudly.

"Can you win one for me?" she asked, rather drunkenly. Before Hank could answer a guy appeared and yanked her away by the arm.

"Maybe next time!" Hank called out after her, laughing.

While we milled around the front of The Showcase Theater, Ronnie was sweet-talking a pair of young cuties from Pasadena. "You must be pretty good with a gun," I heard one of the girls say to him. I couldn't hear Ronnie's response as his back was to me, but he undoubtedly was regaling them with tales of his dexterity with firearms.

The Monkees show was okay if you didn't take it too seriously. Davy sang all the hits, from "Last Train to Clarksville" to "I'm a Believer" to "Stepping Stone," and the four of us danced ourselves silly, even holding up the stuffed animals high in the air while we moved to the music. I could see my mom near the front of the theater, dancing and singing with all her heart. You gotta love a mom who digs The Monkees.

The drive home was a relatively quiet and solemn affair. Ronnie and Weddy, burned out from all the weed they had smoked throughout the day, were asleep before we even left the parking lot. Hank and I chatted quietly for a bit, but eventually even he nodded off, and upon seeing the comforting lights of the Valley after we passed through the Golden State and San Diego Freeway split, I joined my friends in a peaceful slumber, none of us waking up until my mom pulled into our complex and gently alerted us that we were home.

Chapter Five

The final couple of weeks of the school year flew by, and before we knew it, the last day of school was here. I woke up extra early, took a shower, blew dry my hair for that perfect feathered look, and dressed up in a pair of nice jeans with a tucked-in short-sleeved shirt with multi-colored, horizontal stripes. I also picked out my favorite leather belt, brown and wide with pairs of holes running throughout to match up with the two-pronged buckle. My Superstars completed the look.

When I got downstairs, my mom was already making breakfast in the kitchen. "Good morning, honey. Excited about your last day of school?" she said as she flipped over the French toast cooking in the pan on top of the electric stove.

"Yeah, really excited," I answered.

"Well, you look very nice," she responded, giving me the once over. "How about some breakfast?"

"I really gotta go, Mom. Hank and I want to get to school early and get our yearbooks." I was psyched to participate in the annual ritual of having kids "autograph" my yearbook. Last year, I barely knew anyone well enough to even ask them to sign, but this year I had plenty of friends, and was particularly looking forward to seeing what Natalia was going to write; we had promised to save a whole page in our yearbooks for each other.

"But I got up extra early to make you a nice breakfast,"

she implored. "Come on, sit down. It's almost ready," she continued, pointing over to the empty chair at the kitchen table, where a place had already been set for me, complete with a glass of orange juice.

I grudgingly capitulated, and after wolfing down a couple of pieces of French toast in record time, I flew out the door. "Bye, Mom! Thanks for breakfast!" I slammed the door behind me, so enthusiastic to get to school that I didn't even wait for her to respond.

As I reached the front gate to our complex, Hank was there waiting for me. "Sorry," I said as I walked up. "My mom made me eat breakfast."

"That's okay," Hank said. "I just got out here myself. We should be able to make the seven-ten bus if we jam."

We hustled up Lindley to Ventura where, sure enough, the 7:10 RTD pulled up within moments. It was perfect timing. Settling into our seat, Hank and I discussed the main topic of the day: which girls were we going to ask to sign our yearbooks?

"Well," I began, "obviously Natalia is number one on my list."

"Obviously," Hank reiterated. "But if I know you, you're going to try to fill up every page in that book."

"After my pathetic attempts to get people to sign last year, you're right on the money!" I laughed. "Who are you going for?"

"Allison specifically asked me to save a page for her," Hank began, "but I'm also going to go up to Charlotte and see if she'll sign."

"Really? Charlotte Horner? You're a brave man, my friend." Charlotte was probably the most popular girl in the whole school, a ninth grader whom Hank knew from

Band. Hank played the trumpet, and Charlotte played the saxophone, so they had become somewhat friendly with each other, though I had a feeling Hank might be overestimating the depth of their relationship.

When we arrived at school we were surprised to see how many kids were already there; apparently, we weren't the only ones with the "let's get to school early" idea. Lines had already formed at tables where teachers sat with stacks and stacks of yearbooks, handing them out to those who had already paid, and making sure nobody tried to snake a yearbook without paying for it.

It was a typical last day of school, with both teachers and students getting along famously, a loose, friendly vibe washing over the whole campus. Even Principal Carter was in a good mood, standing by the front gate and welcoming everyone as they came to school, something he had only done two or three times all year, and only on days when parents were visiting for some special event or morning assembly.

Scenes of laughter and kids rushing up to one another, open yearbook in hand, were spotted throughout the campus and continued from the opening bell to the closing one. "Hey, will you sign my yearbook?" must've been repeated a hundred thousand times that day.

The truth was, you could really ask anyone to sign, because who was going to say no? It would be rude and totally uncool. Of course, if you asked someone who really didn't know you all that well, or didn't even know you at all, you were likely to discover something like this autograph from Darlene, a girl who I actually thought had a crush on me, written in the corner of a miscellaneous page:

Douglas—
Even though I don't really know you, you seem like
a nice guy and I enjoyed being in English class with
you. Maybe next year we can become better friends.
Have a good summer.
Darlene

It could be a harsh awakening in some cases, but gen-erally people were nice and let people down easy when it was apparent that they really wanted nothing to do with them and didn't consider them a friend or even an acquaintance.

Then, of course, there were the friends who just couldn't resist getting in a couple of digs:

Douglas,
You think you are good in basketball, but you are
the biggest gunner I've ever known. The next time
you are shooting with three guys in your face, think
about passing me the ball.
Your friend,
Alex

It was true I was a gunner, but the reason I didn't pass the ball to Alex was because, while his defense was solid, his offense sucked, and passing him the ball invariably re-sulted in a turnover.

Ronnie, of course, relished writing in yearbooks, as it was the perfect outlet for his warped sense of humor:

To my good buddy Douglas,
Knowing you this past year has been as much fun
as getting my eye poked out with a sharp stick. You
think you are good with girls, but I know what they

all say behind your back. Especially Natalia. You
are the worst basketball player I've ever seen and
I look forward to kicking your butt in 1 on 1 over
the summer. I'd tell you to stay cool this summer,
but you are the uncoolest guy I have ever met. Just
kidding. Weddy is the uncoolest guy I've ever met.
Here's to a fun-filled summer. Maybe we can go to
the beach together. Or not.
Your friend (sometimes),
Ronnie

Another guy who I barely knew went around signing
everyone's yearbook he could get to on the "In Memori-
am" page, simply writing:

Wish you were here.

As the early afternoon rolled around, I still hadn't
seen Natalia and was worried that maybe she hadn't come
to school. Finally, as I was walking to my last class, I heard
her call my name, and my heart skipped a beat. "Hey, you,"
I said. "Where have you been? I haven't seen you all day."

"Oh my God," she rolled her eyes. "First I was late because my sister insisted on making my mom take her to
school first."

"Really?" I said. "But her school is way out near Topanga. She always drops you off first."

"Exactly!" Natalia said. "But my sister had something
she insisted she had to do before school, so I had no choice
in the matter."

"That's a drag," I empathized. I had had plenty of experiences with older siblings' desires taking priority over
mine.

"Anyway, my whole day just sort of fell apart from

there. I couldn't even get my yearbook until after second period," she frowned.

"I'm sorry," I said, taking her hand. "Do you want to sign my yearbook?"

"Of course! But can we do it after school? I have something special I want to say, but there's not enough time before our last class."

"Sure!" I said, excited and wondering what special message Natalia was planning to write. At the same time, I realized I had better start thinking about what I was going to write in her yearbook.

"Cool," she turned, hurrying off in the other direction. "Meet me on the senior quad?"

"Sounds good," I called off after her. There was a tradition that the senior quad was opened up to eighth graders after the final bell on the last day of school as a taste of the power we would hold once school started up again in September.

I ran into Hank and we headed over to our final class of the year: Filmmaking. It was by far our favorite class of the day, full of offbeat, creative kids and the hippest teacher on campus, Mr. Paulson, a tall, slim, gay English teacher with a wide, thick horseshoe mustache that reached down below the cleft of his chin. His mane of blond hair was cut into a perfect shaggy do, complete with wispy spikes on the top. He favored tight, flat-front jeans with zippers on either side of the crotch, and plaid shirts buttoned down to just above his navel.

Hank and I had made two spectacular Super 8 silent films this past semester, one animated and one live-action. The live-action film took up the bulk of our time, as it was like a half-dozen movies in one. We called it "What

If?" and the idea was a series of sketches portraying historical events and what *would have* happened *if* things had gone differently. For instance, one scene featured a title card that read:

HENRY FORD INVENTED THE AUTOMOBILE

Then we cut to Art, as Henry Ford, stepping into his car and driving off. This was followed by another title card that read:

WHAT IF GERALD FORD HAD INVENTED THE AUTOMOBILE?

Cut to Art, as Gerald Ford, mounting a tricycle on the sidewalk and riding away.

It was a lot of fun to make, and it generated a lot of laughs in the class. There were "What If?" scenes substituting George Wallace for Abraham Lincoln and their different responses to slavery, Richard Nixon for George Washington and their different reactions to getting caught chopping down the cherry tree . . . well, you get the gist. Mr. Paulson absolutely loved it, found it hilarious, and gave both of us an A+. The only problem was we had spent so much time on "What If?" that we barely had time to make our second film, and Mr. Paulson required you to make two films of at least five minutes apiece in order to pass the class.

So just a couple of weeks ago, Hank and I got together to figure out what the hell we were going to do. We had to come up with an idea and shoot a five-minute film that weekend, get it into the photo developing place by the end of the day on Monday in order to get it back on Wednesday (if we paid extra to rush it), edit it on Thursday, and turn it in by the deadline this past Friday.

"We have to think about something that would be easy to do, not nearly as complicated as 'What If?' was to make," I suggested.

"You know," Hank said, "we've always had a pretty easy time making stop-motion stuff. Why don't we do that?"

It was a brilliant idea. Hank and I had messed around with my Super 8 camera a bunch of times and had experimented with stop-motion animation as well. One of our great triumphs was "The Blob Who Ate the World," in which a Blob made out of a lump of clay slowly eats his way across the globe. Literally. We actually used a globe and as the Blob would pass over, say, Australia, we'd make Australia disappear through stop-motion animation, turning it into nothing but blue ocean on the globe. We thought it was brilliant, of course.

"Okay," I said, "let's do it. What should we do? What's the story? What's the subject?"

"How about sports?" Hank said. Another great idea. We both loved sports. And then it occurred to me: The 1976 Olympics were coming next summer, and the hype had already begun. Bruce Jenner and Shirley Babashoff, a local SoCal girl who was the most dominant swimmer in the world, were going to be the superstars, and their faces were already being plastered all over newspapers and magazines.

"Why don't we do an animated Olympics?" I asked.

"That'd be cool. But how are we going to do it? Draw it?"

"No, no," I said, shaking my head, "that would take way too long. We have to use figures to represent the athletes."

"Would we make them out of clay?" Hank asked.

"We could, but that might also take too long."

"Well, then what can we use? Toy soldiers? Or dolls?"

Once again, as Mr. Paulson would say, "The doors of perception opened up to me."

"I think we should do something funny. Like, let's use peanuts and call it 'The Peanut Olympics.' We can paint each peanut a different color to represent their country—blue for the U.S., red for Russia, white for Japan, yellow for Sweden, and green for Kenya. That sort of thing."

"Ha! That's classic!" Hank roared. We spent the remainder of the weekend filming "The Peanut Olympics" in my bedroom and my bathroom. For the swimming event, we took my mom's glass Pyrex baking dish, placed it on a striped towel, and filled it with water. We then took Scotch tape and ran strips of tape lengthwise following the stripes to create an invisible way to keep the peanuts in their lanes. We started the race, and while I took a frame or two at a time, Hank used a little stick in between shots to move each peanut up a bit in the water.

We had very successful running events where the peanuts raced around the oval track, but our biggest challenge was the high jump. We created a set consisting of a white foreground and background by using a white sheet and a piece of white foam core board. In between stop-motion shots, we then placed books beneath the peanut, simultaneously raising it up and moving it toward the high jump itself. It was incredibly effective, and on final viewing the peanuts truly looked like they were jumping high into the air, but once they actually reached the high jump, we couldn't figure out how to get the peanuts over the bar. You couldn't push them over because our fingers or stick or whatever we might use to give them a shove would be visible to the camera.

That is, until Hank came up with a fantastic idea: "I'll stand off screen holding your blow dryer, and as soon as you say go, I'll turn it on and blow the peanut over the bar." It was yet another effective solution and appeared to work brilliantly.

We finished the film after school on Monday, and Art drove us over to the little film hut at the corner of Corbin Plaza, getting us there moments before they closed. Hank and I each breathed a sigh of relief; we had met our deadline.

Upon getting the film back, we discovered a couple of flaws that we hadn't anticipated. First, the swimming race was so fast, maybe six seconds tops, that when we added a soundtrack that we recorded on my Panasonic cassette tape recorder and played it back during the showing of the film, our announcing of the event sounded like one of those guys on the radio trying to get in thirty seconds of legal jargon at the end of an ad in, like, two seconds. The other thing that didn't quite pan out was that when the peanuts got blasted by the blow dryer at the top of their high jumps, they wobbled back and forth for a bit before finally falling over the bar. It wasn't exactly the smoothest of effects, but it generated more than its fair share of laughs.

All in all, though, the little hiccups gave the film a certain charm, and once again Mr. Paulson awarded us an A+. He was especially impressed with our creativity in crunch time, as he was more than aware that we had spent far too much time on "What If?" and had left ourselves with little room to create a second film.

"Hello, boys!" Mr. Paulson said as we entered the class. "How are my favorite filmmakers?" We were the first ones to arrive, so he felt free to say that, though everyone in the class knew we were his favorites anyway.

"Hi, Mr. Paulson," we said in unison.

"Since it's the last day of school, I have a question for you: What was your favorite thing about this class?"

"I loved making the films," was my immediate response.

"And I thought that director dude you brought in to talk to us was really cool," Hank added.

The "director dude," Hank was referring to was Roger Corman, who was a friend of Mr. Paulson's. As he was mostly known for making rowdy biker and sexy nurse films, there were more than a few parents who questioned Paulson's judgment in bringing Corman in to talk to us, but we all thought he was totally cool, and it turned out a bunch of famous actors had gotten their start in Corman's B movie productions, including Nicholson and Fonda. Hell, even Coppola and Scorsese worked for him when they were first starting out.

"Nice!" Mr. Paulson said, stroking his mustache and smiling widely.

"Hi, Mr. Paulson!" Just then, Sandy, whose two films were both about the plight of the American Indians, walked in the door.

"Hey, Sandy," he replied. "We were just talking about this past semester. What was your favorite part of the class?"

"Definitely watching 'The Peanut Olympics," she laughed. Like I said, our films were really popular with the other kids.

"Speaking of which," Sandy said, holding out her yearbook to me, "can I get an autograph from the genius of the class?"

"You're too kind," I said, blushing.

"What am I?" Hank blurted out. "Chopped liver?"

"No, no," Sandy said, reaching out and grabbing his arm. "I want you to sign, too! It's just, you know—" Sandy didn't continue, but instead simply smiled at me.

I always thought Sandy might have a little crush on me, but I was never too sure. Today confirmed it. It's funny how the last day of school always made people a bit more bold. Guys who always wanted to tell girls how they felt about them and girls revealing their true feelings to guys always seemed to happen with regularity on the final day of the year. Often times, these feelings were divulged in the autographs themselves, and today with Sandy would be no exception.

> *Dear Douglas,*
> *It's been soooooo much fun being in filmmaking class with you this semester. Your films were brilliant! I especially loved The Peanut Olympics. So funny! I hope we can continue to be friends next year. What are you doing this summer? Maybe you can come to a rally with me. Call me! 555-7673.*
> *Love,*
> *Sandy*

The truth was, Sandy was a little bit too intense for my taste. She was really into all of these different causes— the Indians, the environment . . . she even refused to eat grapes because of something to do with the farm workers not being treated right. I respected everything she was doing, but I wasn't into hanging out at rallies listening to a bunch of speeches and waving banners around. It just wasn't my scene; I doubted I'd be calling her.

During filmmaking class, Hank and I also exchanged autographs. Hank wrote:

Douglas,
It's been great getting to become close friends this
year. Let's have a blast this summer and rock this
school as 9th graders!
Your friend,
Hank

The shortest autographs were usually the ones from your closest friends. We were around each other so much, and talked to each other practically every single day, so what could we possibly write in our yearbooks that hadn't already been said or implied?

The final bell rang, and madness broke out all around the school. Everywhere you looked, kids were tossing papers from their notebooks in the air and throwing away textbooks and supplies and printed and graded assignments into the overflowing trash cans that dotted the campus. It seemed like every other kid was holding a portable radio with "School's Out for Summer" blasting out of every single speaker, over and over again. Screaming and hugging and running like wild coyotes was very typical behavior.

I spotted Natalia from across the senior quad, and we ran toward each other, meeting perfectly in the center of the grass and throwing our arms around each other and kissing each other deeply on the lips. We eventually found a quiet corner near the cafeteria where we could sit down and write autographs in our yearbooks. Each of us had saved a whole blank page for the other.

Dear Natalia,

My life has changed in so many ways since I first met you. The sky seems bluer, trees are greener, the air even seems cleaner. When I listen to songs on the radio, they often remind me of you, or of us. Whether it's Van Morrison singing "Crazy Love," or George Harrison on "Something," or Joe Cocker wailing through "You are So Beautiful," I think of you every time I hear the songs.

I can't wait to spend the summer with you. We can go to the beach, the movies, or just hang out around the complex. Oh! And I really want to have a picnic with you at Balboa Park. We can spread out a blanket beneath the cherry trees and, well, you know . . .

You truly are so beautiful to me.

Love,

Douglas

When we were finished, we exchanged each other's yearbooks. I started to open mine.

"Don't read it now!" Natalia demanded. "It's embarrassing!" Her beautiful skin turned bright red.

"Okay," I said, smiling. "I'll wait until I get home." We kissed each other goodbye and then headed our separate ways; our parents had each parked on opposite sides of the school. As I walked off the campus and straight into summer, a certain calmness fell over me, as if the knowledge of lazy mornings and afternoons combined with late evenings enjoying the warm Valley air would recharge my batteries, feed my soul before I began the new challenges that ninth grade would pose.

That evening, while lying in bed, the lights out, the

sliding glass door to my bedroom open and the smell of jasmine filling the air, I put on my eight-track of the Beach Boys' *Endless Summer*. I kept the volume purposely low, the band's angelic harmonies lightly floating in the darkness, the music the perfect backdrop as I flicked on the Ray-O-Vac flashlight I always kept by the side of my bed— once you've lived through a major earthquake like the '71 Sylmar quake, you'll never sleep without a flashlight nearby again—nervously reached for my yearbook sitting on the nightstand, and turned straightaway to the page Natalia had signed. I had waited all day and night to read it; I wanted the moment to be just right. "In my room," indeed.

Dear Douglas,

I can't believe we only just started hanging out together earlier this year! It feels like I've known you my whole life. You are the sweetest, kindest person I've ever met. And you are such a good listener! I feel like there is nothing I can't tell you, and you are so good at helping me through tough times, like when things get difficult with my parents or my sister or even with Vicki. I am sooooo lucky to be your special friend.

I hope we can spend some time together this summer. I know you know I will be working at my dad's shop, but we'll still find a way to hang out together. I really enjoyed dancing with you at Lee's bar mitzvah—you are such a good dancer! Really! You are!

Well, that's it for now. I can't wait to see what the future brings! I love you!

Love,

Natalia

Chapter Six

Riiiiiinnnggg. *Riiiiiiinnnngggg.* Somewhere deep in my consciousness, I heard a telephone. I fought the temptation to open my eye to catch a glimpse of the clock. Just a bit more sleep, I told myself.

"Douglas! Hey, Douglas!" my mom yelled from downstairs.

I guess catching a few more winks was now out of the question.

"It's Hank. Get out of bed and pick up the phone. It's already past ten."

Past ten? What day was it anyway? Summers are so great. I swung my legs over the edge of my bed—it was the same single bed with a trundle underneath for sleepovers that I had been sleeping on since first grade—and made my way out into the hallway to pick up the phone.

"Hello?" I grumbled.

"Hey, Douglas. It's Hank!"

"Well, aren't you the chipper one. Already had your Wheaties, I take it?"

"Breakfast of Champions! But that was hours ago. I've already been to the gym for an early morning practice with Coach Olsen."

"Yeah, yeah, we all know what a stud you are," I said only half-jokingly. Hank's parents had arranged for him to work with one of the assistant coaches for Woodrow Wilson High over the summer, and he was more determined than ever to one day be a star for their varsity team.

Hank had killer handles. He could cross you over, put the ball between his legs, dribble behind his back, and go in for a reverse layup like it was nothing. He was the Pete Maravich of the playground.

"How'd that go?"

"Pretty good, I guess. Though it's weird, I've been having all of these strange aches all over my body."

"From what?" I asked, twisting the phone cord in my fingers.

"Who knows? Coach said it might be growing pains."

"Growing pains? You?" The one knock on Hank's basketball potential was his size. He still hadn't had a solid growth spurt, and as a five-foot-five fourteen year old, he didn't appear to have much of a future in the sport once high school was over.

"Very funny. It's not like you're touching the rim these days."

"I still have a couple of inches on you, but I'll be lucky to get a place on the bench on the B or C team. Meanwhile, you'll probably be starting on varsity as a freshman."

"Yeah, well, we'll see." Hank was nothing if not humble about his skills. "Hey, I was calling to see if you wanted to head over to The Sixth Chakra today. I need to pick up a present for my sister. Her birthday's tomorrow."

The Sixth Chakra was a groovy, hippie shop down Ventura Boulevard deeper into Encino. I loved going there and would look for any excuse to visit. "Sure. When do you want to go?"

"I don't know. I'm ready when you are."

"Give me thirty. I'll meet you out in front of the building." I hung up the phone, stretched my arms, scratched my belly, and debated going back to bed for another fifteen or twenty minutes.

"Douglas?" my mom cried from downstairs. "I'm making some eggs and toast. Would you like me to make you some?"

Let's see, eggs and toast or another catnap? It was after ten, and I'd be out for a while with Hank. "Sure, Mom. I'll take some. I'm just gonna get ready. Be down in ten."

"What are you doing today?"

"I'm going to hang out with Hank," I answered as I shuffled into my bathroom, the deep brown pile of the shag carpeting massaging my toes. Looking into the mirror, what was reflected back to me was a typical teenager—a bit of acne, braces on my teeth, some baby fat still hanging around my face. Why did God decide to heap so much abuse on teenagers? Is there really any reason why he couldn't have simply given us a pass on the awkward-looks phase? Wasn't it bad enough that we had to go through all of the emotional roller coasters associated with our teenage hormones? Why heap this physical abuse on us as well?

Speaking of abuse, I took off the head gear I was forced to wear on a nightly basis under penalty of death personally administered by Dr. Savage, my uptight orthodontist, sliding the wire through the brackets, and swallowing the excess saliva this morning ritual always seemed to produce. For some weird reason, brushing my teeth actually seemed to bring me and my long-suffering mouth relief, the cold water and minty Aim toothpaste swishing around somehow easing the mild pain of the annoying small cuts and irritations caused by all of the metal in there. I switched out my rubber bands, sprayed on some deodorant, ran the vented brush—ideal for maintaining the perfect feathered look—through my long brown hair and headed back to my bedroom to throw on some cut-offs and a Stones shirt my sister Julie had given me after she saw them at The Palladium during their '72 American tour in support of *Exile on Main Street*. I was just a little too young for that one, and when my mom found out about the riots and arrests that marred many shows later in the tour, she felt good that she had stuck to her guns and refused to let me go, even though the L.A. show was, by all accounts, relatively calm, or at least as calm as a Stones concert could possibly be. Anyway, I figured that if we were heading over to The Sixth Chakra today, I should try to look cool, even if I wasn't actually cool.

As I slipped the shirt over my head, I made my way over to my stereo and threw in an eight-track of Neil Young's *After the Gold Rush*. Most of my friends didn't give a shit about Neil—they were more into Elton John and Zeppelin—but I grew up on the music of the sixties and early seventies because I had an older brother and sister who pretty much dictated what music was playing at any given time around the house, or out by the pool, back when we had a pool when my parents were still together in Northridge.

I knew the lyrics to this whole album—and *Harvest* as well—from front to back. They, like so many others—the Beatles, the Stones—had been ingrained into my brain after years of repeated listening, even if it was simply background music during much of that time, something I'd hear coming from Julie or David's room, or on their car radio, or from someone's transistor radio by the pool or at the beach.

I sat on the bed, pulling my socks on and slipping my feet into a pair of Superstars. To my right was a wall covered by cork panels, where I could pin up various sports memorabilia—newspaper and magazine articles, cards, programs . . . basically anything I could stick a push pin through. There was the headline from the *L.A. Times* the day after the Lakers won their record-setting thirty-third game in a row during the 1971–72 season. Jerry West's basketball card from the following year. An autograph from the Globetrotter's Meadowlark Lemon that my dad got for me when he saw him on a plane. I also had some posters of famous athletes taking up significant real estate: Wilt Chamberlain dunking over Jabbar, Muhammad Ali standing triumphantly above Sonny Liston, O.J. Simpson in full Bills' regalia cradling the ball in his right hand while cutting across the field.

On the wall behind me, above my closet doors, were a line-up of pivotal *Sports Illustrated* magazines, which I had cleverly strung ribbon through, and then hung the tied ribbons from nails I had hammered directly into the plaid wallpaper-covered walls, much to my mom's dismay. These included the issue celebrating Bill Walton's dominant game against Memphis State in the NCAA Championship, another one featuring Ali's stunning win over George Foreman, Mark Spitz with his seven gold medals around his neck, and the Lakers victory over the Knicks in the 1972 NBA championship.

"Douglas? What's taking you so long? Your eggs are getting cold."

"Okay, Mom, be right there," I said as I bent down to tie the laces of my shoes. I turned Neil off, headed out my bedroom door, and bounded down the stairs, ready for whatever the day was gonna bring.

I entered the kitchen, and my mom opened the oven where she'd been keeping my eggs warm and pulled out the plate and placed it on the table. "Don't complain if your yolks aren't quite as easy as you normally like them," she frowned.

"Don't worry, I won't," I said, looking down at two very overcooked eggs. "These look great," I lied.

"Say," my mom said as she stood at the sink, washing the pan she used to cook my eggs, "Art ran into Lew Farmer early this morning, and Lew told him that there was quite a ruckus over at the Guinzburg's place a couple of nights ago. The police even showed up."

"Really? Natalia hasn't said anything to me about it. You sure Lew knows what he's talking about?"

Lew Farmer was a former child star whose career petered out before he even reached the age of thirty, and yet his townhouse was filled with memorabilia from the movies he made when he was a kid. Well into his seventies by now, Lew spent his days spying on his neighbors and filling the courtyards of the Encino Royale's complex with gossip, rumors, and innuendos, while sitting on his centrally located patio with a small glass of sherry every afternoon beginning precisely at 4:00 P.M., and stopping anyone and everyone who walked by to tell them which neighbor recently broke an HOA regulation, or who was getting a divorce, or who just bought a fancy new car with money earned in some illicit fashion. And if you weren't able to pull yourself away from Lew after he was through reciting the recent wave of sordid events, he'd go on to regale you with the same tired tales of the golden age of Hollywood and his life acting alongside the likes of Mickey

Rooney, Jackie Coogan, and Coy Watson that you'd likely already heard several times over.

"Well, you never know with Lew, but Art said he seemed pretty certain that the police were definitely at their door. Apparently there was a big fight with a lot of screaming and yelling."

"From whom?"

"I'm not sure. Probably Mr. Guinzburg. Have you ever seen him get upset? He's always seemed pretty calm to me. Though he definitely has a bit of an edge to him."

"He's pretty strict," I admitted, "but other than that he seems okay to me, and Natalia's never really complained about him. Anyway, Lew Farmer should find a new hobby."

"That's true!" my mom laughed. "He's such a *yenta!*"

After gobbling down my scrambled eggs and draining a glass of orange juice in one, long gulp, I leapt up from the table and headed out the door. My mom, turning around from the sink where she had been doing dishes, cried out, "Jesus, Douglas! Where's the fire?"

"Sorry, Mom. I told Hank I'd meet him out front, and I'm already late."

"It's not healthy to eat so fast! And you didn't even clear your dishes!"

"Sorry, Mom," I cried out as I slammed the door behind me. As soon as I stepped outside, I could tell it was going to be a hot one today. Maybe even triple digits, though the news said something about mid-nineties. God how I loved the Valley heat. I remember visiting Seattle one time on a trip with my dad and thinking, *Christ, how do people live up here? It's always cold and drizzly.*

After growing up in the Valley, I've discovered there are two types of weather I could never survive long-term:

Cold, drizzly weather, and hot, humid weather. Southern Californians need their dry sunshine, and we just can't survive humidity. It's like our kryptonite. We simply melt into a puddle of sweat and tears when we visit places like New York in the summer. Gross. I once had a friend in grammar school who moved to Chicago. We kept in touch for awhile after he moved, and even though he was initially terrified at the thought of living through a brutally cold Chicago winter, the one thing he complained about after he had been there for awhile was the summer heat and humidity.

"At least in the winter you can throw on layers of clothes and get warm," he'd tell me. "But in the summer, there's no way to escape the heat except by staying indoors and running the air conditioning. But the problem with that is when everybody in the city does it, the electrical grid goes down, and then you don't even have air conditioning to give you relief."

Mental note to myself: Never visit Chicago in the summer.

"About time," Hank teased as I approached the front gate to the complex.

"Sorry, my mom forced me to eat breakfast before I went out."

"You bring anything for me?" Hank kidded.

"I thought about it, but scrambled eggs don't really travel too well." I smiled.

As we made our way up Lindley toward Ventura, sweat was already starting to form on our brows. "It's too hot to walk all the way over there today. Let's take the bus."

"Sorry, but I don't have any money for the bus."

"What do you mean? How could you not have any

money for the bus?"

"I need to save everything I brought for my sister's birthday gift."

"Couldn't you have at least gotten some extra pocket change from your parents?" I asked.

"My mom had a doctor's appointment this morning, and my dad wouldn't give me any money today. Said my sister didn't need any more crap from 'that ridiculous hippie store.'" Hank did a dead-on impression of his dad. In fact, Hank could pretty much do an impression of anyone: Nixon, Howard Cosell, even Mick Jagger.

Hank's dad was old-school: a crew-cut wearing, staunch conservative Republican. He still swore allegiance to Nixon even after all that had happened—"It was all just a liberal conspiracy," he'd say of Watergate—and absolutely hated it when Hank would do his Nixon impressions. "Show some respect for the greatest president in the history of this country!" he'd shout at Hank. He also couldn't stand The Sixth Chakra. "Bunch of hippies selling drug paraphernalia," is how he referred to the store.

I have to admit, though, that his characterization of the store was pretty accurate. It *was* run by a bunch of hippies, and they *did* sell bongs and pipes and elaborate hookahs and such, but there was a bunch of other cool stuff in the store as well.

"Fuck, Hank. It's too hot to walk. I guess I could lend you the thirty-five cents."

"Why don't we just hitch-hike? It'll be easy to catch a ride. It's just a couple of miles down Ventura."

My parents weren't crazy about hitchhiking, though my brother did it all the time when he was growing up. I'd done it on occasion, and it had always been mellow.

"All right," I said, hoping we were making the right decision.

When we reached Ventura, we crossed the street, walked down a ways past the bus stop, and stuck out our thumbs. Within a few minutes, a red Dodge Dart pulled over to the curb. Hank and I ran over to the passenger-side window, which was already open.

"Hi, boys! Where you going?"

As we lowered our heads to look inside, we were pleasantly surprised to see a very attractive lady, maybe a little younger than our moms, dressed in a skimpy dress that revealed her legs well up to her thighs.

"Ummm," I stammered, staring at that space where the tops of her thighs came together.

"We're just going a couple of miles up Ventura," Hank said coolly.

"Well, hop on in. I'm going to work at Encino Hospital, so I can take you at least that far."

"Oh, we're not going that far. Just over to The Sixth Chakra," I clarified.

Hank gave me a quick elbow to the ribs, and as we opened the rear door to the car and climbed into the back-seat he whispered, "Don't tell her that! She might not want to take us there."

But he was wrong.

"I love that place!" she said delighted. "In fact, I bought this dress there! What a trip!" She laughed and brushed a few strands of her long, straight blonde hair away from her face.

"Are you a doctor?" I asked as she pulled away from the curb.

"Who? Me? Ha, that's a laugh. Yeah, just call me Dr.

Sunshine."

"Dr. Sunshine?" If she was joking, I wasn't quite getting it.

"That's my name," she said, smiling back at us with a mouthful of pearly whites. "I used to be a raging hippie, as if you couldn't tell."

Hank, always the smooth one with the ladies, piped up in his distinctive fashion, "Well, I think it's a beautiful name. It suits you well."

"Well, thank you, young man." I could see her green eyes in the rearview mirror, flashing at us.

As we pulled up to the stop light at White Oak, the Stones' "Satisfaction" came up on the radio. Uh-oh, I thought. Here comes Hank's imitation.

"And a man comes up and tells me," he snarled, "how white my shirts can be."

"Wow! You're amazing!" Sunshine laughed. "How'd you learn to do that?"

"I'm a man of many talents," Hank bragged.

"Oh, I see." Sunshine smiled.

"He's the best junior basketball player in the entire Valley," I said proudly.

"Is that so?" Sunshine said. "Well, I don't know much about basketball, but I do know rock and roll, and I think you might have quite a future ahead of you as a singer. I want you to promise that you won't forget me when you become rich and famous."

"Oh, don't worry about us," I said before I even knew what I was saying. "We'll never forget you." As soon as the words were out of my mouth, I turned fifty shades of red.

"Ah, aren't you just the cutest," Sunshine said somewhat dismissively, immediately making me feel not a day older than my thirteen years. To add insult to injury, Hank gave me another elbow jab to my ribs along with a "what-the-fuck?" look.

Trying to rapidly change the subject, I asked, "So if you're not a doctor, what do you do at the hospital?"

"Oh, it's very exciting," Sunshine said sarcastically. "I work in billing. I'm the one who calls your parents when their bill is overdue. It's actually a huge drag of a job, but it pays the bills."

"But if you hate it so much," Hank asked, scratching at a mosquito bite on his cheek, "why don't you just quit? Doesn't your husband work?"

"Husband?" Sunshine laughed in a way that wasn't really quite a laugh, but was more like revulsion. "I've already had two of those, and I'm not looking for another! The third time is definitely not going to be the charm for this girl!"

Hank continued to pry. "You have any kids?"

"Kids? No, no kids," Sunshine said distractedly as she changed lanes. We were approaching Louise, and she was getting ready to pull over and drop us off.

"Well, listen you two," she cautioned as she reached the curb. "Don't be buying any of that drug paraphernalia in there. You're too young for that stuff. Take it from someone who knows. It'll destroy your ambition, and you'll end up working in the billing department at a hospital for shitty pay."

"Okay, ma'am, don't worry, we won't," I said.

"Who you calling 'ma'am'? I ain't that old!" she laughed.

"Sorry, Sunshine," Hank quickly replied. "You'll have to excuse my friend, here. He's got manners disease."

"All is forgiven," Sunshine smiled. God she was beautiful. "You kids are cute. I'll pick you up anytime."

And there it was. The kiss of death. "You kids." Well, there went any fantasies about making it with Sunshine one day.

"Thank you for the ride, Sunshine," Hank said as we shut the door behind us and bent down for one last look at our Ride Goddess.

"Thanks, Sunshine," I called out as she pulled away, her Dodge Dart spewing black exhaust out of the tailpipe.

"Jeez," I said, "I think she needs an oil change."

"Hell, I'll change her oil," Hank mused.

"She was pretty beautiful, huh?" I said, the two of us still watching as her car faded into the distance.

"A hundred percent total fox," Hank declared. "No wonder she's already had two husbands."

"And probably quite a few boyfriends as well," I surmised.

"That's for sure."

We headed on over toward The Sixth Chakra, the giant oak trees surrounding the property providing much-needed shade and relief from the rapidly rising temperature. As Hank and I walked along, we both fell into a little shuffle, so much fun to do because you could watch the fine dust from the Valley floor kick up in clouds lighter than cotton candy. Who cared if they were making my white All-Stars filthy? Mom would clean 'em, though she'd chastise me first.

Once you passed through the oak trees—all told, the property that The Sixth Chakra sat on was several acres—you came through a cut-out in a hedge and the first thing that came into view was the Ken Kesey-inspired psychedelic bus. It wasn't a carbon copy of the legendary Further bus, but an inspired homage. And the best thing was that the owners of The Sixth Chakra kept the door open so that any customer was free to hang out inside the bus, which always had music playing, and was outfitted with Indian rugs, bean bag chairs, and couches of various shapes and sizes. People would generally kick back in there to smoke a joint or share a bowl. They didn't let you eat in there because hippies were such slobs, but they were cool with pretty much anything else. Oh, and absolutely no alcohol, though The Sixth Chakra's customers definitely preferred grass, acid, and shrooms anyway.

"You want to check out the bus?" I asked Hank.

"Let's do it after. I gotta pee."

The first thing to hit you when you walked in the door of The Sixth Chakra—which was actually just a converted ranch house from the twenties—was the smell of the patchouli incense. The musky scent burning throughout the house combined with the structure's own musty smell—from what was probably decades of mold and rot in the old wood framing—to create an immediate sensation that absolutely repelled some folks, but made others feel strangely calm and peaceful. It was always pleasant inside the walls of The Sixth Chakra, even when the heat was triple digits outside. Well shaded and apparently well insulated, the vibe at the store was always cool, calm, and, well, given the general spaciness of the employees, maybe not collected, but definitely contented.

"Hey, guys!" a dude with long dreadlocks arranging some hand-made greeting cards on a rack smiled as we walked in through the barn-like door. "Welcome." He was wearing a hand-made name tag on the pocket of his shirt that read, True.

"Thanks," Hank and I self-consciously muttered. We were always the youngest people in there. Oh, occasionally we'd see some burn-out from our grade or even the grade below us buying a bong, but generally speaking, the customers in here were a lot older than either of us.

"Can I use your bathroom?" Hank asked right away.

"Uh, yeah, sure. Back there to the right," True said warily.

"Don't worry," I said, reassuringly, "we're gonna buy some stuff."

"Cool," he said, stroking one of his long dreadlocks and going back to his greeting cards.

I immediately headed to my favorite part of the store: the blacklight poster room. "Hey, Hank," I called out as I walked by the restroom door, "I'm going into the poster room."

"Be right there," Hank replied.

The poster room was in an old barn that had long ago been connected to the house, and featured an incredibly cool collection of blacklight posters. It was, of course, dark in there with the exception of the blacklights. You pulled back a heavy curtain to gain access and entered a high-ceilinged room that featured couches along three walls, with dozens of posters hung at different angles on an enormous fourth wall that sat in front of you as you lounged on one of the sofas.

I was particularly enamored of a poster of Jimi Hendrix where it looked like his giant 'fro was on fire. The colors—a pastiche of electric oranges and yellows and greens and purples—were beyond wild, and the image just leaped off the wall in the black light. But they could turn almost anything into a blacklight poster, and so in addition to musicians like Hendrix, there was Mickey Mouse, marijuana leaves, and peace signs. The Zig-Zag man was ubiquitous, with several posters referencing him. As were the Beatles, from *Yellow Submarine* to *Magical Mystery Tour* to *Sergeant Pepper*.

Images from movies like *Easy Rider*, *The Endless Summer*, and *Bonnie & Clyde* were popular. Hell, even Tricky Dick Nixon got his own blacklight poster, though of course its tone was mocking. And then there were just the pure psychedelic manifestations of an LSD trip, wild posters filled with images of mushrooms, trolls, dragons, rainbows, and pits of fire. There was some far-out shit in that room, let me tell you. And the posters sold really well, because the images on the walls in the room were always changing, which kept the inventory fresh and encouraged repeat visits.

"Jeez," I said as Hank pulled back the curtain, "what the hell were you doing in there?"

"Huh? Oh, I ran into Ronnie. He's in the head now. He'll join us in a second."

"Ronnie's here?" I asked incredulously.

"Yeah. Funny, huh? His mom's at the beauty parlor across the street, and he has to go to the dentist afterward. Instead of waiting in the parlor or the car, he figured he'd kill some time over here."

"Hey, guys!" Ronnie burst through the curtain, throwing it aside with wild abandon.

"Ronnie, chill out," I scolded. "This is a mellow place, don't kill the vibe."

"Oh, yeah, yeah, right, right. Sorry," Ronnie whispered, now overdoing it one-hundred-fifty percent the other direction as he tiptoed over to a couch and very cautiously sat down. "I forgot how sensitive these hippie types can be," he said sarcastically, continuing to whisper.

Ronnie wasn't as in tune with the whole sixties thing as I was. He didn't have the benefit of having siblings a lot older than him, and his parents weren't into the hippie vibe at all. His dad was a car mechanic who rode a Harley with a Valley motorcycle gang on the weekends, and his mom never seemed to get out of her robe and always had a glass of white wine in her hand no matter what time of day it was. But with one slightly older sister and two twin brothers who were only eleven months younger, Ronnie was sort of the black sheep of the family, the kid who wasn't the baby for very long, and who happily abdicated his responsibilities as the oldest male child to his sister and younger brothers many, many years ago.

"Damn. I wish I could just stay here instead of going to the dentist," Ronnie said as he kicked back on the couch, lying on his side and staring at the wall across from him. "Maybe I won't go back to the salon."

"Won't your mom freak out?" I asked.

"Nah. She knows I don't want to go to the dentist," Ronnie said, continuing to stare at the posters.

"I fucking hate the dentist," Hank said contemptuously, after silence had hung in the air for a beat too long.

"Do you ever think Dylan looks like a woman?" Ronnie asked.

"What?" I asked, exasperated.

"Look at him," Ronnie said, pointing his long finger at the poster of Dylan on the wall opposite of him.

"Well, it's only because they got him at a weird angle, in profile. And he was in his 'Jew-fro' phase, which was sort of a woman's haircut," I pointed out. I loved Dylan. I even defended him for releasing *Self-Portrait* and *New Morning* and *Pat Garret and Billy the Kid*. And now that he'd just put out *Blood on the Tracks* and *The Basement Tapes* back to back, he was on top once again, the darling of both critics and audiences alike. While I was never able to see Dylan in his prime back in the sixties, my brother and sister did take me to the Forum to see him with The Band early last year—my mom loved Dylan and had no problem with me attending the show—in what would eventually be released as the *Before the Flood* album. And while I knew I was catching him toward the end of his career—I mean, the dude was going to be forty in a few years—he was still amazing, and seemingly at the top of his game. Who knows? Maybe he'll be like one of those old blues or jazz guys and continue to play well into his seventies or even his eighties. Ha! Can you imagine that? Bob Dylan still playing rock and roll as an old man, using a cane or a walker to get onto the stage? That'll be the day.

After a few more contemplative minutes, Ronnie announced, "Okay, I'm officially bored. Anyone want to walk around the store with me?"

"I'm gonna chill in here for a few more minutes," I said.

"Yeah, me too," Hank joined. Hank was a good friend. He had come to the store with me, not Ronnie, and even though I knew he didn't enjoy the blacklight room quite as much as I did, he remained loyal and stuck by me.

"Ronnie's a piece of work," Hank laughed after Ronnie had left. "He's a lot of fun to be around, but you certainly can never just have a mellow moment with him."

"Yeah, seriously," I added, falling silent and staring

off into the neon colors of a gorgeous naked woman with a strong resemblance to Linda Ronstadt, standing alone in a field of green grass and brilliant pink-purple flowers with bright yellow centers, and the words, "The Burden of Life Is Love" rising up from the grass. The Linda lookalike was buck naked, with her back to us so that you could see her beautiful ass, but she was turned enough to the left that you could also clearly see one of her perfectly shaped breasts, her long, dark hair falling below her waist, but pulled back off of her face so that you could ruminate on her delicate features and sly smile as she looked down her long arm toward her hand where her finger touched a flower that wasn't actually a flower, but was a peace sign, growing right there among the other flora.

I didn't really know if love was actually a burden or not. I thought of Natalia and whether she could ever become a burden, and I just couldn't imagine how that could ever happen. Peace and love, isn't that what they say? How could love ever become something that wasn't peaceful, that actually turned into something so toxic that it became a burden to one lover or the other? In the case of my mom and my dad, sure, they divorced, but they still loved each other. Their love had never become a burden. Or had it?

"You awake?"

"What? Huh?" Hank was on his feet, standing over me, waving his hand in front of my eyes.

"You totally zoned out. I thought I had lost you for good."

"Oh, sorry, I was just staring at that poster over there," I said, pointing toward the woman in the field of flowers.

"Yeah, she is one hot mama," Hank said. "Come on,

let's go see what Ronnie is up to."

"Sure thing," I said hopping up off of the couch and taking one more glance at my flower girl on the wall.

We spent the next thirty minutes or so wandering around the store, checking out the latest in hippie fashions, such as handmade beaded necklaces, studded leather belts with peace sign buckles, and paisley scarves. Of course there was a huge section of candles, All personally crafted from the finest natural ingredients, as the sign read. With all of the candles burning in bedrooms and bathrooms these days, it's no wonder the fire department was experiencing record numbers of calls for home blazes. Not to mention the rising numbers of adults, even people my parents' age, who were now regularly and casually smoking dope, another potential fire hazard. I saw Jerry Dunphy covering the story on the evening news the other night:

> From the desert to the sea, to all of Southern California, a good evening. Our top story tonight: fires in your neighborhood. What is causing the dramatic increase in fires in suburban homes? We'll have that story and much more coming right up. But first, President Gerald Ford is in the news once again for yet another faux paus . . .

Ronnie, of course, spent his whole time at The Sixth Chakra in the head shop section of the store. He must've held every bong and pipe in the place and had to be reminded on several occasions by True to not actually put his lips on the merchandise. The Sixth Chakra, while not primarily a head shop, did have a pretty solid collection of smoking merch. In addition to the pipes and bongs, there were hookahs, rolling papers, grinders, seed removers . . . and then there was all of the coke paraphernalia, which had started to appear a year or so ago, but had now taken over an entire case as cocaine had become an extremely popular drug with the wealthy Hollywood crowd, many of whom lived right here in the Valley, south of boulevard, of course.

There were spoons of various shapes and sizes, mirrors, and more glass vials than you ever thought possible. Silver and glass seemed to be the main theme running through all of the coke products, although the occasional gold spoon showed up here and there. Snuff cases were popular as well, usually engraved with an old-style Western motif.

Meanwhile, Hank was over checking out the turquoise jewelry. This section rivaled the drug paraphernalia as the most popular part of the store, with its multitude of glass cases filled with all kinds of rings, bracelets, necklaces, earrings, and belt buckles. All of it was made by one of two different tribes out in Arizona, who were probably earning a small fortune as turquoise jewelry was all the rage these days with both women and men.

As I approached Hank, I saw he was looking at a pair of silver-and-turquoise earrings. "You thinking of buying those?" I asked.

"Thinking about it. My sister's been wanting a pair like these for a while."

"Looks good. I like how the pieces of turquoise form a little flower," I said.

"Yeah, they're cool, aren't they? I'll take them," Hank said to the woman helping him. She was a petite girl, with wispy blonde hair and a pretty smile.

"Great! I'll ring you up over here."

As Hank walked over to the cash register, I stayed behind looking at the rings. I had been thinking about buying something for Natalia, maybe even asking her to officially be my girlfriend, to go steady with me, and there was a particular ring in the case that was speaking to me, telling me that it was meant for her. It was a decent-sized ring, certainly more expensive than the earrings Hank was buying for his sister, with two triangular pieces of turquoise in the center, separated by a thin band of silver. It was a supercool design, with a simple pattern stamped into the edges; I was certain that Natalia would love it.

"Is there something you'd like to see?" I looked up to see the girl with the pretty smile standing in front of me, apparently finished with Hank's purchase. Hank had by now joined Ronnie in the bong section on the other side of the store.

"Yes, please," I said in a soft voice so as not to attract Ronnie or Hank's attention. That ring on the second shelf, the one on the end," I said, pointing directly at it.

"Nice choice," she smiled as she pulled it out and handed it to me. "It's Zuni. Is it for someone special?"

"Yeah, it's, ah, it's for my girlfriend," I answered, trying to sound as mature as possible. "Well, it's for someone who I'm hoping will be my girlfriend anyway."

"That's so sweet," she said, placing her hand on top of my hand, which was holding the ring out in front of me. Her nails were painted white with tiny yellow daisies on the tips. "I'm sure she'll love it. And I'm sure she'll say 'yes,'" she smiled. Wow. What a smile.

"Um, how much is it?"

She took the ring from my by-now sweaty palm with

her delicate fingers and looked at the tag. "Eight-fifty," she said. "But I can give it to you for eight," she whispered, and then she winked at me, in a way I'd only seen in movies, sending a bolt surging through my heart.

"Cool. Thank you. I don't have that much money on me right now, but I can come back later."

"Would you like me to hold it for you?"

"Sure. That'd great."

"What's your name?" Damn. Her eyes were so blue they just mesmerized you.

"My name? Oh, Douglas."

"Nice to meet you, 'Oh Douglas,'" she laughed as she extended her hand, her dimples now showing as she smiled. "I'm Saffron. I'll put it back here with your name on it." She glanced over at True, who was appearing more and more agitated by Ronnie, who had now been joined by Hank, and then whispered once again, "Just make sure to ask me to get it for you when you come back so that I can save you that fifty cents."

"Will do," I whispered. "And thanks." I smiled.

"You know what? I'm done." True had apparently had enough, and his voice was now raised well above the threshold of hippie mellow. "I've shown you every god damn pipe and bong in the store—some of them twice—and I bet you don't even have a dollar in your pocket!" he said, his voice now something just short of a yell. He was demonstrative enough, however, that his long dreads were flying this way and that.

"Hey, *mellow out*, man," Ronnie said in his best sarcastic voice. "I'm not trying to bring you *down*, brother. Anyway," Ronnie said as he turned away from True, "I'll just go over to Captain Ed's, where they appreciate my business." Ouch. Captain Ed's was definitely the top head shop in the Valley and had a far superior collection than The Sixth Chakra.

"Whatever, dude," True said, shaking his head.

Hank and Ronnie headed out the door. "Sorry, man," I said to True and Saffron. "He can be an ass sometimes. He's having a rough time at home with his parents. You know, divorce and all that," I lied.

"No worries," Saffron smiled. "Have a good day, and see you again soon."

"Thanks. You, too. I'll definitely be back for the ring." The truth was, I could've bought the ring right then and there. I had two more fives in my pocket, but I really didn't want to do it in front of Hank and Ronnie. While they were generally supportive of my relationship with Natalia, once they found out I was giving her a ring and asking her to be my girlfriend, I'd never hear the end of it. Plus, if she turned me down, it'd be "no harm, no foul," as Chick Hearn liked to say. They wouldn't even know about the ask, and I wouldn't have to tell them about the denial. Better to come back and buy the ring when I was alone and then go present it to Natalia without saying anything to the guys.

As I walked out the door, the Valley heat was there waiting for me. It seemed like the temperature had climbed twenty degrees from the time we had entered the store, and the fierce light from the sun caused me to momentarily shade my eyes with my hand while they adjusted to the onslaught of the heat and glare.

"Hey! Numb nuts!" I looked over to the bus and saw Ronnie hanging out the window. "Get your sorry ass in here, you faggot." He always had such a beautiful way with words.

I walked over to the bus, so many clouds of dust coming off of my shoes that my white socks were now turning a light shade of brown. Before I even climbed the steps I could smell the skunky scent of pot; Ronnie had lit a joint and was blowing a huge cloud of smoke toward me. "Come on, you pussy. Get with the program and take a hit."

"No thanks, I'm good," I replied. It was my standard answer, and Ronnie had heard it a hundred times.

"What the fuck is with you, dude?" Ronnie asked as he passed the joint to Hank, who proceeded to take a tiny hit and quickly give it back to Ronnie. Hank was what was known as a classic lightweight. He'd take a small hit here and there, but wasn't anywhere close to the level of Weddy and Ronnie. He could never be the elite athlete he aspired to be if he were to rise up to their class of stonerdom.

"Leave him alone, Ronnie," Hank admonished.

"You're such a drag, Douglas," Ronnie said as he leaned back into the purple bean bag chair, closed his eyes, and blew another gigantic cloud of smoke into the air. "One of these days you'll come around. I'm sure of it."

I plopped down on a gold couch across from him. "Yeah, I know. I'm a real drag, buddy," I agreed sarcastically.

"Seriously, though, dude," Ronnie said through squinty eyes. "When are you going to get off your high horse?" Ronnie began to laugh hysterically. "Get it? *High* horse!!"

I didn't even bother to answer Ronnie, as he had heard me explain my position plenty of times before. The truth was that I had watched several of my brother's and sister's friends become total burn-outs who'd done absolutely nothing with their lives since graduating high school other than do drugs and, in some cases, sell drugs.

First it was Brad, who was one of David's best friends, and then Wendy, who was close to Julie. Both of them were once gregarious, outgoing kids, always the life of the party. They both started with grass, then alcohol, then acid and shrooms, but I think it was the Quaaludes that really did both of them in. Take enough 'ludes and your brain simply becomes like mush. I watched as both Brad and Wendy—who didn't even really know each other because of their age difference—went from being normal, bright kids to true dopeheads who you could barely understand since their speech was always so slurred while they were high, which seemed to be a twenty-four/seven addiction.

Brad had resorted to staying in his room for long stretches of time, the blinds closed on his window overlooking the street where we would play ball back in the Northridge days. Meanwhile, the last report on Wendy was that she was living in a sketchy part of North Hollywood, turning tricks on Van Nuys boulevard to support her various habits. The simple fact was seeing what drugs did to Brad and Wendy was enough for me to want to stay clean, at least for now, until I was older and could potentially handle everything better.

Some kids, even Natalia on the phone just the other night, have asked me why, given how I felt, I hung out with people who did drugs, but the truth was so many kids smoked pot or ate shrooms or dropped acid that it wasn't easy to find friends who were clean. Or at least kids who I'd be even remotely interested in hanging out with. Maybe I just found kids who did drugs more interesting than kids who didn't. Or maybe our tastes in things, our sense of humor, and our views on life were just more aligned. Besides, it didn't bother me to be around people getting high; I'd been around it my whole life. It was just part and parcel of growing up in the Valley in the '60s and '70s. We were all kindred spirits.

"Whatever, dude," Ronnie said. "All I know is I'll be kicking back this summer getting high while you'll be schlepping paper in your dad's warehouse."

"Actually, I think I dodged that bullet," I said.

"Really? That's great!" Hank responded enthusiastically. He knew how badly I *didn't* want to work for my dad this summer. "What happened?"

"My mom convinced my dad that I had worked so hard during the school year that I deserved a break."

"Hah!" Ronnie guffawed. "What a load of crap!"

"Hey, I—"

"Oh, shit!" Ronnie suddenly shouted, jumping up from the beanbag after glancing at his watch before I could defend myself. "I was supposed to meet my mom back at the beauty parlor ten minutes ago. She's gonna kill me. I'm going to be late for the dentist. See you guys later!" he cried over his shoulder as he bounded off the bus.

"And there goes Ronnie," Hank smiled. "He's so full of it. Just a few minutes ago he was bragging that he could skip the dentist, and his mom wouldn't even care."

"Yeah," I agreed, "he's always full of shit. But it's hard not to like the guy. He can be so damn funny. And no one else has your back like Ronnie."

"That's for sure."

Hank and I both leaned back at the same time, him on a bright green bean bag and me on the gold couch, and stared at the painted ceiling of the bus in silence for a while. Someone—nobody remembers who anymore—got the brilliant idea to paint the ceiling in the style of

Michelangelo's Sistine Chapel, only God was a Maha-rishi-looking dude in a white robe with tons of beads around his neck and flowers in his hair, and instead of touching the finger of some super-ripped dude, he's pass-ing a hippie with long stringy hair dressed in tie-dye from head to toe a big, fat doobie. And surrounding God aren't a bunch of angels, but a bevy of beautiful women who look like classic Southern California beach babes—thin and wispy, with blonde hair and a handful of sun freckles around their noses.

Other parts of the ceiling pictured various characters from popular culture. There was Mr. Natural, Alfred E. Neuman, even Yogi Bear getting a blow job from Judy Jet-son. And, of course, all of the major dead rock stars were up there in various places around ceiling of the bus: Hen-drix, Janis, Morrison . . . the usual suspects.

"Hey, Douglas?" Hank woke me from my reverie.

"Yeah?"

"You think Bill Walton has ever been inside this bus?"

I looked up above where Hank was sitting, and there was Walton, who some artist had decided to picture float-ing above a basketball hoop, wearing a Grateful Dead tie-dye shirt and tie-dyed shorts, socks, and shoes, a ball in one hand and a bong in the other, his long, red hair pulled back in a ponytail. A green bandana adorned with yellow marijuana leaves was tied around his head.

"Maybe," I said, "back when he was at UCLA."

"I bet he used to come into The Sixth Chakra, and they honored him at some point by putting him on the wall of the bus."

I nodded in agreement, though I wasn't sure how Walton would feel about this particular depiction of him.

"Yeah, probably," I said. "Hey, you want to hang out in here any longer? It's getting sort of hot."

"Yeah, we can head out. What do you want to do?"

"I don't know. Want to check out the newsstand?"

"Sure," Hank agreed. Out of all of my friends, Hank was the most easygoing, and was usually agreeable to whatever anyone else wanted to do. "Should we try our luck hitching again?"

"I think one Mrs. Robinson for the day is enough for me. And it's too hot to walk. Let's just take the bus."

"Okay," Hank said. "But I think I'm twenty cents short." I looked down to see one lonely dime and one lonely nickel in the palm of his hand.

"That's okay, I'll give you the money."

"Thanks, buddy," Hank said as he stood up and flashed five fingers at me—code for our secret "Soul Brother #5" handshake—which we proceeded to perform flawlessly.

The bus ride up Ventura to the newsstand started out uneventfully, just the usual mix of Mexican housekeepers, local junior high and high school kids, old people who couldn't drive anymore . . . Of course, there's always the loud guy, and this ride proved to be no exception. But he was a sports guy, just going on and on about the Dodgers, so it wasn't too annoying. Not like a Jesus freak, conspiracy theorist, or cult member. That's when you'd hop off the bus early, maybe at Zelzah even, or White Oak if the person was a total nutcase.

"I'm telling you," the Dodgers fan was saying to no one and anyone at the same time, "they should give this guy Lasorda a chance to manage the team. Alston's too old for these kids." Like I said, he was loud and obnoxious, but what he was saying actually made sense. I didn't know who this Lasorda guy was, but Alston was definitely ready for the old folks' home, and the Dodgers had a young team filled with a bunch of promising talent: Yeager, Cey, Russell, Garvey, and Baker were all only, like, twenty-eight years old.

"Alston should be sitting at home collecting social security!" the Dodgers fan yelled. "Bring in a young manager who can relate to these guys and nurture their talent."

"Hey!" Hank yelled back.

"What?" the Alston hater glared back at him.

"Hank," I whispered loudly, "what are you—"

"How old is this Lasorda guy?" Hank smiled.

"Oh, ah, Lasorda! Young. Younger than Alston, that's for sure!" And the Dodgers fan laughed a big, hearty laugh as the bottom of his button-up, short-sleeve shirt, which had already pulled up and out of his pants, now exposed his rather large belly. On a dime he sobered up and his tone grew serious, contemplative even: "Mid-forties, I believe. Yes, forty-six, I think. Maybe forty-eight."

We stood up from our seats just as the bus had to swerve around an illegally parked Datsun, and I inadvertently knocked Hank back into the seat and the wall beneath the window.

"Jesus, Douglas!"

"Sorry, man. She swerved."

"I had no choice," the driver cried out from nowhere.

"Oh, yes, I know that, ma'am. I didn't mean to imply—"

"Is this your stop?" she cut me off with plenty of attitude, but I knew better than to mess with an RTD driver. We used the buses all the time, and the drivers had seriously good memories. Good luck getting them to pull over and pick you up if you were on their bad side and you were sitting alone on Wilbur and Ventura and there was only one bus that stopped there per hour. You'd end up having to walk over to Reseda and catch a ride from there with a different driver.

The door in the back opened, and I immediately hopped out onto the sidewalk. "Go Dodgers!" I heard Hank scream from behind me as he followed me out with an athletic leap of his own.

"Yeah, baby!" The Dodgers guy was sticking his face, reddened from his soliloquy, out of the window, pumping his fist and arm out as the bus pulled back into traffic and disappeared down the boulevard.

We headed over to the newsstand, and I once again admired the signage on the liquor store next door that essentially formed the back wall of the stand. There was a large neon clock that was brightly lit up at night with the words Time to Buy looming over it. The clock was surrounded by neon stars, one of which was falling to the earth. And then, across from the clock, about ten feet away, in the same red-and-white color scheme, was a giant arrow that rose down from the sky, curving in the direction of the liquor store, with, in fact, the word Liquor lit up at night in the same bright neon. In small letters, off to the side, Encino Spirits, the name of this fine establishment—and I should mention that it did carry a high level of quality merchandise, especially California wines, which had suddenly become a revolutionary sensation at dinner parties throughout Encino—was subtly announced, well, as subtly as you can announce something in neon.

"You looking for anything in particular?" Hank asked as we approached the long racks of all manner and type of magazines and newspapers. The stand as a whole was a pretty ramshackle affair, with a peeling roof made out of tin or aluminum, and a raised wooden cashier's stand at one end where the clerk sat. You'd basically make your way down the stand from left to right and end up at the cashier. Of course, you could always just dash in and head straight for what you wanted, but only newbies started at the cashier's stand and made their way to the *back* of the place. There were also racks outside of the metal over-hang, just in front of where you parked. It could get a little precarious looking at those publications, depending on how fast someone pulled into a spot off of Newcastle.

"Thought I'd pick up a *Herald*, see what Krikorian has to say about the Lakers trade," I said. "Maybe see if the new issue of *Baseball Digest* came in. You know, the usual stuff."

"I don't know how anyone could disagree with getting Kareem," Hank said, pulling out an issue of *Screw* maga-zine from the adult section. "Even if you have to give up your whole team, and they only gave up half of it. I heard this guy on The Steamer's show yesterday saying it was the worst trade in Lakers' history. Ridiculous."

"Hey!" the guy behind the cash register shouted out. "Are you over eighteen?"

"Yeah," Hank immediately shot back, looking the guy straight in the eye. "My birthday was a few months ago." This was actually true, but Hank had turned fourteen, not eighteen.

"Bullshit!" the guy said, not buying any of it for a sec-ond. "Put that magazine down, and get out of there!"

"Aw, can't a guy have any fun around here?" Hank said in his best Beaver Cleaver voice. I laughed at Hank's dead-on impression. Hank put the magazine back and moved along.

I found my *Baseball Digest*—this week's issue featured Pete Rose on the cover (and even though I was a Dodgers fan, who didn't like Charlie Hustle?)—and indeed Krikorian was weighing in on the Lakers' options during the off-season now that the Kareem trade was complete, so I picked up this afternoon's *Herald*, and then for good measure I grabbed a copy of *Mad* magazine with the venerable Alfred E. Neuman standing among and above a sea of black umbrellas on its cover.

Before heading back to the Royale, we popped into Nick's Sub Shop to grab a couple of meatball subs to take home. Nick's was great: a classic sandwich joint with a loyal following. Hank's tab was growing, but his credit was as good as gold with me. I mean, how many friends will you ever have who would be willing to master seven secret Soul Brother handshakes with you and only you?

Chapter Seven

A few days later, Hank, Weddy, Ronnie, and I made plans to go see *Jaws* in Westwood. Normally, we'd just go see a film at one of the many theaters in Encino, Tarzana, Woodland Hills, Canoga Park, or Reseda, but this movie was a phenomenon, and we wanted to see it on a big screen, and Westwood had the best theaters in town. None of our parents were available to drive that day, and none would've approved of us taking the RTD all the way into Westwood—well, Ronnie's parents probably wouldn't have cared, but the rest of ours would—so we all came up with an agreement that we'd tell our parents we were walking over to Balboa Park to play basketball for the day. There was a 1:00 P.M. showing, and we knew we had to get there by 11:00 A.M. to make sure we'd get a ticket, so we agreed to meet up at the corner of Ventura and Zelzah at 10:00 where we could catch the 10:06 bus into Westwood.

The great thing about taking the RTD into Westwood was that it picked you up right on Ventura and literally dropped you off a short block from the Fox Theater where the movie was playing. It was a longer ride than by car since the driver would take Sepulveda to Sunset instead of the San Diego Freeway, but we would still make it there in a little under an hour. From Sunset, the driver would head through the ritzy homes in Bel Air to Hilgard, then down to Le Conte and over to Westwood Boulevard, finally dropping us off at the corner of Westwood and Weyburn, where we would walk the short block to the Fox.

As we approached the theater, we were shocked to find a line that already stretched down the block toward Le Conte. There must've already been a couple of hundred people there.

"Shit," Ronnie said. "I can't believe all these fucking people are here already."

"Don't worry," I reassured him, "the theater's huge."

"Yeah," Hank agreed, "we'll be fine. That's why we came down here so early."

"Okay," Ronnie calmed down, "but why don't you guys go get in line, and I'll buy the tickets. You can pay me back later."

"You sure?" I asked. "I'm happy to go to the box office with you."

"No, I think it'll be better if I'm the only one that comes and joins you in the line. Otherwise, people might get uptight since you're not supposed to get in line until after you've bought a ticket." He was right on that point; the theater had even erected a little sign that stated as much.

"Yeah, you're right," Weddy added. "Come on, guys." And with that, Ronnie headed over to the box office while Hank, Weddy, and I walked past the long line filled with people seemingly of all ages and colors. There were tons of kids like us, but also lots of adults, both young and old, and people from all over L.A.—black, white, Chinese, Mexican . . . I guess everyone was interested in a movie about a renegade shark.

We took our spot at the end of the line, and that's when the questions started. Hank led off: "You think Ronnie's up to something?"

"I don't know," I said, "but I was thinking the same

thing."

"Oh, mellow out," Weddy said. "He's not trying to pull anything."

"Weddy," I put my hand on his shoulder, "it's Ronnie. Of course he's up to something."

"He probably has some free passes or something and wants to make a few bucks off of us," Weddy admitted. "It's no big deal, right? I mean, do you really care if Ronnie gets the money or if the theater gets the money?"

"I guess not," I replied, though I wasn't really sure how I felt about it. I knew Ronnie and his family weren't as well off as our families, so I just went along with it. Hank did the same. "Still, it would've been nice if he just would've been straight with us," I couldn't help but add.

"Okay, boys," Ronnie said as he returned. "We're all set."

"What do we owe you?" Hank asked.

"Two and a quarter. We can settle up at the snack bar," Ronnie replied.

"Can I have my ticket?" Hank persisted.

"They're safe in my pocket."

Hank frowned.

"What? You don't trust me?" The edge was back in Ronnie's voice.

"It's fine, Hank," Weddy stepped in before anything escalated. "Ronnie, let's go smoke a J in the alley behind the theater. Hank? Want to come?"

"I'm good," Hank said. "I'll just hang here with Douglas."

As Ronnie and Weddy walked up Broxton toward the back of the line and then into the alley that ran directly behind the theater, parallel to Le Conte, Hank turned to me and said, "I don't like the smell of this. Ronnie's up to something."

"Yeah, I know, but it's probably like Weddy said: Ronnie must have some passes or something he's just trying to make a couple of bucks from."

"Whatever," Hank said, looking up ahead in the line to see if there was any movement. "I wonder when they're going to start letting people in?"

"I'm guessing we still have a good half-hour at least, maybe even an hour." Hank proceeded to engage me in a battle of Rock, Paper, Scissors, and I proceeded to cream him like I always did. Throwing down yet another rock when Hank went with scissors, he finally threw up his hands and yelled, "How the fuck do you do that? You outfox me almost every single time."

"Remember what Sun Tzu said: 'To know your enemy, you must become your enemy.'"

"Give me a break," Hank sighed. "Don't be bringing Mr. Lincoln's crap into this."

It was true. During Power Reading, we spent a whole week on Sun Tzu's *The Art of War*. Mr. Lincoln said that when he was a jockey, he took Tzu's lessons to heart and it led him to a great deal of success. I don't really think anyone in the class understood what Sun Tzu had to do with horse racing, and I wasn't really sure what he had to do with Rock, Paper, Scissors, either, but that one line from *The Art of War* had stuck with me and it seemed like a good time to use it.

"Hey, boys!" Weddy had a shit-eating grin on his face and his eyes were once again just two reddened slits on his face.

"Did we miss anything?" Ronnie added.

"Just me kicking Hank's butt at Rock, Paper, Scissors."

"I'll take that as a no," Ronnie said, smirking. I'm sure he considered Rock, Paper, Scissors child's play, and Ronnie wasn't really into anything that was too kid-like.

"Oh, fuck," Weddy suddenly called out, looking ahead toward the box office. "What the hell are they doing here?"

I followed Weddy's gaze only to see Moose and Clark heading away from the box office and toward us and the back of the line.

"Just ignore them," Hank advised. But, of course, that would be impossible.

"Well, well, well," Ronnie piped up, "look who's here."

Moose, immediately recognizing Ronnie's voice, picked us out from the line and while he was still a good twenty feet away, yelled, "You gotta be kidding me!"

"What are you assholes doing here?" Clark asked as they approached.

"We're going bowling," Ronnie replied sarcastically to The Big Lefty. "What the fuck do you think we're doing here, moron?"

Turning his attention to Weddy, Clark said, "I'm going to do my best to ignore this dork and ask you if you'd be so kind as to allow us to join you in this here line."

"Ha!" Ronnie immediately shot back. "Fat chance. Go drag your sorry asses to the back of the line."

"Sorry, guys," Hank interjected. "These guys behind us would have a fit."

"It's a big theater," Weddy added. "You're early enough. You'll be fine."

"Gee, thanks, guys," Moose said sarcastically as he and Clark continued past us toward the back of the line.

"Goodbye, La—"

"Ronnie!" Weddy cut him off, "come on, dude. Don't you ever stop?"

"Not with those assholes, I don't," Ronnie said proudly.

We killed the next half-hour or forty-five minutes checking out the girls in the line, seeing if there was anyone we knew from school. At one point, after the munchies had kicked in, Weddy and Ronnie walked over to Stan's Donuts and came back with a Stan's original Peanut Butter and Banana Donut for each of us.

"Ummmm, sooooo good," I said, biting into the still warm, creamy center. "What do we owe you? Who paid?"

"My treat," Weddy said. "My mom gave me some extra money today."

"Cool! Thanks, Weddy," Hank said.

We continued eating our donuts in silence, relishing every bite. It must've had an effect on the people around us because, before we knew it, everyone seemed to be chowing on Stan's up and down the line. Finally, we saw some activity up toward the front of the line, and we started moving, slowly shuffling our feet and inching toward the theater. The line had grown to gargantuan lengths behind us, continuing all the way up Broxton and turning and running down Le Conte.

"I hope this shark's worth it," Hank mused.

"You kidding?" Ronnie said. "I hear the shark is badass. This is gonna be great!"

"I agree," Weddy said. "Besides, what would you rather see: *Bug*, a movie about a bunch of giant, mutant cockroaches, or *Jaws*, about a killer shark?"

"You've got a point, Weddy," I laughed. We all looked across the street toward the Bruin Theatre, where *Bug* was playing and seemingly no one was going inside. It was supposed to be the big movie this summer, but it had gotten horrible reviews while *Jaws* was killing it at the box office.

As we approached the door, Ronnie dropped a bomb. "So here's the deal," he began. "I only bought one ticket for myself, and I'm going to go inside while Weddy takes you around the back, and I'll let you in from there."

"What?" I said, my jaw dropping.

"You've got to be fucking kidding me, Ronnie!" Hank followed.

"Weddy, are you in on this?" I asked in disbelief.

"Well, not exactly, but—"

"What the fuck, Ronnie?" Hank was mad. "I didn't come all the way down here to get thrown out of the theater. Why the fuck didn't you just buy the god damn tickets like we asked?"

I had never seen Hank so angry, and I was pissed off, too.

"Will you guys relax? I've done this a million times. I already showed Weddy where to go. Just follow him."

"Fuck," Hank and I both said in unison. We really didn't have much of a choice at this point. The movie was sold out, so the only chance we had was to blindly follow Ronnie's plan.

"I'll see you in a sec," Ronnie assured us as we stepped out of line and followed Weddy around the front of the theater, down Weyburn, and eventually made our way into an alley that ran along the side of theater, parallel to Broxton. There was a series of doors and loading docks leading into the theater, and Weddy stopped in front of one particularly nondescript door.

"He said to wait here," Weddy instructed.

"Weddy, what the fuck is the matter with you? Why did you agree to go along with this idiotic plan? You're smarter than that!" Hank, still angry, chastised.

"I really didn't have much choice," he answered. "Ronnie didn't even tell me what he was planning to do until we went to get donuts and by then it was too late to do anything about it because the tickets had already sold out."

"I hope this works," I said, looking up and down the alley nervously. After what seemed like an eternity—far longer than "a sec," as Ronnie had promised—the door slowly crept open and there was Ronnie, shushing us and waving us in silently. Once we were all inside, everything went pitch black. "Follow me," Ronnie said.

"Follow you where?" I whispered. "I can't see a fucking thing." Just then, Ronnie reached ahead of him and slowly pulled back a curtain, revealing a bit of light from the theater. He waited until a group of people, about six or eight strong, walked in front of us and then said, "Now!" We bolted out from behind the curtain and followed Ronnie as he walked directly behind the group, seamlessly merging the four of us in with them, as if we were all friends. He even turned and followed them down the row where they had chosen to sit, and after they had picked out their seats, we simply sat down next to them. They didn't seem to care or notice, and nobody else did, either.

"This good?" Ronnie asked, gesturing to the screen. We were a little closer than I preferred, and a little bit off-center for my taste, but we were in and the seats were filling up quickly.

"Perfect!" Weddy said, laughing. Hank didn't respond and was obviously still upset by Ronnie's whole charade.

"Ronnie's an ass," I whispered to him, "but I think

we're cool."

"So stupid," was all Hank could say, shaking his head. "And if he thinks I'm paying him two-and-a-quarter for the ticket, he's out of his fucking mind."

Just before the movie started, we saw an usher walking around with four people, looking for open seats. There was one that was open, and one of the group of four sat down in it, but the usher had to lead the other three out of the door. Hank and I looked at each other, feeling bad that we had obviously stolen their seats. Weddy was watching as well and he leaned over and whispered, "Well, they probably bought the last tickets, so if we had bought our seats, they wouldn't have gotten in anyway."

I doubted that was true, but they probably were toward the end of the line, so it made me feel a little bit better about what we had done. As the lights came down, Ronnie leaned over and said, "Enjoy, boys!" Hank and I just rolled our eyes and sat back, letting our anger and irritation float away as we leaned back into our cushy red velvet seats and prepared ourselves to be entertained by a killer shark.

When all was said and done, the movie was fantastic, one of the most thrilling, we all agreed, we'd ever seen. Everyone in the theater, us included, had leaped out of our seats and screamed at the top of our lungs on numerous occasions. The shark, while a bit silly, had nevertheless scared the shit out of us. "When that dude's head showed up underwater!" Ronnie said with as much excitement as I'd ever seen him muster, which was saying something, "I almost shit my pants!"

"I loved when the shark hit that guy's cage from behind. Fuck!" Hank shouted with a mixture of true horror and unabashed glee.

"What a great movie," Weddy kept saying over and over again. "What a great fucking movie."

"Scariest thing I've ever seen," I agreed.

"Although," Weddy said in all seriousness, "*The Exorcist* was pretty fucking scary."

"Nah," Ronnie responded as we walked toward the bus stop, "I don't believe in that devil crap. Now a shark—*that's* something I can believe in. I ain't ever going swimming in the ocean again!!"

We all laughed and laughed, joking about never even going into a *swimming pool*, much less the ocean, again. Fortunately, the bus arrived sooner than later, and we spent the bulk of the ride home revisiting our favorite parts of the movie. "How about when Chief Brody is throwing shit in the water and he turns to look back at his guys right when the shark jumps out of the water?" I asked.

"I loved that part!" Weddy said.

"Me, too," Hank agreed.

"I loved when the chief has the shark in the sights of his gun and he says, 'Smile, you bastard!'" Ronnie yelped.

"No," I corrected, "he says, 'Smile, you son-of-a-bitch!'"

"Yeah," Weddy added, "that's it. That's the line."

"No," Ronnie insisted, "he said 'bastard,' not 'son-of-a-bitch'."

The bus driver's voice suddenly came on the speakers. "Can you boys please keep it down back there? The whole bus can hear you."

"Shit," Weddy whispered.

"We're sorry, ma'am," Hank called out.

"You guys are wrong," Ronnie whispered. "It's bastard!"

"Whatever, Ronnie," I waved him off. "Who cares? Whatever he said, it was funny."

"Agreed," Ronnie smiled. "Hey," he continued after a few moments of silence, "is it cool if we settle up now?"

"Sure," Weddy said. "What do we owe you?"

"Well," Ronnie replied as if he had given this a great deal of thought, "the tickets were two-twenty-five apiece, right?"

"And?" Hank said, already sounding irritated at what was coming next.

"So, I was thinking maybe you guys would pay me a buck fifty each?"

"You're out of your fucking mind!" Hank was trying desperately to keep his voice down but was having tremendous difficulty doing so.

"I got you guys in for free!" Ronnie argued.

"Exactly," I said. "Why should we pay you anything?"

"Well, Ronnie did have to buy his ticket," Weddy pointed out, always the reasonable one.

"Fine," I offered, "how about the three of us pay for Ronnie's ticket. We'll each give you seventy-five cents." I looked at Hank. "You cool with that, dude?"

"Yeah, I guess so," Hank responded, reaching into his pocket and handing Ronnie three quarters.

Ronnie begrudgingly accepted the change. "Whatever . . . ungrateful assholes. Last time I ever do you a favor."

"We didn't ask you to do a favor for us, Ronnie," Hank shot back.

Weddy and I each handed Ronnie a dollar and, in order to lighten the mood, I said, "Keep the change, Ronnie."

"Me, too," Weddy joined in.

"Gee, thanks," was Ronnie's sarcastic response to

what I thought was a nice gesture on our part.

The movie had been so much fun that nothing—not an argument over how much we owed Ronnie, or whether Chief Brody had said "bastard" or "son-of-a-bitch"—could ruin the high the movie thriller had delivered, and on the walk home, after splitting off from Ronnie and Weddy, who had, of course, gone off to smoke a doobie, Hank and I were still buzzing.

"God, I love a good movie," Hank said.

"I know," I agreed. "Hey, I heard *Walking Tall Part 2* is coming out in a couple of weeks. Wanna go see it?"

"Hell yeah," Hank smiled, "I love Sheriff Pusser. Dude is badass with that club."

"I know! I wouldn't want to fuck with that guy."

"But I betcha Ronnie would take him on!" With that, Hank and I doubled over with laughter, shaking so hard neither of us could get the key in the front gate. Finally, Hank managed to do it, and we waved goodbye to each other and went to our own homes.

That night, before I went to bed, I decided to give Natalia a call. "Hello?" a gruff voice answered.

"Uh, hi, Mr. Guinzberg. It's Douglas. Is Natalia home?"

"Isn't it a bit late to be calling?"

"I'm sorry, sir, Natalia told me it was okay to call up to ten o'clock during the summer." There was no response.

"Natalia! Phone!" Mr. Guinzberg shouted. After a few moments of stressful silence, she picked up.

"Hello?"

"Hi Natalia. It's Douglas."

"Dad, can you please hang up?"

"Nine o'clock, young lady."

"What?"

Her dad repeated the directive. "No phone calls after nine o'clock. You know that."

"Dad, it's summer. Mom said I could talk to friends until ten. *Permiso? Por favor?*"

"*Ni a palos!* Nine o'clock," he repeated. This was followed by a stern "click" as he got off of the line.

"Sorry about that," Natalia apologized. "Rough day at the pharmacy."

"I hope I didn't get you in trouble," I said.

"Oh, don't worry about him," Natalia replied in her sweet voice. "My mom will take care of it. How are you? What'd you do today?"

I recounted my adventures with Hank, Weddy, and Ronnie in Westwood; meanwhile, Natalia told me about her day working at her dad's pharmacy and her trip to the orthodontist. "It looks like I'll be joining you in the braces brigade," she said.

"Welcome to the club!" I offered.

"Fortunately, he said I'd only have to wear them for a year. Eighteen months at the max."

"You're lucky," I said while adjusting my headgear. "I'm looking at three years minimum."

"Oh, you poor thing," Natalia said sympathetically.

"Do you have to wear a headgear?" I asked, still struggling to get the headgear in a comfortable position. Whoever thought it was a good idea to put kids in these things and then make them sleep with it must've been a sadistic bastard.

"No, he didn't say anything about that. Why, do you have to wear one?"

"No," I lied, quickly realizing that the last thing I wanted was to put an image of me wearing a headgear into

Natalia's head. "Fortunately, my teeth aren't that bad." The bitter truth was that my teeth were awful. The teeth on the bottom row were so twisted it was amazing Dr. Savage thought he could ever straighten them out. The top wasn't so bad, but my adult teeth were really slow to come in and there just wasn't enough room for them. Before the whole process started, I had to have thirteen—thirteen!—teeth taken out. Most of them were baby teeth, but they even pulled a couple of adult teeth to create space. "Now, count backward from one hundred," I remember the nurse saying after they had given me some sleeping gas. "One hundred, nine—" and I was out. Okay, okay, it didn't exactly happen like that, and yes, I stole that joke from Bill Cosby's "Tonsils" routine, but I did go under quickly, and the next thing I remember I was on a small bed in the dental surgeon's office, waking up from the sleeping gas, my mouth feeling swollen from all of the Novocain.

Thankfully, since we had only become friends earlier this year, Natalia didn't remember seeing me in seventh grade, when I used to have to wear my headgear twenty-four/seven. I mean, seriously, what evil orthodontist decided it was okay for kids to wear a headgear to school? Talk about public shaming. "Hey, Douglas," the mean kids would tease, "do you need your feedbag yet? Should we attach some reins to that bridle?" The cruelty of those kids was relentless.

When we first moved here, being "the new kid" was tough enough. But the bullying and even anti-Semitism I encountered at my new school was brutal. Days after I first arrived, I was walking from one class to another when I suddenly noticed a few pennies at my feet. I ignored them and continued walking when suddenly a few more pennies were rolling around me. "Hey, Jewboy, aren't you gonna pick them up?" A group of boys I recognized from my grade were standing off to the side of the walkway, laughing. I ignored them and kept walking, but it was the most bizarre behavior I'd ever experienced. At my old school in Northridge, I was practically the only Jewish kid in the school, and nobody ever said one word about it. Then I moved to Encino, where ninety-eight percent of the kids at my new school were Jewish, and suddenly I was being teased for being Jewish. *Huh?* What was the logic to that one? My dad said the kids throwing the pennies were all just self-hating Jews, whatever that meant. At the time, I generally took it all out on my mom, staring daggers at her for selling our old house, moving us into this much smaller townhouse, and forcing us to do it during the middle of seventh grade. The only good to come out of it was that we were now just a few blocks away from my dad and my stepmom, so I was able to see them a bit more—at least when my dad was at home and not in the office.

In fact, between the throwing of the pennies at my feet, the teasing about my headgear, and my "husky" body, I was one miserable hombre when we first moved to Encino from Northridge.

It got so bad that one night about a year ago I simply ran away from home. I was missing my friends from grade school, didn't have any new friends yet at my new school, and my dad had recently announced he was going to marry his girlfriend, Cindy (now my stepmom), which really drove home the finality of my mom and dad's divorce even though my mom had already been seeing Art for quite some time. As a little kid, though, you tend to hold onto this fantasy that your mom and dad are somehow going to make things work, get back together, and all would be well once again. But now that my mom *and* my dad were in serious relationships? Well, I guess the reality of it was too much for me to handle, and so I ran away. I mean, I didn't really run away, I just spent the night in the sauna back by the pool. Still, I was gone all night, my mom and dad were in a panic, my brother and sister were searching the neighborhood all night long . . . hell, my mom even called the police!

By the time I reappeared in the morning, everyone was super pissed off. There wasn't a lot of sympathy for me or what I had done or why I had done it. Instead, my mom simply signed me up to see a shrink. At first, I actually didn't mind going. Dr. Spangler was a decent enough guy. He had long gray hair and always wore a sweater, even when it was triple digits outside. Mostly, we'd just play darts for an hour and talk about stuff. I didn't really get the point of the whole exercise, but it made my parents feel better about themselves to have me going there, so I just went along with it. But after about six months or so, I had begun making new friends and was adjusting to my new life in Encino, and I started dreading the sessions. Finally, one day while I was playing a game of Whiffle ball in the alley behind our townhouse with Hank, Weddy, Ronnie, and some other kids from the complex, my mom shouted out the window that it was time for me to go to "my appointment."

"What appointment?" Hank asked.

"Oh, I just have to go the doctor for a check-up," I answered.

"But if you leave we won't have enough players for the game," Weddy complained.

"Mom, please," I begged, yelling up to her in the window, "can't I just skip it?"

"Douglas, you know we can't just skip it. We have an appointment."

"Sorry, guys," I said. "Gotta go."

"That sucks," Ronnie said. I have to admit, walking away from that game and having my new friends sorry to see me go—even if it was just because they needed an extra body—sure did feel good. I hadn't had that since the move from Northridge. And that day was a turning point in other ways as well, because it would be the last time I'd ever have to see Dr. Spangler, who pronounced me cured of my melancholy and free to continue on with my life without his assistance.

"Thank you, Dr. Spangler," my mom said as we left his office for the last time. "We really appreciate all of the work you did with Douglas."

All of the work? What a racket. A guy gets paid thirty dollars an hour just to sit and play darts with kids all day. Sounds like a pretty cush job to me.

After a few more minutes of small talk with Natalia— she told me that she was going shopping for earrings this weekend with her older sister, Catalina (a truly beautiful girl who was by far and away the smartest kid at her high school, a private girls school where Natalia would probably end up going), as Natalia had gotten her ears pierced awhile back for her thirteenth birthday—we made plans to go to Topanga Plaza on Sunday and said our goodnights.

"Sleep tight," Natalia said, yawning.

"You, too," I yawned in kind. "Oh, I almost forgot. I've been meaning to ask you . . . my mom said that Lew Farmer told her that the police came to your house a few nights ago. Is that true? What happened?"

"What?" Natalia responded incredulously. "Lew said that? That guy should mind his own business. The police came to the Baxter's house next door. I think their car was broken into while they were at Sav-On or something."

"Yeah," I replied, "Lew's an idiot. One time, he told everyone that my mom had left my dad and shacked up with a much younger guy. What he failed to realize was that Art was seven years *older* than my mom!"

"He's a jerk," Natalia said sullenly.

"Hey, sorry, I didn't mean to bring you down. Lew's not worth getting worked up about."

"No, I know, you're right," Natalia replied, sounding more like herself. "Enough about Lew. Sweet dreams and I'll talk to you soon!" she said cheerily.

I put on my best Robert Redford voice and purred, "Good night, Natalia. Sweet dreams." I swear I could feel her blush through the phone cord.

I hung up the phone and turned on my clock radio to see what KMET was playing. I loved my Panasonic clock radio. It had a rack of small metal numbers that would flip over as the minutes and hours went by. The radio dial was illuminated in this sort of futuristic green Fluorescent color that glowed in the dark. And it had a sleep feature where you could turn on the radio when you went to sleep and it would go off automatically twenty or thirty minutes later so that you could fall asleep to the sounds of Neil Young, or the Eagles, or whoever the DJ was playing.

Tonight it was Elton John, and as "Someone Saved My Life Tonight" played softly beside my ear, that tinny but somehow comforting sound coming out of the tiny speaker on the clock radio, I thought about my upcoming date with Natalia. We'd do a little shopping—me at the

Wherehouse record store, she, undoubtedly, at one of the numerous jewelry stores in the mall—followed by lunch near the rain fountain, a faux water feature made out of wire and drops of glycerin that actually looked like real raindrops falling from the sky. Afterward, we'd hit the ice rink, where we'd hold hands, and I'd pick Natalia up off the ground after she'd fallen, pulling her close to me and kissing her on the lips the way that I imagined more experienced lovers did it.

As my eyes closed and I started to drift off to sleep, Van Morrison came on the radio. "And it stoned me, to my soul," I began to softly sing, my mouth barely moving. God, I loved Van the Man. David turned me onto *Astral Weeks* when I was about six years old, and it's always held a magical place in my heart. I took a deep breath, exhaled, thought once again about kissing Natalia, and succumbed to the sandman while Van serenaded me into a deep slumber.

When I woke up the following morning, Natalia was still at the forefront of my mind. In fact, I swear I could smell her lemon lotion on my pillowcase. Wishful thinking, I know, but a boy can dream, can't he? I decided that today would be the day I would go back to The Sixth Chakra to buy the ring.

We were in the middle of one of our runs of June Gloom, when fog and low clouds would cover the Southland, keeping temperatures relatively low. Of course, in the Valley, it would always burn off at some point, but often not until the early- or mid-afternoon, which meant that temperatures would stay in the seventies for much of the day. Taking advantage of the brief respite from the heat—July through October would present no such relief, with temperatures at least in the high eighties and many,

many days in the nineties or hundreds—I decided to ride my bike over there.

Hopping on my blue Schwinn Stingray, with the sparkling blue banana seat for extra comfort, I headed up the alley behind our complex, cut through one of the apartment buildings and over to Newcastle where I crossed Ventura and then rode south of the boulevard to Valley Vista. I could take Valley Vista, a lightly traveled alternate to busy Ventura, all the way to White Oak, where the street would turn into Rancho. Then it was just a few more blocks to Louise, where I'd hang a left and head back toward Ventura and The Sixth Chakra.

It was a quiet morning, a Tuesday in late June. The Jacarandas were nearing the end of their flowering season, and there were piles of indigo flowers all over the sidewalks, parkways, and gutters lining the streets. Back East, they get piles of snow, but here in Southern California, our streets fill with mounds of spent Jacaranda flowers. Pretty nice deal, I'd say.

The neighborhood in this part of Encino was a tight-knit community of people who bought tract homes in the fifties and sixties for thirty or forty grand, and raised families in the small, three-bedroom, two-bath homes with a front and back yard and a handful of fruit trees. I knew a bunch of kids who lived around here and had been in several of their homes, but they all pretty much looked the same to me. "Cookie-cutter" homes, my mom called them. The only difference was that some dads decided to fill the backyard with a small pool, others decided to just get a small above-ground pool, while most just preferred to enjoy a small patch of grass, a flower garden, and the aforementioned fruit trees, and call it a day. Everyone, of course, left room for their Weber charcoal grill.

I approached The Sixth Chakra from the back, jumped off my bike, and ran the chain around a small tree, weaving it between both wheels and around the frame and locking it with my key. Bikes were always getting stolen, and you had to really be vigilant and not let your guard down for a second or your bike would be gone. I had learned this the hard way a few years ago back in Northridge, when Greg Steiner's older brother stole this same bike out of our garbage can enclosure on the side of our house.

My best friend at the time, Nick Einhorn, lived across the street. He was standing at his kitchen window making a milkshake in the blender, when he looked out and saw Greg's brother and a friend wheeling my bike out of the area where we kept our trash cans and where I often parked my bike. He picked up the phone and called me to tell me what was happening.

"David!" I yelled. "Greg Steiner's older brother is stealing my bike!!"

David, who loved a good fight, leapt up from the couch and ran toward me as I headed down the back hall and out the door that led to our driveway. As soon as we got outside, we could see the two thieves riding down the street toward the acres of open land behind our house. David, a stellar athlete who was in great shape at that time as he was playing multiple sports at Granada High, took off running.

"Hey assholes! Drop the bike!" I heard him shout.

Steiner's brother and his friend turned and looked back with horror in their eyes; they were only about fourteen at the time, and David was sixteen or maybe even seventeen at that point, so he was a lot bigger and stronger than they were. They quickly picked up their pace, peddling as fast as they could, trying to get to the field where they could hide among the trees, the tall weeds, or even the patch of cornfield on the other side of the property, but David was fast and was gaining on them. I was falling further and further behind, and when they turned the corner and headed into the field, I lost sight of all of them. Eventually, the thieves not only ditched my bike, but they ditched the bike they had brought with them, and they ran off and hid somewhere. David never found them, but after a few minutes he reappeared, a huge smile on his face as he wheeled both my bike *and* their bike alongside him.

"Did you see those pussies run?" David laughed.

"Thanks, man," I said, taking my bike. "I owe you one."

That night, my parents called Steiner's parents, and they made Greg's older brother and his friend come to the house and apologize before picking up their bike which, it turned out, had also been stolen. I later heard that the parents of the kid whose bike was also stolen had not been as cool as my parents and that they pressed charges with the police, and Steiner's brother and his friend ended up spending three months in Juvenile Hall. Evidently, it wasn't the first time they'd been caught stealing. Greg and I remained friendly, and the topic was never really brought up between us since my family had been cool about the whole thing. And once his brother got out of Juvi, he also didn't seem to have any problem with me whenever I'd see him around the neighborhood. I don't think he ever learned his lesson, though. The last I'd heard, he had dropped out of high school and was trying to live a life on the rails, like some sort of hobo.

The Sixth Chakra was quiet today, and when I walked in, the only person in the store was Saffron, and damn if she wasn't looking even more beautiful than when I was in here the last time.

"Oh, hey!" she said as I entered, smiling broadly at me. "I was wondering when you'd come back. Douglas, right?"

I couldn't believe she remembered my name. "Ye-ye-ah," I stammered. "Saffron, right?"

"Very good!" She continued to smile and looked at me with her blue eyes, melting me to my soul, before reaching down beneath the counter to grab the ring. "I think it's so cute that you're giving a girl this ring!" she chirped.

And there it was again: "Cute." Another dagger to the heart.

"Um, yeah, I really like her," I said.

"Well, I know I said I'd give you the ring for eight dollars, but because I'm in such a good mood today, how about if I let you have it for seven-fifty? That'd be a whole dollar off of the normal price."

"That'd be great!" I said. "Thanks so much!"

"My pleasure, sweetie." After she had given me my change and as I was turning to walk out the door, she demanded, "Now you make sure you come back at some point and tell me whether or not she accepted your proposal, you hear?"

"Okay, I promise. I'll be back." And who wouldn't want to come back to visit someone like her?

"See you later," she called out.

"Bye," I said, backing out the door and taking one last glance at this true Southern California beauty. I pulled the ring out of the bag and rolled it around in the palm of my hand, imagining it in all its glory wrapped around Natalia's finger. She was going to love it.

On the way back home, I decided to vary my route a

bit, cutting off of Valley Vista onto Enfield, which I'd take down to Santa Rita and over to Lindley. Enfield was a very quiet side street, and as I rode down it, I could see a group of kids up ahead playing baseball. I slowed down as I approached, not wanting to mess up their game. Suddenly, one of the kids who I recognized as a guy who was in ninth grade when I was in seventh grade, shouted out, "Are you coming through, or what?" He was notorious at Cabrillo and held the record for most days in detention in one semester—fifty-two, I believe.

"Sorry, I was just—" My foot slipped off the pedal and I almost fell off my bike.

"Come on, dufus," Mr. Detention yelled, "we're trying to play a game here. Can you believe this idiot?" He turned and looked at his friends, kids I also recognized as being part of the "rough crowd" at school.

I began to pedal when suddenly one of the kids reached out and grabbed my arm, jerking me to a stop. "Hey. Isn't this guy friends with that Ronnie asshole?"

"Oh yeah," Mr. Detention said as he moved toward me. "What's your name, kid?"

"Um, Douglas."

"And, Um Douglas," he turned and laughed at his friends, waiting until they recognized his joke and laughed in kind before returning to me. "You know this guy, Ronnie, right? You're friends with him, right?"

"Yeah, I sort of know him," I said, not wanting to reveal too much at this point. My heart was pounding, and this was not going well.

Mr. Detention suddenly sucker-punched me right in the stomach, knocking the wind out of me. It was a well-known that he was a Bruce Lee freak—he was usually wearing some kind of T-shirt featuring the karate legend—and was supposedly a fifth-degree black belt himself. I gasped for air, tears welling up in my eyes. "You tell that little fuck that I didn't appreciate the way he and his dad talked to me and my dad when I saw him at Flooky's, and that he might think he's tough when his dad's with him, but the next time I see him without his dad around, he's gonna get what's coming to him. You got it?"

"Yeah," I said, barely able to get the words out. "I got it."

"Now get the fuck out of here," and with that he shoved my bike forward; I was barely able to hang on and start pedaling, but pedal I did, riding as fast as I could and not daring to look back for the rest of the ride home.

This certainly wasn't the first time Ronnie's big mouth had gotten him into trouble, and it certainly wouldn't be the last. I wondered what had happened. Ronnie had never mentioned anything to me about it, but then again, this was probably just another minor skirmish, a regular occurrence in Ronnie's life. And when his dad was with him, anything could happen. His dad was well-known in the Valley, having been born and raised here and remained here as an adult. He was a badass juvenile delinquent as a kid, and while he was a respectable car mechanic at this point and didn't seem to live a life of crime as far an anyone knew, he was still a badass. One of two men I knew with tattoos on their arms, the other being Hank's cousin who was in the Marines.

While Flooky's was a great place to go to grab a hot dog and fries, it also had some batting cages, so I can only imagine whatever happened between Mr. Detention and his dad and Ronnie and his dad also involved baseball bats. Ronnie had gone to Vegas with his family to stay with a relative for a couple of weeks, which meant I had to wait to talk to him about the incident with Mr. Detention and his gang, but once I found out he had returned, I called him immediately.

"What an asshole," Ronnie said when I told him about the sucker punch Mr. Detention had delivered to me. "I'm sorry he did that to you," he offered by way of an apology.

"What the hell happened at Flooky's?" I asked.

"Nothing! It was so stupid," Ronnie insisted. "My dad was in the Koufax cage, and after he finished one round, he decided he wanted to do another round now that he was warmed up and feeling it. That asshole's dad tried to insist that you couldn't do two rounds in the cage in a row while someone was waiting, which is total bullshit. My dad told him to 'fuck off,' there was a bit of shoving between the four of us, and a couple of bats even got raised into the air, but there happened to be an off-duty cop in the Gibson cage right next to us, and he broke it all up. My dad proceeded to step back into the Koufax cage and crush every single pitch that came at him."

Ronnie's dad had once hoped to become a pro baseball player, "but it just wasn't in the cards," was all Ronnie would ever say about his aborted career. I wasn't happy that I had somehow been dragged into this skirmish, but I will say that there is no rule at Flooky's that you can't do more than one round in the cage while someone is waiting, so Ronnie's dad was in the right. Still, why did seemingly every minor confrontation involving Ronnie or his dad have to end in a major argument or even violence?

Chapter Eight

July Fourth was here before we knew it. None of us had any big plans, so Weddy, Ronnie, Hank, and I decided to go over to Balboa Park to spend the afternoon playing ball and then watching the fireworks at night. The truth was, I'd secretly made plans to hook up with Natalia, who was going to be there with her parents. We agreed to meet at the big Ficus tree in front of the swings just before the fireworks were to begin. I hadn't told any of the guys of my plan, and just figured I'd be able to sneak away once it got dark.

Things had been going pretty well between the two of us. We had had a great day together at Topanga Plaza, and while Natalia's summer job at her dad's pharmacy made it hard for us to spend a lot of time together, we did try to see each other for a few minutes almost every night between when she got home from work and when we each had to go inside to eat dinner with our families. Her mom and dad were pretty strict, and I got the sense that they didn't want anything serious to develop between the two of us.

I still hadn't given Natalia the ring I bought for her. The day at Topanga Plaza just didn't seem right—after all, there is *nothing* romantic about a mall, though I was tempted to do it when we were in the ice rink, until, that is, we ran into some kids we knew and hung out with them for a bit—and there was never enough time to get into anything serious during our brief chats after she got home from work. So, I had decided that, being July Fourth and all, today would make a great day to give Natalia the ring and ask her if she'd like to go steady.

I was notably nervous the morning of the Fourth and must've changed my clothes a hundred times. I had to balance looking nice for Natalia with all the stuff I'd be doing with my friends the rest of the day, most importantly, playing basketball at the park. I ultimately decided that I had to wear my Superstars, but could forgo any kind of basketball trunks for a pair of dark blue denim shorts with fringe at the bottom. I brought a white T-shirt to play ball in, and wore a light blue-and-orange striped Hang Ten shirt for the rest of the day. I purposely placed Natalia's ring in my pocket as soon as I was dressed, just to be safe and make sure I didn't forget it.

The rest of the morning and early afternoon seemed to drag by. There were some old *Twilight Zones* on TV that helped kill a couple of hours—David and I had probably watched every episode together several times over, with Burgess Meredith as the bookworm wandering around in a post-nuclear wasteland ranking as my favorite show, while David preferred the one featuring Telly Savalas being driven crazy by a spooky talking doll who keeps threatening to kill him—but three o'clock took forever to arrive, especially since I had been dressed and ready to go since late morning. Hank, Weddy, Ronnie, and I had decided that we'd first grab some subs at Nick's and then head over to the park. There was going to be a stage set up, and several bands were going to play, and there was sure to be plenty of action on the basketball courts.

It was a typically roasting Fourth of July, with temperatures close to a hundred degrees by the mid-afternoon, so by the time we made it up Lindley to Nick's and then back down Lindley toward Burbank, we were already sweating.

"Damn, it's hot," Weddy complained.

"We should take Killion instead of Burbank," Hank said. "It's cooler."

"Fuck that," Ronnie demanded. "It's much farther. You have to go around and up to Margate and all that shit."

"Yeah, but at least there's trees and shade along the way. And Burbank, with all the cars . . . it's just much hotter."

"You do what you want," Ronnie waved him off. "I'm taking the shortest way there."

The real reason Ronnie didn't want to go the back way was because then we'd pass right by his parent's place on Yarmouth, and he didn't want to chance running into them. I knew this, because earlier, when I went outside to meet the guys, Ronnie was the first one there and he told me he had just gotten into a huge fight with his mom. His eyes were red, and it looked like he had been crying.

"Hey, Hank," I said. "Let's just take Burbank. It *is* shorter."

"Alright, whatever," Hank replied. Ronnie shot me a quick look of thanks that neither Hank nor Weddy saw. As we crossed Burbank, a car had pulled a few feet into the crosswalk, so Ronnie did his best Dustin Hoffman imitation, slamming his hands onto the hood of the car and screaming, "Hey! I'm walkin' here!"

Hank, Weddy, and I were mortified, terrified that the guy behind the wheel was going to jump out and beat the crap out of us. Instead, he must've been a *Midnight Cowboy* fan because he just sat in his car and laughed hysterically.

"Jesus, Ronnie," Hank said. "You're going to get us killed one day."

"What's a matter?" he said, maintaining Hoffman's New York accent. "Haven't you ever seen *Midnight Cowboy*?"

"You're not the only one with Z channel, Ronnie," I countered

"Whatever. Lighten up. It was funny!"

"Hey! Look! Santa Rosas!" Weddy was pointing excitedly toward a plum tree that was on the other side of a cement block wall. A few of the branches were hanging over the sidewalk, but the only fruit we could see was clearly in the owner's backyard. But that didn't matter to Weddy. "Quick," he said sotto voce, "give me a boost."

Ronnie bent down and offered his hands clasped together about knee high. Weddy placed his tennis shoe into the improvised step, and Ronnie helped lift him up the wall. By just sitting on the wall facing the yard, Weddy was able to grab eight or ten ripe Santa Rosa plums off of the tree before you could say "lickety-split." He tossed the plums down to us quickly, and we caught every one of the precious cargo, and after Weddy hopped back down, we took off racing up Burbank. A couple of blocks later, we figured we were safe even if the owner or a neighbor had seen us, so we slowed down and started enjoying our bounty, the dark, purple juice running down each of our chins.

Out of all the incredible fruit grown in the Valley—peaches, nectarines, apricots, pomegranates—nothing could touch a Santa Rosa plum. And I'm not even counting the wide variety of citrus that grew all around us, because citrus was a second-class citizen when compared to the stone fruits. The unique sweet and sour taste of a

Santa Rosa was incomparable, and they were always at their peak ripeness right around July Fourth, so juicy that shirts worn around that time of the year inevitably ended up with a few stains here and there from the stream of juice that would squirt out whenever you'd take that first bite of the plum. Of course, if you wanted to play it safe, you could always just shove the whole plum in your mouth, you just had to be careful not to swallow the pit.

As we approached Balboa Park, we could see it was packed. There didn't appear to be any spaces left in the parking lot, and hundreds—thousands?—of people were spread out all over the place. There were a multitude of games going on—people were playing softball on the baseball fields, volleyball over on the volleyball courts, and of course every basketball court was at least two or three games deep.

"We better go call a game and then eat lunch," Hank suggested.

"Where do you want to play?" I asked. Hank was good enough to play on any court, even with the bigger, older guys. I noticed that some pretty skilled players were running full court with the Jackson brothers. Jermaine, Jackie, and Marlon were out here a lot. It was no big deal, there were all kinds of stars living in Encino, and you'd see them everywhere—the deli, the car wash, and, yes, even on the basketball courts. In fact, the great John Wooden could be seen early every morning on his daily walk around the park. "I don't know if I have the energy to hang on court one," I said. "It's too fucking hot."

"Yeah," Weddy concurred. "I don't want to push it too hard. It's a holiday after all." Weddy never pushed it too hard. In fact, even though he probably had the athleticism to be a varsity-level player, he rarely put it on display. The simple fact was that he just didn't care enough, would rather go get high. I fell somewhere in between Weddy and Hank. I didn't have the drive or talent of Hank, and I probably wasn't as naturally gifted as Weddy, but I generally outplayed him because I was such a pure shooter and was willing to hustle when necessary.

"Court two looks good," Hank proclaimed confidently. I looked over and saw a group of kids around our age playing. They seemed like decent players, but nobody in the same league as Hank. We were sure to dominate. Hank walked over, found out who had the next game and the one after that, and then told them we'd be taking the third game down the line.

We all sat down beneath the shade of some Eucalyptus trees and watched the games while eating our submarine sandwiches. I had brought along a cold can of Hawaiian Punch, which went down nice and smooth in the summer heat. When it got to the game before ours, we started paying closer attention, especially when one team began pulling away from the other, and it became obvious who we'd be matching up against.

"I'll take the kid with the cut-offs," Hank said, pointing to the best player on that team. "Weddy, you take the dude with the 'fro, Ronnie you can take their center, and Douglas you can take the blond guy." After the current game was over, Hank would ask the tall skinny kid who was the best player on the losing team to play with us, and he could guard the other team's fifth player.

"Sounds like a plan," I said agreeably. Hank always knew best when it came to matching up on the court.

"Ronnie, you think you can handle that guy? He's

pretty big. . . ." Weddy asked.

"You kidding?" Ronnie was obviously offended by Weddy's doubtful tone. "That clown's a dufus. I'll destroy him," Ronnie said confidently. Offensively, Ronnie couldn't destroy anybody; he had a crappy shot and couldn't dribble worth shit. But he was a very strong defender and a damn fine rebounder.

"Just box him out," was all Hank said. He knew Ronnie's strengths and limitations.

I was a great shooter from the outside, could pass and handle the ball adequately, but that was about it. I didn't rebound much, unless it was off of a long bounce, and my defense was, well, adequate at best. But when I got hot, I could hit several shots in a row and either get you back into a game quickly, or help you build an insurmountable lead. I was especially good when I got to play with Hank—though he made everyone he played with better—because he was terrific at driving the lane and kicking it to me in the corner. I loved baseline shots and could drill them from as far back as the very corner of the court.

Back when Jimmy McMillian was with the Lakers, he was one of my favorite players, and I used to imitate his deadly corner shot. The more I pretended to be Jimmy Mac on the court, the better my shot from the baseline became, eventually becoming my best shot, my secret weapon. I'd just park myself in the corner and wait for Hank to drive and kick it out to me. Since my man would invariably cheat toward helping his teammate guard Hank as he drove to the basket, I was usually left wide open and I'd make the guy guarding me pay for leaving me to go double-team Hank. If he didn't drop off of me to help on Hank, Hank would just continue straight to the basket, where he could beat his guy nine times out of ten. Our opponents were damned if they did, damned if they didn't, and could rarely figure out a way to stop us.

As I said, Weddy had talent, but you never knew if you were going to get the Weddy who was focused and keen on winning, or the loafer Weddy who would barely get up and down the court, spending much of the game between the two tops of the key and just not doing a whole lot. Fortunately, today, in spite of his stated ambition of taking it easy, Weddy was playing well, and we were able to hold the court for five straight games. Hank was a genius for picking up the tall, skinny kid, as he was able to give us some more presence inside, especially against the teams who had some considerable size of their own. Ronnie did his Maurice Lucas imitation, and Hank just dominated anyone who tried to guard him. I hit my usual assortment of outside shots, including plenty of open looks from the corner, and as I said Weddy was solid until the latter part of the last game when he threw the ball away on three consecutive possessions down the stretch, and we lost our fifth game by a bucket.

"Sorry, guys," Weddy said as we walked off the court.

"Don't worry about it, Weddy," I consoled him. I was done anyway.

"Yeah," Ronnie agreed. "I couldn't have played another game. Five is plenty. It's too fucking hot. Let's go get high."

"I'm up for that!" Weddy said, in what would not rank as a big surprise.

Hank still hadn't said anything. I knew how competitive he was, and how much he hated losing, even a stupid game in the park, but he was also such a nice friend that he wasn't about to come down on Weddy for blowing a pick-up game. Especially after we had reeled off four wins in a row.

"You okay?" I asked Hank.

"Yeah, just not crazy about how I played. Too many stupid turnovers. I don't know what's wrong with me. I don't seem to be able to control my dribble like I used to. And my shins are killing me."

"Are you kidding? You dominated out there. Besides, it's probably just growing pains. You seem like you've already shot up a couple of inches this summer."

"I know," Hank replied, smiling. "It's crazy."

I offered up our Soul Brother #3 handshake, which featured a meeting of the back of our hands followed by the wiggling of all five digits, and we walked over to the area where people were relaxing in front of a stage watching a band play. I didn't recognize the name of the group, but there were so many bands in the Valley—many of them quite good and featuring very talented musicians—that it was hard to keep up with them all. I knew The Sylvers were supposed to headline the night—Foster Sylver went to our junior high—but that was still a couple of hours away.

We picked out a spot on the grass and settled in. All around us were the usual assortment of Valley denizens—neighborhood families with little kids, large groups of Mexicans celebrating together around kegs of beer, hippies and stoners smoking joints . . . it was a mellow, celebratory scene, with plenty of kites and balloons dotting the blazing blue sky. The band onstage launched into a cover of "Smoke on the Water," and Weddy lit one up.

"Bah, bahh, bahhh," he sang between hits. "Bah, bahh

... bahhh–bahhhh!"

"Shut up and quit bogarting the joint," Ronnie admonished. The two of them continued to pass it between them; I abstained as usual, and Hank was passed out on the lawn, recovering from the basketball games where he definitely exerted himself twice as hard as any of us.

We basically just hung out there for the next couple of hours. The day's heat finally giving way to a beautifully balmy evening. Several bands came and went, each more faceless than the other. By the time The Sylvers came on, the sun had begun to set and the crowd had swelled in anticipation of the fireworks. Everyone seemed to dig their R&B, Jackson 5-like sound—a relief after hearing generic cover band after generic cover band take the stage earlier in the day—with many getting up off of their feet to dance. Even though it wasn't my favorite type of music, I had to admit that Foster and his siblings were pretty talented kids. Not in the league of the Jackson 5, of course, but talented nonetheless.

About fifteen minutes before the fireworks were supposed to start, I told the guys I had to go take a piss and took off to get together with Natalia over by our appointed meeting spot. As I approached I could see she was already there waiting for me, which made my heart glad. I reached down into my pocket and fingered the ring, making sure it was still there, even though I'd already done that fifty times this afternoon and knew it was safe and secure. When she finally saw me coming, Natalia smiled that lovely smile of hers and ran toward me, leaping into my arms and kissing me all over.

"I didn't know if you were going to come," she said.

"Why wouldn't I come?" I asked sincerely.

"I don't know. I just didn't know," she repeated, smiling.

We held hands and walked around a bit, chatting about our respective days. Hers had been fairly dull as she had been with her family for most of the afternoon and evening. I told her about our basketball games, and she was disappointed that she didn't get to see me play. "The next time you play, you have to promise to tell me so that I can come and watch."

"Okay," I promised, but I doubted I'd do it as I'd never hear the end of it from the guys.

All around us, people were settling in, anxious for the fireworks to begin. I glanced over and happened to catch a glimpse of BJ Turner, the hottest chick in ninth grade last year, straddling an older guy I didn't recognize, pinning down his shoulders while kissing him madly. BJ had quite the reputation around school. Aside from being a classic Southern California girl, the type the Beach Boys always sang about, with a perpetually tanned and trim body, long bleached blonde hair, pouty lips, and just flat-out beautiful tits, she was known as "BJ" not because of anything to do with her name, which was really Alice, but because of her reputation of giving the best blow jobs at school. All of the jocks talked about it incessantly, so it was common knowledge. Hell, it was even rumored that she provided the service to Mr. Knightly, the theater teacher who kept a van on campus and used to "entertain" his favorite acting students within its curtained-drawn windows. The tales around school about what went on in that van were legendary, and mostly revolved around sex, drugs, and rock and roll. It was hard to believe everything you heard, but there was no doubt that Knightly had a thing for his young female students, and with his beard and long hair—he was definitely more artist than teacher—the junior high school girls were attracted to him as well.

"Who you looking at?" Natalia queried.

"Oh, I just noticed BJ over there," I said, pointing over to the girl of every Cabrillo boy's dream. She was now adjusting her tube top and swatting away her latest beau's hands as they reached up to touch her breasts.

"What a slut," Natalia said, her mood suddenly darkening.

"Yeah, I know," I said. "Hey, what's the matter?" Natalia had let go of my hand and was walking away from me, her pace quickening. "Natalia! Hey, wait up!"

I rushed back up to her and noticed a couple of tears running down her cheeks. "What's the matter?" I asked. "Are you okay?"

"I don't like it when you look at other girls," she said.

"Huh? But I was just, I mean—"

"You were fantasizing about her, weren't you?" Natalia demanded. Jeez, I had never seen her like this.

"What?" I said incredulously. "Fantasizing? I don't know what you're talking about. Come on, Natalia," I said, wrapping my arm around her. "You know you're the only one for me."

She turned and looked at me with her deep, dark eyes. "Really? Do you really mean that?"

"Of course I do," I answered softly, and then I kissed her gently on the lips. Wiping the remaining tears from her cheeks, I kissed her again, and she smiled.

Was now the right time to give her the ring? I started to reach down to put my hand in my pocket.

"I'm sorry," she said. "Sometimes I can get a little

jealous."

"It's okay. I understand," I lied, bringing my hand back up and wiping a few strands of hair away from her eye. I really couldn't for the life of me figure out why she would get jealous just because I happened to spot someone from school at the park. Hell, it wasn't like a guy like me would ever have any chance with someone like BJ anyway. I mean, she was in the Hall of Fame of hot chicks. I decided to hold off on the ring for a bit, not quite sure if this was the best moment to pop the question.

The fireworks started, and we sat down on the grass, me sitting behind Natalia, she leaning back into my body while lying between my legs. My arms were wrapped around her, and I had easy access to her neck, which I kissed incessantly, the fireworks bursting in the sky above us. Occasionally, when one of the loud sets sent booming echoes across the sky, Natalia would startle and jump even deeper into my body, imploring me to hold her even more tightly. I happily obliged, inhaling the smell of her hair, the scent of lemons wafting into my nose. I knew she used a shampoo made with lemons, and I imagined being in the shower with her, rubbing our bodies with lemon-scented soap and shampoo. I felt my dick start to get hard and thought about moving her hand toward it, but then thought better of it. As I had found out at the movies a few months back, Natalia just wasn't that type of girl. My God, just look at how she had reacted to BJ a few minutes ago.

I again thought about whether this was the right moment to give her the ring but, honestly, the booming from the fireworks was so loud that I didn't think she'd be able to hear me, and I didn't just want to hand her the ring, I actually wanted to tell her how I felt about her, and take my time asking her if she wanted to be my girlfriend.

My hand held hers, and she began stroking it lightly with the fingers of her other hand, which made my heart race. I looked up at the exploding fireworks in the sky, smiled, and kissed her lightly on top of her head. Life was good, and even if I were presented with three wishes from a magical genie in a bottle, there really wasn't anything I'd change at that very moment in time.

"Natalia! What the hell do you think you're doing?" Before the fireworks had even ended, our reverie was broken by the booming voice of Mr. Guinzberg, which even rose above the bursting fireworks. Natalia leaped out of my arms and onto her feet as if she'd been shot out of a cannon.

"Oh, hi Daddy. Look who I found on my way back from the bathroom!" Evidently, Natalia had used the same excuse to get away from her family as I had used to escape my friends.

"Hello, Mr. Guinzberg," I said nervously, once again butchering his name which I had actually gotten pretty good at pronouncing as of late.

"Let's go, young lady," was all he said as he led her away. I could also make out "I'm very disappointed in you," as Natalia turned to look back at me and mouth the words, "I'm so sorry," before disappearing into the crowd.

The fireworks were over even before I made it back to my friends. "What the hell happened to you?" Ronnie asked. "Did you fall in the toilet?"

"Yeah, Douglas, where were you? You missed the fireworks." Hank added.

"Sorry, guys," I answered solemnly. "I ran into Natalia

and watched the fireworks with her. . . . That is, until her dad found us and yanked her away from me."

"What an asshole," Weddy sympathized. "What's his problem with you anyway?" The guys had heard me complain in the past about how strict Mr. Guinzberg was with Natalia.

"Who knows," I answered glumly. "I don't think it's necessarily just about me. I think he's just overprotective. He pulls this same shit with Natalia's older sister as well."

"Sorry, dude," Hank said, putting his arm around my shoulders. "I'm sure he'll loosen up the more he gets to know you."

"I hope so," I replied, but deep down I knew that I probably wouldn't be seeing much of Natalia for a while.

Chapter Nine

The summer days began to fly by. Long stretches of boredom would be broken up by late mornings and late afternoons—early-to-mid afternoons were just too brutally hot—spent by the pool in the back of the complex. I had been correct about Natalia; her dad had really tightened the screws on her, and our time together had become extremely limited, restricted to no more than ten minutes on the phone—"Time's up, Natalia!" I'd hear Mr. Guinzberg roar in the background every time we'd be just getting to the crux of something important, something deep, our feelings for each other—or a few minutes outside, usually when I had left the house to go walk L and Natalia would sneak out of her house for a few minutes to join me on Lindley. We'd kiss like mad, terrified that Mr. Guinzberg would come tearing out the front gate, a lion protecting his young, until Natalia would suddenly break away from me, nervously racing back to the den before she was found out.

There was a rotating assortment of characters out by the pool, some were daily regulars, others, like me, floated in and out depending on the heat and the level of inertia one was experiencing that day. Sometimes, after taking L out for her morning walk and seeing the temperature already up into the mid-eighties by 9:00 A.M., you just knew you might as well crank the AC and see what was on TV. Hell, I even got caught up in *The Young and the Restless*, with its stories about rape, alcoholism, and having sex before marriage. To most people's shock, they even had a couple of lesbians on the show. I thought it was all silly fun, though they were actually trying to get viewers to talk about things that weren't normally discussed openly, which I guess was cool.

Fortunately, today wasn't going to be too hot. Mid-nineties, tops, maybe even high-eighties. And it was a *dry* heat as Valley natives liked to say. For the most part, I loved the heat, loved getting a deep tan. My skin would turn incredibly dark during the summer, only lightening up when I forgot to use after-sun lotion and I would peel, sometimes literally taking my fingers and grabbing a chunk of skin on my arms or stomach and just stripping it off of my body. My dad said that some of our ancestors came from a couple of the Mediterranean countries—I'm not exactly sure which ones—and that's why we had skin that browned so easily in the sunlight. By the time I hit the pool, most of the lounges were taken, but there was a spot open next to Jake, one of the regulars at the pool. "Hey, Jake. Anyone sitting here?"

"All yours, my man." Jake was well-oiled up today, the bottle of Hawaiian Tropic sitting close by on the small, square glass table that sat between our lounges. He easily had the hairiest body out here, the type of guy who had to shave his neck all the way down to his upper chest and back, and the Hawaiian Tropic made all of his little hairs glisten in the sun. Jake wasn't originally from America, but he wasn't Mexican, either. I really didn't know where he was born, but I'm sure it wasn't anyplace I had ever heard of. His parents, who he still lived with even though he was several years older than my brother and sister, owned a small jewelry store in Beverly Hills, and Jake worked there off and on when he wasn't getting fired by his old man.

"You want to play?" he asked, picking up the dice to the backgammon set that sat on the ground next to his lounge, and shaking them in his hand with what was definitely a manic energy for this early in the day. Jake was insane when it came to backgammon. He played it nonstop, every day, from nine in the morning to six at night and sometimes seven or eight, even in the darkness of the early summer nights, as long as there was someone hanging out by the pool willing to play with him.

But play "with" him was a bit of a misnomer. Because Jake was such a control freak that if you didn't make your move within three seconds of rolling the dice, he would thrust his hand toward the board, pick up a couple of your round pieces, and move them for you. "That's the move you want to make," he would say with authority. The thing of it was, he was always right. The dude was a killer backgammon player, and I actually learned a lot from him. But as to whether it was any fun playing with him? Well, let's just say at least it killed some of the boredom of the day.

"Sure, but let me take a dip first," I responded.

"I'll be here," Jake said, picking up the bottle of Hawaiian Tropic as I turned to go jump into the pool. The seventy-eight-degree water hit me like a cool mist floating over my body. My long, brown hair immediately lost its feathering and became straight, hanging down my neck toward my shoulders. My capacity to hold my breath was pretty good because of all the basketball I played, so I headed underwater down to one end of the fairly large pool—not Olympic-sized, but certainly much larger than anyone would ever have in their own home—executed a mediocre flip turn even though I was imagining I was Mark Spitz as I did it, pushed off and headed for the other end. My legs were always pretty powerful, and so I always had a good deal of momentum coming out of my Spitz-like fantasy turn. Once I reached the other end, still underwater, I went for one more flip turn—somewhat better this time—and then pulled up about mid-pool like a turtle sticking his head out of the water, slowly and gracefully, took an easy, deep breath, and flipped over on my back for a couple of strokes.

There weren't too many folks in the pool at this point—it always ebbed and flowed throughout the day—just a couple of young kids playing in the corner of the shallow end, and Mr. Grigoryan and his daughter, Jenny, hanging out mid-pool, holding onto the side. Mr. Grigoryan was infamous around the Encino Royale for having been caught taking a bath in the Jacuzzi on numerous occasions. And not just him, but his wife and kids as well. They'd bring their soap and shampoo and just go for it, somehow thinking their soap and shampoo bubbles were the same as the foam bubbles that were generated by the Jacuzzi.

Mr. Grigoryan claimed their bathing behavior was tied to an old Armenian family tradition, but the Association wouldn't have any of it. They had fined him on several occasions, but when that didn't stop him, they threatened him with serious legal action—something to do with a health code violation, I think I heard Art say—and that finally seemed to put an end to it. Ever since then, the entire family had become something of a pariah around the Royale, and nobody talked to them much. Truthfully, though, they were always a bit weird. Mr. Grigoryan had a normal job, he was a CPA at one of the Big Eight firms, but everyone in the family just seemed a little off. Jenny was in Special Ed at school, and her older brother, who was high-school aged, went to some special school that nobody had ever heard of. Plus, the whole family had a weight problem. Mr. Grigoryan was one of those men who wore his swimsuit—and his pants—way above his belly button so that he could fit his really, really large mid-section below his waistband or belt. Sort of like Jackie Gleason or Archie Bunker. Meanwhile, Jenny always wore a skimpy bikini—it was yellow with little daisies today—on her baby-fat-filled frame. Odd, to say the least.

I took a deep breath, brought both my arms up through the water and above my head, drifted underwater, began to let out all of my air, and slowly fell toward the bottom, hundreds of air bubbles trailing the way above me as I made my way down, weightless, like an astronaut. I'd always found the bottom of the pool a calming, sacred spot. If I were to have a place of worship, this would be it. The air was still, the silence was perfection, and the zero-gravity sensation made the whole experience magical no matter how many thousands of times I had done it throughout my life.

I'm a Pisces, and not just my astrological sign, but my rising sign as well, making me a *double* Pisces. Before the divorce, my mom had really gotten into astrology, took a class at The Learning Tree, and started charting everyone in the family. Anyway, my point is that I'm a Pisces through and through and absolutely love the water—pool, lake, river, ocean, you name it, I love it—and feel most at peace when I'm in or near some kind of H2O.

In fact, last summer, a couple of the younger kids around the complex took to calling me "Fish," because

I did spend so much time in the pool. It wasn't exactly a name that appealed to me—after all, when I think of "fish," I think of the trout my dad, brother, and I caught up in the Sierras a few summers ago, the poor creatures hanging off of a hook, looking at you like they had no idea what just hit them. Fortunately, Hank, Weddy, Ronnie, and the other guys my age never really heard the younger kids using the name, so it never stuck and, more importantly, I didn't get teased with it by the gang.

"Hey, Douglas! Douglas!" Just moments after I came up from my reverie at the bottom of the pool and broke through the surface of the water, I heard Bobbi calling out my name. I looked around, the bright sunlight reflecting off of the water playing nasty games with my eyes. Finally, while shading the sun with my hand, I saw her standing by the side of the pool next to Weddy.

"Hey, Bobbi! Hey, Weddy! What are you up to?"

"Not much," Bobbi replied. "We just took a walk up the alley to the liquor store to grab a coke." Whenever anyone around Weddy used the term "took a walk," it was code for "went to smoke a joint."

"Sounds good," I said. "A little wake and bake?"

"Ha!" Bobbi laughed. "That was hours ago."

"Oh, right," I smiled.

"Hey, man," Weddy said in his best stoner voice, "Ruth told Bobbi to bring some friends by for some late-morning treats. Interested?" Was I interested? Bobbi's grandmother was the Ruth behind Ruth's Bakery, probably the greatest bakery in the Valley. She lived in the condo part of the complex, up on the top floor, with a nice view looking north past the 101 Freeway toward Chatsworth and Granada Hills. At night you could see the L.A. Aquaduct up in Sylmar, the entire run of free-flowing water lit up by a series of lights that ran alongside the Cascades, as it was known. This was the spot William Mulholland famously said, "There it is. Take it," as they opened the spigot and let the water flow down the hillside toward the Valley. I wrote about it last year in a paper I did for Mr. Karp's history class.

"Sure! You going up now?"

"Yeah, man, I got the munchies something serious!" Weddy giggled.

"We'll wait for you over by the clubhouse," Bobbi added. Bobbi was sweet. She visited for about a month every summer from Arizona. Bobbi was older than we were—she'd be starting eleventh grade in the fall—but seemed to enjoy hanging out with a slightly younger crowd. All of us were looking forward to next summer, because by then Bobbi would be driving, which would open up a world of possibilities—we'd already made plans to go to Magic Mountain, for instance. Oh, and the drive-in movies as well.

After pulling myself out of the pool and toweling off, I told Jake I'd be back in a bit for our backgammon game and headed over to where Bobbi and Weddy were patiently waiting in the shade of the clubhouse. We took the elevator and went on up to Bobbi's grandmother's place. As soon as the elevator doors opened, the smell of baked goods began wafting from beneath Ruth's front door and into the hallway. It wasn't like Ruth baked all of her goods from her little condo kitchen—her bakery had professional ovens and all of that stuff—but she would experiment with new recipes at home, so there was usually something delicious-smelling in the air whenever you entered her home.

"Hello, kids!" Ruth enthusiastically welcomed us as we walked through the door. Ruth was a tiny Jewish woman, with red hair she kept impeccably coiffed and dyed through regular visits to the hair salon right next to her bakery. "Help yourselves."

Two of the most magical words as were ever spoken. Ruth waved her arm toward the dining room table where there sat an assortment of baked goodies like you've never seen: giant black-and-white cookies sat next to various types of rugelach, chocolate babka, macaroons, hamantaschen, and the pièce de resistance, the thing Ruth was most famous for, her upside down, chocolate chip cupcakes. Picture the lightest, fluffiest chocolate cupcake you've ever tasted, filled with delectable chocolate chips, served upside down and dredged in a fine coating of powdered sugar. Nobody knew if the secret was some special ingredient or what, but no other bakery in the world could make a cupcake that could even touch Ruth's version. And there wasn't even any frosting!

"Oh my God," Weddy said, a huge smile spreading across his face. "This looks amazing."

"Eat! Eat!" Ruth admonished. Truth be told, none of us needed any encouragement.

"Thank you, Ruth," I said.

The three of us got to work, and Ruth genuinely enjoyed watching us eat. Weddy, of course, had the munchies something serious, and he ate with reckless abandon.

"Doesn't your mother feed you, Weddy?" Ruth asked.

Weddy could only giggle, shoving the remains of a cupcake into his mouth. "Sorry, Ruth," I replied for him. "He was raised by wolves."

"I was not," Weddy said in a muffled voice, crumbs

spilling from his mouth.

"That's true," Bobbi chimed in, "he was actually raised by chimpanzees."

"Very funny," Weddy managed to squeak out.

"There's no rush," Ruth advised. "Take your time. You can eat all day for all I care. I just don't want you to get a stomachache."

"Thank you, Grandma," Bobbi said as she picked at a black-and-white cookie. Bobbi had access to these goodies twenty-four/seven, so you rarely saw her eating much of the treats.

"So," Ruth looked at me and Weddy, "what are you planning on doing with yourselves this summer?" Her Jewish accent was fairly thick as she had been raised in Poland and spent over two years in a concentration camp. She normally wore long sleeves, even on the hottest days, and today was no exception. However, one time I happened to see her getting into the Jacuzzi and caught a glimpse of the tattooed number on her forearm. I had seen these on older Jewish adults a few times in the past, and it was always a stark reminder of how much evil some people are capable of inflicting upon the world.

"No real plans," Weddy said without a trace of irony.

"I might work in my dad's warehouse," I lied.

"That's good, Douglas," Ruth beamed. "Hard work is good for the soul. As for you, young man," she turned toward Weddy and her voice grew stern. "You're too young to not have any plans. When you're old like me, you can have no plans, but when you're young, it's important to have plans."

"Yes, ma'am," Weddy stammered, his high definitely becoming quickly bummed out.

"Don't worry, Grandma," Bobbi chimed in, "I'll keep him busy and out of trouble."

"You? You're another one," Ruth said, grabbing some milk from the refrigerator and pouring us each a small glass. "I promised your mother and father that you would study for the SAT while you were here, and I haven't seen you crack that book open once."

"Not true," Bobbi said. She took a sip of milk and continued. "I've been working on my vocabulary."

"Oh yeah?" Ruth challenged. "Tell me one word you've learned this summer."

"Okay. Supercilious."

"What? What kind of word is this?" Ruth asked incredulously.

"It means someone who thinks they're better than someone else," I piped up.

"Oh, look at Mr. Smarty Pants over there," Ruth laughed. "Well, okay, shoot me for caring. And one word does not make a difference on your SAT scores," she admonished, directing her attention back to Bobbi.

"I've learned much more than one word, Grandma," Bobbi said. "And, yes, Douglas is very bright, and he's going to be a famous writer one day."

"Oh really?" Ruth turned to me. "Well, I've got a million stories I could tell you. Have you ever met my brother, Bobbi's Uncle Marty?"

"No, I haven't."

"Yes, you have," Bobbi stepped in. "He was the one cooking hamburgers at the grill last summer when your family joined us for that barbecue by the pool."

"I remember that!" Weddy suddenly woke up from his food-induced coma. "He was the funny guy who turned the ketchup bottle upside down and when he took off the cap the whole bottle poured out onto his plate."

"Exactly," Bobbi said.

"Well," Ruth continued, "he escaped from a camp and walked over a hundred miles in the snow before he collapsed along the side of a road. Fortunately, some local Polish farmers saw him before the Nazis did and they took him in and hid him in their barn until the war was over."

"Wow. That's incredible," I said, reaching over and picking up a rainbow sprinkle cookie.

"You should write about that one day," Ruth directed, looking me straight in the eye. "So that nobody will forget what the Jews endured at the hands of those bastard Germans."

"Oh, I don't think anyone will ever forget," I said innocently.

"Don't you believe it, Douglas," Ruth said forebodingly. "They're already forgetting, and in another twenty or thirty years, there will be plenty of people who will have forgotten. In fact, there will be plenty of people who will say the whole thing never happened. That it was a hoax. You mark my words, young man." Ruth grew quiet and stared out her window at the view across the Valley.

I didn't know quite what to say. It seemed ludicrous that such a horrible event in history could ever be forgotten.

"Can I have some more milk, please?" Weddy broke the silence, and we couldn't help but start laughing hysterically when we turned to look at him and saw a nearly perfect milk-moustache above his upper lip.

"Yes, yes, of course," Ruth replied as she broke out of her tired reverie. Bobbi took Ruth's arm and rubbed it gently as she walked by and they exchanged a loving look, Ruth softly placing her hand, covered with veins and liver spots, on top of Bobbi's.

"I love you, Grandma," Bobbi said.

"And I love you too, my sweet girl."

Bobbi *was* sweet, and I enjoyed her visits almost as much as Ruth did. It was a bummer she lived in Arizona and not in Southern California. Her dad was a pilot, and for some reason he was based out of Phoenix. She used to complain about Arizona, and at one point there was some discussion of her moving in with her grandma on a permanent basis, but for some reason that never happened, and she never really explained to us why the plan fell through. There was a certain sadness about her, maybe it was the small folds of skin beneath her blue eyes that gave her sort of a mournful look. Not that she was depressing to be around or anything like that, quite the opposite actually. She was always agreeable and generally went along with the wishes of the others in the group, but you just knew that deep down inside it was killing her to be living in Arizona and not here in Encino with her Grandma. Nobody really knew what exactly was going on in her home, but something told us all wasn't hunky-dory.

After an hour or so of stuffing ourselves silly, we said our thank yous and goodbyes to Ruth and headed back down to the pool. Bobbi and Weddy went into the clubhouse, and I made my way back to my lounge next to Jake, where he promptly kicked my ass in a game of backgammon. I didn't mind, though. With the lingering taste in my mouth of freshly baked pastries and cookies, nothing could ruin the moment, not even a whipping from Jake.

Chapter Ten

By the time August rolled around, David was well set-tled into his apartment with Sam, and Mom had long transformed his old bedroom into a combination TV and pool table room. In fact, just a day or two after David had finished packing up the rest of his stuff and got out of the house, Mom and Art and I were already negotiating the stairs while carrying our brand new RCA TV into our brand new game room. The pool table soon followed, a used Brunswick in great shape that Art had managed to get from a guy who owned a busy car repair shop on To-panga in exchange for some auto parts that he desperately needed and that Art happened to have in stock. Surpris-ingly, David didn't seem to care that his bedroom had been transformed into a pretty cool place to hang out and play pool and watch TV, as he was stoked about his "bach-elor pad."

"No more Mom bitching at me about my dirty laundry or my unmade bed or the dishes in the sink. I can do what-ever the fuck I want," he said proudly. In reality, however, he'd still been a regular fixture at our house, bringing over his laundry and eating plenty of meals at our table, and of course Mom was absolutely okay with all of it. "And if I want to get high, or have a girl spend the night," he contin-ued, "there isn't anybody around to tell me I can't do it."

In order to afford the apartment, David had reluctant-ly agreed to take a job at my dad's company, learning the ropes as the low man on the totem pole in the marketing department. Additionally, my dad made him promise that starting in September, he had to take two business classes a semester at Pierce, the local junior college, and he had to take them at night so that they wouldn't interfere with his job. "But Dad," David complained, "when will I have time to study? And when will I have time to have any fun?"

"Maybe you should've thought about all of this when we were encouraging you to go to college after high school like your sister did," was my dad's only reply. In the fall, Julie would be finishing up her final year at UCSD, where she was pre-med. My dad and mom were justifiably proud of Julie—"our daughter is studying to be a doctor!" they would tell anyone within earshot—and I thought she'd make a fine pediatrician as she was always great with kids. In fact, she was spending her summer down in San Diego working in a pediatrician's office, so she was well on her way to achieving her goal.

"Well, I'm not Julie," David sulked.

"Damn right, you're not," my dad said snidely. "But if you keep your nose to the grindstone and work hard you might still be able to make something of yourself."

"Good luck with that," I murmured under my breath.

"Fuck off, Douglas," David shot back.

"Douglas, what are you planning on doing with your life?" Crap. I shouldn't have opened my mouth. Now I was in my dad's sights.

"Well, uh, you know, I do love to write," I stammered, knowing full well that this wouldn't satisfy my dad, who was a businessman through and through.

"Tough way to make a living, Son."

"Yeah, but I hear that all the kids who go to law school

have strong writing skills, so maybe I'll do that."

"Well, law is an admirable profession," he smiled. "And it can be very lucrative. Just look at Jerry Solomon. He's made quite a living chasing down ambulances," and then my dad laughed and laughed. Mr. Solomon was a well-known personal injury attorney—you could see his face, or his "punim" as my mom would call it, on bus benches throughout the Valley.

When his laughter subsided, my dad said, "I'm just kidding, Son. I think it'd be great if you became an attorney. What kind of law are you interested in practicing?"

What kind of law? Was he joking? What the hell did I know about the different types of law besides what Mr. Solomon did? "Uh, I'm not sure, Dad."

"Well, it's never too soon to start thinking about it. Maybe I'll set up a meeting with you and Merv Sanders. He'd be a good guy to talk to."

Great. Merv Sanders was my dad's attorney. Nice guy, but I really had no interest in sitting in his office talking about the different kinds of law. Merv was fat—I mean, really fat—and he had this annoying habit of picking his teeth with a silver toothpick. Undoubtedly, I'd have to endure not only the law talk, but sitting across from him while we ate pastrami sandwiches he'd undoubtedly bring in from Jerry's Deli—his office was in Northridge and he was a regular at Jerry's—and I would have to look at him as he talked and ignore the mustard smeared around his mouth. However, when he would start to pick out pieces of meat stuck between his teeth once he had wolfed down his sandwich, I would be forced to avert my eyes.

"Do you enjoy speaking in front of people, Douglas?" he'd ask. "Do you enjoy a good argument? If so, then maybe you have a future as a trial attorney."

I could envision the whole lecture from the beginning to its merciful end. "Would you like a little rugelach for dessert?" Merv would ask, pulling out an enormous bucket from the cabinet behind his desk. Even though I'd be stuffed from the gigantic sandwich from Jerry's, I'd accept a couple of pieces, knowing that at least this meant our lunch hour "talk"—in which I'd uttered no more than a few words—would be coming to a close. "Gotta get back to making some dough for the donuts," Merv would say, awkwardly rising up from his chair with a fair amount of difficulty due to his weight and shuffling over to show me the door.

"Yes, sir," I'd politely reply. "And thank you for the time you spent with me. It was very inspirational and gave me a lot to chew on," I'd say without a trace of irony. Then I'd head out the door and get into my mom's car where I'd have to undergo the third degree from her.

"So what did you talk about? What did Merv have to say? You know he's a very brilliant lawyer and that was very nice of him to spend time with you." I'd make a couple of general comments to satisfy her curiosity while sitting there staring out the window, wondering if my friends were still swimming in the pool or if they'd all gone inside to enjoy some AC and TV for the afternoon.

With David now out of the picture, the house was a lot more mellow, just me, mom, Art, and L, and no more screaming matches between my mom and David, or me and David, or Art and David. Hell, even L had taken to growling at my brother before he moved out.

That night there was a party at some rich kid's house over on Shoshone, just on the other side of White Oak.

That part of Encino wasn't "south of the boulevard," but it contained some really big homes, some with pools *and* tennis courts. The kid went to Pershing High, so we obviously didn't know him, but someone in Weddy's apartment building knew him well and told Weddy he could come and that it was cool if he wanted to bring a few friends. Around eight o'clock that evening, Hank and I met out front and walked over to Weddy's apartment. From there we stopped by Ronnie's place. He was waiting outside as usual—none of us had ever stepped foot in his apartment and Ronnie assured us nobody ever would. "It's just a complete nightmare," was all he would say. "I wouldn't want to put anyone through it. Even you guys," and then we'd all laugh uncomfortably in an attempt to break the tension.

"So what's the story with the kid throwing the party?" Ronnie asked.

"Supposed to be cool," Weddy said, pulling on a joint that he had lit as we walked from Ronnie's building over to the party. "And my buddy said there'd be both junior high and high school kids there so we didn't have to worry about being the youngest ones at the shindig. I think the kid throwing the party has a younger sister around our age."

"Cool," Ronnie said with his typical braggadocio, "though older chicks dig me, too."

"Yeah," Hank said. "Remember that retarded girl who wouldn't leave Ronnie alone that day we all went to Busch Gardens? She was older, wasn't she, Ronnie?"

"Fuck off, Hank," Ronnie said sullenly. But the rest of us laughed our heads off, remembering how excited Ronnie was that day when this girl started showing interest in him while we were in line for the log ride. Every time we'd pass her in line, she'd smile and give him a wink. "This is it, boys," Ronnie had said. "I'm gonna get laid today!" The girl was sort of cute and was definitely older than we were as her tits were just too big for a girl our age, but I did notice there seemed to be something off about her. This was confirmed once we got off the ride and there she was, waiting for Ronnie.

"Hi!" she said to him, smiling broadly.

"Hey there," Ronnie said calmly, trying to be cool about the whole thing. "I'm Ronnie."

"I'm Renee!" she squealed. "Ronnie and Renee! How do you like that?" Her energy seemed to be a bit over the top, but Ronnie was so horny all the time that he was game for anything.

"Wanna go for a walk?" Ronnie asked.

"Sure!" she replied excitedly. "Where do you want to go?"

"I don't know," Ronnie said, putting on his best Paul Newman-like charm. "I thought we could find someplace secluded, where we could be alone."

"Like the bathroom?" she suggested.

"Well, I, uh, I guess so," Ronnie said, obviously starting to wonder if all was right with this girl.

"Renee! Renee!" A woman was walking around nearby, obviously searching for Ronnie's new sweetheart.

"Over here, Mom! Come meet my new boyfriend!"

By now, Weddy, Hank, and I had quickly made ourselves scarce, scurrying away into the crowd. Ronnie, unfortunately, couldn't move as his new girlfriend had locked arms with him and was proudly marching her new catch over to meet her mom. Suffice it to say that her mom didn't take too kindly to Ronnie, and after extricating her daughter from him, she scolded our friend and threatened to call the police on him for taking advantage of a retarded girl. For weeks after that, we all called him, "Retard Loving Ronnie," which pissed him off to no end but brought howls of laughter from anyone around who knew the story.

We wound our way through the neighborhood streets and over to White Oak, finally heading down Weddington to Shoshone. As we got closer, the activity definitely began to pick up. Cars were parked all over the place and kids were streaming toward a big, white house that was all lit up. The Stones' "Brown Sugar" was pouring out of every open window and door. There was a large half-circle driveway in front, and kids stood around in groups, holding red cups filled with beer or wine or some form of alcohol, and joints were being freely shared all around us.

"This looks like the place!" Weddy smiled. "Let's go grab ourselves some refreshments." We headed back through the house—probably the largest home I'd ever walked into, with a huge two-story living room filled with paintings and antique furniture, and out into the backyard where several kegs were set up by the pool. I hadn't done a ton of drinking in my life, but I did enjoy a beer from time to time, though after my dad's wedding to Cindy—where I drank several rum and cokes and passed out spread-eagle on an ottoman directly in front of a piano where a horde of drunken adults were gathered around, playing and singing Sinatra standards in off-key voices that did absolutely nothing to disturb my drunken slumber—I generally avoided hard liquor and stuck with an occasional beer or a glass of wine with dinner if it was a super special occasion and my dad insisted on me trying some amazing Cabernet

he had decided to drop a couple of Jacksons on to cele-
brate David's graduation from high school, for instance,
or Cindy's thirtieth birthday.

Red plastic cups in hand, we settled in with a small
crowd around a fire pit. I always found it funny that here in
Southern California, after a day spent bitching about how
hot it was, we loved to then huddle around an open gas fire
pit, fake flame, lava rocks, and all, even though the temperature still hadn't dropped below the mid-seventies.
One of the great things about having Hank, Weddy, and
Ronnie as friends—besides, of course, just having friends
at all—was that all three of them were pretty good with the
girls. Don't get me wrong, I was no slouch when it came to
girls, but I was more the shy, sensitive type who took a bit
of time to get to know. And because of my tendency to be
a bit overweight—though I had been dropping the pounds
this summer, Ruth's baked goods notwithstanding—girls
didn't generally just walk up and start talking to me. But
Weddy had that easygoing, stoner appeal, not to mention
that people generally congregate around the guy with the
joints; Hank was your classic, good-looking SoCal surf-
er-looking dude (even though he didn't surf; none of us
did out of fear of getting our butts kicked by the dickwads
from Malibu—"Valley Go Home," my ass), and Ronnie, of
course, always maintained supreme confidence with the
ladies, even when he sounded like an idiot.

Sure enough, within moments of Weddy lighting up a
reefer, two pretty cute girls who must've been at least fifteen and maybe even sixteen, sidled up next to us.

"Hey guys," the blonde with the cowboy hat said, "I'm
Christina." Her hair went all the way down to her waist
and she was wearing tight jeans and cowboy boots.

"Hey, Christina." As usual, Ronnie led the way. "I'm Ronnie. Want a hit?" he asked, holding the joint out in front of her.

"Sure! This is my friend Alexandra." Christina took a pro's hit off of the J and passed it to Alexandra.

"Hey, Alexandra. I'm Weddy."

"I'm Hank."

"What about you?" Christina said after a few moments of silence.

"Oh, sorry," I said, the beer starting to dull my senses. "I'm Douglas."

"So where do you guys go to school?"

"Cabrillo," Ronnie answered.

"Wait," Christina said, sounding alarmed. "How old are you guys?"

"Ha! Jail bait, babe!" Alexandra cried out to her friend as they exchanged fist bumps followed by the opening of their palms and the wiggling of their fingers as their hands retreated from each other. It soon became clear that these girls were going into eleventh grade next year, and Christina was already driving. They went to Reseda High and were clearly from "the other side of the tracks." Christina apparently lived on a small farm with horses and other farm animals, while Alexandra lived in an apartment with her grandmother somewhere near Sherman Way and Wilbur, apparently not too far from Christina's place where she evidently spent a lot of time. Christina had dark eyes and a somewhat sad look about her, even though she was nice and actually seemed to have a pretty good sense of humor.

A couple of hours into the party, the police made their customary visit with the typical consequences: After looking inside over the shoulder of the host and seeing kids of all ages drinking alcohol, smoking pot, and doing God knows what else, they told the guy whose house it was to get everyone out of the front yard and street and into the house. As usual, all the cops cared about was that whatever was going on was going on behind closed doors. As long as there wasn't a ton of kids hanging outside in front the house and loitering in the street near their cars while drinking and smoking, everything was okey-dokey. What really upset them was when a party just got totally out of control and there were so many people that the house was full, and the backyard was packed, and there were dozens and dozens of people partying out front. That's when the neighbors would really get pissed and start bitching at the cops to do something. I remember David telling me about a party over on Topanga just south of the boulevard that got so big there were *hundreds* of kids partying in the street in front of the house, and the cops had to bring in a helicopter to disperse the crowd.

By now most of the guys were pretty drunk as they'd moved on to their third or fourth beer. I, being the lightweight I was, had barely touched my second beer, which had grown warm in my hand. The girls, who were still hanging out with us, were more stoners than drinkers, so they, too, hadn't been drinking all that much. I actually really liked Christina, who was totally different than any girl I'd ever hung out with. She really did grow up on a small farm and took care of a lot of the animals. She'd raised pigs, chickens . . . had even milked cows and rode horses since the time she was three years old. School and college didn't seem to hold much of an interest for her, though she did allude to possibly going to Pierce to study animal husbandry after she graduated high school; by the same token, she even talked about dropping out and just starting the program a year or two early.

I'm not sure what she saw in me, but Christina seemed to like me as well; I don't know if she had ever really hung out with someone like me before, either. "You're a pretty smart kid, aren't you?" she said after I had told her about some of the various businesses I had run during my lifetime: the car washing business, the dog poop scooping business, the weed-pulling business, etc. And then came the inevitable, "You Jews are pretty good at making money, aren't you? I haven't really known too many Jews in my life," she added.

"You see," I joked, trying to make light of the situation, "we really don't have horns." I was no Woody Allen, but I certainly didn't mind borrowing his humor.

"You're funny," she said, pushing the side of her body into mine. "I like you."

"I like you, too," I responded. "Cheers!" We clinked our plastic red cups together and took sips of our beers, both making a face as the piss-like warm Budweiser touched our tongues. Just at that very moment, someone shouted "The last keg is out!"

"Bummer!" Ronnie shouted in kind.

"That's a drag, man," Weddy added.

"Hey, I don't mind running up to the liquor store to grab a couple of six-packs if you guys want," Christina offered. "Douglas, want to come?"

"Sure!" I blurted out without thinking.

"They'll sell you beer?" Weddy asked, surprised.

"No, silly," Christina smiled. "But I have my ways," she teased, batting her long eyelashes and sashaying her hips.

"Anyone want to pony up some cash?" The guys reached into their pockets and came up with a few dollars and some change. "Well, I don't know if that'll buy us *two* six-packs, but I'll see if I can scrounge up a couple more bucks on my way out. Come on, Douglas." Christina locked her arm into mine and began to lead the way toward the front door.

"See you, Douglas!" Weddy shouted out. I turned to look back over my shoulder and could see Ronnie whispering into Weddy's ear and them both laughing as they watched Christina and me melt into the crowd.

"Beer run!" Christina shouted out, holding her cowboy hat upside down in the air. Several partygoers dropped bills and coins into the hat, and by the time we reached the door, she must've had another five dollars to spend. As we started to walk out, I heard someone shout behind me, "Douglas!" I turned around and saw Vicki, Natalia's best friend, standing with another girl I didn't recognize.

"Hey Vicki! How you doing? Is Natalia here?"

"No, her parents wouldn't let her come."

"That's a bummer."

"Hey," Vicki said, looking past me toward Christina, "who's your friend?"

"Oh," I said, gesturing toward Christina who had broken away and was now standing on the front porch, "that's Christina. We're making a beer run."

"Come on, Douglas!" Christina shouted.

"Sorry, gotta go! See you later."

"Bye," I heard Vicki say from behind as I joined Christina outside.

Things had definitely calmed down out front. There were a few kids staggering to their cars, leaving to go to another party now that the kegs had been emptied at this one. We approached a beat-up, white Ford pickup truck with a spare tire and a couple of rolls of old chicken wire in the back. I hopped in the passenger seat, covered in green vinyl that was torn in several places, and closed the very creaky door. As Christina turned the car over and over again, the engine finally roared to life and the eight-track player belted out "Gimme Three Steps" by Lynyrd Skynyrd.

"You like Skynyrd?" Christina yelled over the music.

"Yeah, love 'em!" The truth was I did actually like them, even if I didn't outright love them. It took a lot of balls to come back at Neil with "Sweet Home Alabama." It'd be one thing to answer back with a shitty song, but that was a home run, a killer song with a killer riff. Even Neil had to respect it.

"I was cutting the rug down at the place called The Jug," Christina sang out.

"With a girl named Linda Lou!" I joined in, and as we made our way up White Oak toward Ventura, Christina turned and smiled at me and gave my thigh a playful squeeze. I was still feeling the effects of the beer or beer-and-a-half I had drunk, not to mention the slight contact high I had undoubtedly gotten from standing around with those guys as they smoked joint after joint. Christina seemed totally fine, maybe an occasional weave over the white dotted line between lanes, but nothing serious. Traffic was light and she had obviously done her share of partying over the years.

I was surprised when she made a left instead of a right onto Ventura.

"Don't you want to go to Time to Buy?" I asked.

"Nah, I like the place over on Balboa."

"Cool," I said.

We pulled into a parking lot, and Christina parked in one of the last spaces, far out of sight of anyone working in the liquor store. "Wait here," she ordered with the authority of someone who knew exactly what she was doing. As she walked from the car over to the brick wall next to the windows in front of the store, she took her hat off, ran her fingers through her hair, and shook her beautiful mane out before placing her hat back atop her head. She then adjusted her jeans, pulling them up tight around her admittedly very fine ass. The pale, greenish light emanating from inside the store lit her from the side, forming a sort of halo around the outline of her body. Sure enough, within about twenty seconds, a guy in a Mustang pulled up. Christina smiled that wide smile of hers, called him over, and he immediately made his way directly to her. After all, what guy could resist a hot chick in a cowboy hat and tight jeans, the boot of her left leg lifted up against the wall, even if he were twice her age?

After some flirtatious talk—I could see Christina reach out and touch the guy's arm and he responding in kind—Christina gave him the money she had gathered and the dude reached into his pocket and slipped her something and went inside. Christina gave me the thumbs-up once he entered the store, and within minutes he was outside with a couple of six packs of Hamm's, handing them off with a huge smile and watching Christina with a lecherous eye as she walked back to the car, purposely swinging her butt to give the guy an extra thrill for doing her a solid.

"Well, that was easy, even for me!" she laughed as she climbed into the truck. "He was a really nice guy, too. Even gave me his card and told me to give him a call anytime."

"Wow, you're good," I said, taking the beer and the business card from her. I glanced down at the card and it read, "Joel Weinstein, Esquire." "Huh," I said, "dude's an attorney."

"Really?" Christina said, grabbing the card back from me playfully. "Maybe I *will* give him a call!" She started laughing hysterically, and I didn't really know if she was being serious or just joking. She definitely seemed like the type of girl who'd been with older guys lots of times. I really didn't know what to say in return, so I piped up with, "The guys will be really excited to see that you scored some beers."

"Huh?" Christina replied, obviously still thinking about her possible future with this Jewish attorney. "Oh, yeah, I know."

There was once again a bit of an awkward silence, and I was trying my best to think of something interesting to say in order to break it. "You ever been to Hawaii?" I asked. For some reason, seeing a palm tree along White Oak had triggered the memory of going to Hawaii when I was nine; it was the last trip we'd ever all taken together as a family.

"Me? Are you kidding? Who has the money to go to Hawaii? Have you been there?" Christina was taken aback by my question, even seemed a bit angry about it.

"Uh, no, no," I lied. "I just saw that palm tree and for some reason started thinking about it."

"I don't even dream about stuff like that," Christina said sullenly. At that exact moment, the Ford started shooting shotgun blasts out of its tailpipe, misfiring for the whole ride back to the party, making conversation difficult if not impossible, but which mercifully came to an end just before we turned the corner and pulled up and parked in a space that had opened up right in front of the house. "Fucking piece of shit car," Christina said as she shut off the engine, climbed out, and slammed the rusty door. "I fucking hate it."

Once again, I really didn't know how to respond or what had triggered Christina's sudden change in mood, so I remained silent and handed her the two six packs as we crossed the driveway and went back into the party, where we were hailed as heroes by our friends and others, Christina's demeanor shifting on a dime as she smiled that pretty smile of hers and handed out beers right and left to those who had contributed to the pot. Soon, she was hanging out with some older guys whom she evidently knew from Reseda, and the truth is by the time Hank, Weddy, Ronnie, and I were ready to leave the party, I couldn't even find her to say goodbye. On the way back home, the guys teased me mercilessly about her.

"What happened, Douglas? Couldn't get it up on the ride to the liquor store so she dumped you for those older dudes?" Ronnie yelled, drunk out of his mind.

"Yeah, man," Weddy's speech was so slow and slurred I could barely understand him. "Weren't you able to satisfy her?"

"Don't pay any attention to them," Hank consoled. "They're just drunk and stoned and being assholes."

"I know," I said, though their words definitely stung a bit. What had happened? Did I say something wrong to make her mad? It was sort of weird how quickly she turned on me and then abandoned me. Oh well, we were too different from one another anyway, and besides, I had Natalia and wasn't even looking to date any other girls.

Thankfully, the teasing stopped when Ronnie had to throw up in the bushes in front of some apartment building on Margate, right under the iron sign on the front of the building that read The Seven Seas. This was yet another Tiki-themed apartment building that dotted the Valley, left over from a time when GIs returning from World War II and who had spent time in the South Pacific yearned for the respite that those establishments had once represented to them during the war.

"Dude, it's on your shoes," Weddy teased. "That's so gross."

Ronnie mumbled a "fuck you" before taking off his formerly white Vans and wiping them on the grass. He then carried them in his hand, holding them gingerly by the inside of the heels with just two fingers, and walking the rest of the way home in his socks. He didn't even say goodbye to us as he trudged up the stairs to his apartment. Hank and I peeled off from Weddy once we reached our building, exchanging a friendly, if tired, goodnight, before splitting off to go to our respective units. Thankfully, my mom and Art were out like a light by the time I got home, so I didn't have to go through the third degree about tonight's activities, and I immediately hit the sack, where I spent the night sleeping fitfully while dreaming about pick-up trucks, Hawaii, cowgirls, and farm animals.

Chapter Eleven

The next morning I was jolted out of my deep sleep when my mom opened up my door and said loudly, "Douglas? Are you still sleeping? It's almost noon! Time to get up. I've been calling out to you for forever. Natalia's on the phone." L burst through the door and jumped on the bed, licking my face.

"L! No! Get down." Of course, L paid me no heed, and continued licking and sniffing me. I petted her and then stretched my arms above my head. "What does she want?" I asked.

"How would I know?" my mom answered. "What am I, your secretary? Get out of bed and go talk to her!"

I let out a big yawn, picked L up and carried her with me out into the hall where our mauve Princess phone lay waiting in anticipation. As I put the handset to my ear I could hear the dishwasher from our kitchen running in the background. "Mom, hang up the extension!" I yelled. After a few moments, I heard the click, knew the coast was clear, and croaked, "Hello?" My throat was parched, and my head was throbbing. I had only had a couple of beers last night, but I was definitely feeling the effects. "Hello?" I tried again, this time the words coming out a bit clearer.

"Douglas? Is that you?"

"Yeah, Natalia, it's me. Sorry, I just woke up and my throat's a little dry," I replied, kissing L on the forehead while I gripped the phone with my left hand and held L tucked securely under my right arm.

"Too much partying last night?" she asked snidely.

"Um, yeah, sort of. I hung out with Hank and the guys."

"Oh, really?" she said curtly.

"Yeah, Ronnie knew of a party over on the other side of White Oak so we went and checked it out."

"How was it? Did you have a good time?" I could tell that something wasn't quite right with her. Her tone was cold and even a bit sarcastic.

"Yeah, it was okay. Mostly older kids, though. We didn't really know anybody there."

"That's not what I heard."

"What do you mean?" I asked, my mind now attempting to replay the events from last night.

"Vicki said she saw you at the party."

"Oh, yeah, right. I didn't really get a chance to talk to her, but we did say hello," I answered.

"She said you were leaving the party with a very pretty, older girl in a cowboy hat." Her voice was now breaking, and it sounded like she was beginning to cry.

"Well, sort of," I stammered. "We just ran out to do a quick beer run. I was only gone like ten minutes."

"Douglas, how could you?" Natalia suddenly screamed out, breaking into hysterical sobs. "I thought you loved me!" she cried.

Wow. I definitely was not ready for this. L, probably sensing my growing uneasiness, started to squirm and scratched my arm with her paws, so I put her down, and she bolted down the stairs for safer quarters. I realized I had to pee in the worst way and began to cross my legs in order to hold it in. "Come on, Natalia," I said in my sweetest voice, trying to calm her down. "There's nothing to cry about. It was just some girl we met at the party, and when it came time to get some more beer I was the one who happened to go with her. It was no big deal."

"Vicki said you had your arm around her and looked like you were having a really good time with her," she countered, continuing to sob.

"That's not true!" I demanded. "I barely even know her and didn't even say goodbye to her when we left the party."

"Do you really expect me to believe that?" she shouted, her tears and sobs now shifting into outright anger.

"Well, yeah, why wouldn't you?" I asked innocently. Damn, I really had to pee. "Hey, can I call you right back? I just got out of bed and have to go to the bathroom really bad."

"Don't bother! I don't ever want to talk to you again!" Click. Dead silence. *What the hell just happened?* I slowly hung up the phone and walked into the bathroom, my mind a jumbled mess of fog, a dull ache, and a growing realization that I might have really fucked up. But had I? I mean, what had I really done wrong? I was very confused and truly didn't understand Natalia's reaction.

Unfortunately, despite my attempts to patch things up with her, Natalia stood her ground and absolutely refused to speak to me or take any of my phone calls over the next day or two. When I summoned up the courage to simply knock on her door, Mr. Guinzburg answered and told me in no uncertain terms that his daughter never wanted to see or speak to me again, which I knew would be impossible since we lived in the same complex and went to the same school. Over the following several days, I tried writing notes, and even put together a nice bouquet of flowers

I picked from some of the gardens up and down the street, but nothing worked, and finally I had to accept the fact that I had lost Natalia for good, and not only that, I was out the seven-fifty I had spent on the ring.

It had been a pretty rough week or so. I didn't feel like doing much, hadn't seen any of my friends, wasn't really into eating anything. I guess the only good news was that I dropped another few pounds during this period. I spent a lot of time in my room, listening to the radio and rolling Natalia's ring around in my hands. It was amazing how many love songs were out there that had to do with the breaking of hearts; I had never really noticed them before, whether it was James Taylor singing one of his many love songs or Bill Withers moaning through "Ain't No Sunshine," or pretty much anything off of Dylan's *Blood on the Tracks*, which had suddenly become my go-to album. I'd listen to "If You See Her, Say Hello," over and over again, and try to figure out how I could get Natalia back while still attempting to understand what it was I did that was so wrong.

There was a light knock on my door. "Honey, are you awake?" my mom asked. "Can I come in?"

"Yeah, I'm awake," I answered. "Come on in."

"How's my boy?" she asked, walking over to me where I lay on my bed and stroking my hair. The morning light was streaming in through the blinds, which I had opened part way when I had woken up an hour or so ago.

"I'm all right," I lied.

"Why don't you get up? I don't want to see you lying in bed all day. It's time for you to go have some fun with your friends. Besides, Lassie hasn't been out yet and I'd like you to take her for a walk."

"Ugh," I moaned, rolling over and putting the pillow over my head. "What time is it?"

"It's after nine."

"Maybe later," I said.

"Come on, Douglas," she said grabbing my pillow and tickling my ribs. I couldn't help but laugh. I was extremely ticklish. She kissed me lightly on the top of my head and offered, "I'll make you French toast if you get up and take her out."

"Okay," I relented. I loved my mom's French toast, and I *was* sort of hungry. Maybe my week-long stomachache was finally going away. Maybe I was finally getting over this Natalia thing.

I threw on some shorts and a T-shirt, grabbed L's leash, and took her outside. It was predictably already warm, just another long, hot, summer day in the making. The walks with L had become much more manageable over the past few months; after I had pulled the baseball bat on Mr. Asshole he had never shown his face again, and L had free reign to poop and pee all over his parkway as she pleased. As I came out the front gate and turned to go up the sidewalk, I noticed an exterminator's truck parked in front of Mr. Asshole's building. A man in a long-sleeved yellow shirt with his company's name and an image of a large rat lying on its back, paws up in the air and eyes crossed out, was just finishing hammering the last of three signs into the grass along the parkway in front of the complex.

The signs featured an image of a dog with a large red circle and a red line placed through it. Beneath the no-dogs picture were the words No Dogs Allowed and Chemically Treated Lawn.

Fuck. Mr. Asshole had ratcheted up our feud to a new level.

"Hey," I said to the exterminator, who was holding a mallet in his hand and looking at the signs, presumably to see if they were straight and well-spaced out along the grass. "Are they allowed to do that on a parkway? I thought it was public property."

The exterminator turned and gave me a "Who the fuck are you?" look. Then, glancing down at my dog, he immediately got it. "'Fraid so," he said. "They're responsible for watering and maintaining the grass, so they can do whatever they want."

"What is that stuff you put on the lawn, anyway?" I asked.

"I don't know. Some combination of chemicals. The company don't tell us. It's kinda like McDonald's secret sauce, you know? But I'll tell you this much: Dogs can't stand the stuff."

"Will it make her sick?" I asked, watching as L wandered toward the parkway. I started to pull back on the leash, but then watched as she sniffed the edges of the lawn and turned away.

"See what I mean?" the exterminator laughed, revealing two very prominent gold teeth. He then began loading up his truck.

"Fuck," I muttered under my breath, and as I walked L past the entrance to the building, there was Mr. Asshole, standing behind the glass doors and smiling at me, Prince by his side.

"Where the hell are you going to take your dog to shit, you fucking asshole?" I shouted. "Now you've ruined it for everyone!" It was true, without their parkway as a place to take your dog, everyone would now have to walk down to the empty lot on the corner of Killion, a weed and flea infested patch of dirt. The parkway, with its fifty feet of nicely maintained grass, was perfect, and as long as everyone picked up their poop, it always remained looking lovely; dichondra was amazing that way, and it was enormously popular throughout the Valley. Even the Krahn's lawn, with two huge Dobermans shitting all over it, remained impeccable as long as I or someone else was there to remove the piles of crap on a daily basis.

After I had taken L down to the corner and back, as I approached our building, I was stopped in my tracks when I suddenly saw Natalia and Vicki walking from the opposite direction, holding tell-tale white bags from Winchell's; they had evidently walked over to Reseda boulevard to pick up some fresh donuts for their morning breakfast. Just as I was about to yell, "Hey, Natalia!" she caught sight of me, said something to Vicki, and the two of them literally ran to the entrance of our complex, disappearing inside the gate before I even took another step. *Great*, I thought. *So this is how it's going to be.*

"Come on, L," I sighed, "let's go in."

When I got back to our unit, the smell of my mom's French toast immediately lifted my mood. "Hi, Mom," I called out. "We're back. And guess what? Mr. A had the lawn sprayed with chemicals to keep all dogs off of it."

"Are you serious?" my mom called out from in front of the stove, where I could see her in her apron, her hair in curlers, and a spatula in her hand. "What a jerk."

"Yeah," I said.

"Ronnie called while you were out. Something about going to the beach. You should call him back. It'll still be a few minutes before your French toast is ready."

"Okay," I answered, releasing L from her leash. She immediately bounded up the stairs toward the kitchen; if there was food being cooked, you could be sure to find L nearby.

I picked up the phone and dialed Ronnie's number, pushing the square buttons quickly with my fingertip which, even though it had been awhile since we had switched from the old rotary phones, still occasionally gave me that thrill over just how fast you could dial someone now, especially when you had to do it over and over again if the line were busy and you had something important to tell the other person.

"Yo!" It was always hard to tell the difference between Ronnie and his dad on the phone.

"Um, hi Mr. Munson. Is Ronnie there?"

"It's me, you dickwad. You still can't tell the difference between me and my dad?"

"No, actually, I can't."

"Oh," Ronnie said. "Well, maybe that's a good thing," he laughed. Ronnie definitely had his own sense of humor. If he found it funny, then it was funny. And if he didn't, it wasn't. There was no gray area with Ronnie. "Hey, man," he continued, "my sister's going to the beach today, and the only way my parents would let her use the van was if she took me and my friends along with her. Want to come? Weddy and Hank are already in."

"Sure," I said. "What time?"

"Be out in front of your building in thirty," Ronnie said, before hanging up abruptly as only Ronnie could do.

"Okay," I said to the dial tone. I sighed and hung up the phone. I really didn't feel like going to the beach, but what the fuck. Maybe seeing Natalia and Vicki dash off into the building like that had finally driven home the reality that it was over between us, and I might as well move on. "Mom?" I called out. "How's that French toast coming along?"

By the time I had scarfed down breakfast, thrown on my suit and a T-shirt, grabbed my towel and boogie board, I knew I was running late, and I doubted that Ronnie's sister would show much patience.

"Gotta go, Mom," I said as I ran out the door.

"Douglas! Don't you want your flip-flops?"

I looked down at my bare feet. "Crap," I muttered. My mom tossed the light blue pair I'd left in the dining room above, and they landed at my feet with a smack. "Nice throw, Mom," I said as I slipped them on and headed out once again. "I love you!"

"Love you!" I heard her yell as I slammed the door behind me.

"You're late, jackass!" Ronnie yelled as I burst through the front gate. He was standing next to the open door of the van, looking at his watch.

"Sorry, man," I said breathlessly as I approached him and climbed in. "You didn't give me much notice. Hi, Marilyn," I said to Ronnie's sister.

"What's up, Douglas?" she purred through squinty eyes as she took a hit off of a joint and handed it to her friend, Julie, whom I had met once or twice before. "Everyone in?" she asked to no one in particular, glancing into the rearview mirror and then shifting into Drive, and peeling off with a squeal down Lindley to Burbank. I assumed we'd head over to Reseda where we'd catch the 101 Freeway to Kanan for the drive through the canyon to Zuma.

I threw my boogie board in the way back with the rest of the gear—towels, coolers, Frisbees, chairs, and other foam boards—and settled into a spot between Ronnie and Hank. Weddy sat across from me. "What's up, fellas?" I said, looking around to each of them.

"Hey, buddy," Hank said. "Long time no see."

"Yeah, where the fuck you been?" Weddy asked as he took a hit off of the joint, which had been passed from the girls in the front, to the other girls—three of them, none of whom I knew—in the middle row of seats, and then back to us.

"I've been around. Just busy," I lied. I still hadn't told any of my friends about Natalia and me.

Weddy gave the joint to Hank who simply reached past me and handed it to Ronnie, who took a huge hit, inhaling deeply.

"No wake and bake, Hank?" Ronnie said while holding his breath, his voice something between a squeak and a whisper.

"Nah, maybe later, thanks." I knew Hank well enough to know that he never liked to get high before he was going to do anything remotely athletic, and Hank loved to boogie board and body surf.

"Pussy." Ronnie suddenly exhaled and began coughing violently, holding out the joint in front of him and pounding his chest with his other fist. "Oh, shit, man," he managed to say. "That was a huge hit!" And then he started laughing as only Ronnie could laugh, somewhat maniacally, which then caused the rest of us to break up.

"Goooood and gooooood for you!" Weddy joked, and that got us going once again. "Hey," he said, once we had all calmed down, "did I tell you guys that my brother's moving back from New York?"

"Oh, yeah?" I said. "That's cool. He's a cool guy."

"He completed his residency and is joining a pretty good cardiology practice in Beverly Hills. His life is basically set."

"Sweeeeeeet!" Ronnie said.

"You'll be there one day," Hank added.

"Yeah, maybe," Weddy said. "Although I don't think cardiology is right for me. I don't have the heart for it." Weddy smiled that contagious smile of his, and we all laughed.

"You should become an orthopedic surgeon," I suggested. "That way you can operate on Hank once he makes it to the NBA and tears his knee up."

"Gee, thanks," Hank said, punching me in the arm.

"Seriously, though," Ronnie added as thoughtfully as he could muster. "You could specialize in famous athletes and make a shitload of money."

"Yeah, that'd be cool," Weddy said, trying to light the roach before finally giving up and tossing it on the dirty floor of the van.

Being mid-morning, traffic was light, and we flew up the 101, making it to Kanan in no time at all. Ronnie's sister and her friends were Zeppelin freaks, so that's all we listened to while we were driving. I had never really been into Zeppelin because my brother and sister always dismissed them as "heavy metal," but I have to admit I was digging some of the stuff I was hearing this morning, especially the slower tunes. Generally speaking, my tastes ran along the same lines as Julie's and David's—all of the great sixties bands with a strong dose of seventies singer-songwriters—Neil, Jackson, Bob, etc.—and country-influenced bands like the Eagles, the Byrds, Creedence, and the Grateful Dead thrown in for good measure. And, of course, we all liked Bowie, who had a unique style that was all his own.

"Hey, Marilyn!" Ronnie yelled out. "We gonna stop at McDonald's?"

"Of course!" Marilyn yelled back. Pretty much every trip to Zuma included a stop at McDonald's on Kanan, right as you exited the freeway; it was super convenient. Even though I had already eaten my mom's French toast, I happily joined in the fun and ordered an Egg McMuffin and a Coke.

Driving through the canyon, everyone was fairly quiet, listening to Robert Plant wail and eating their food. I glanced out the back window on occasion, seeing the dry, brown hills and inhaling the smells of sage and wild onion through the open windows up front. At about the halfway point through Kanan, the Malibu "welcoming" graffiti started to appear on the large boulders that dotted the landscape along with the fronts of a couple of the tunnels: "Valley Go Home!"

The surfers in Malibu were extremely territorial and hated it when surfers from the Valley would come out and try to take their waves off of Point Dume or even over at Zuma One. Zuma One was called Zuma One because that was the number of the lifeguard station in front of the best break at Zuma. We also called it Free Zuma because you could park pretty close to the water for free, unlike the rest of Zuma which had a gigantic parking lot where they charged you to park. We generally stayed away from Free Zuma since we weren't that serious about boogie boarding and none of us surfed. Besides, most of our friends from school hung out by Zuma Three or Four. We were early enough that we'd be able to get a free spot along PCH. It was a hike across the parking lot and the wide swath of sand to get to a place on the beach where we could set up shop for the day near the water, but we could use the money we saved on parking for ice cream or Popsicles or something cold to drink later in the afternoon.

As soon as we parked and gathered our stuff, we split off from Julie and her friends—upon her parents' insistence she had reluctantly agreed to take Ronnie and his buddies along with her, but she drew the line at their request to hang out anywhere near us or to even keep an eye on us. "Meet us here back at the van at three. And if you're late, you'll be hitching home. I don't want to hit any traffic."

"Thanks, Marilyn," Ronnie said sarcastically. "Love you, too." Then, turning to us, he said, "She's such a fucking bitch."

I actually always liked Marilyn and totally understood why she wouldn't want to hang out with her little brother's friends. Then again, I had older siblings and had often been the target of their wrath when my parents made them take me somewhere or watch me and be responsible for me, so I was used to this sort of treatment and disdain.

Weddy pointed to a spot about halfway between the two lifeguard stations, far enough away from both towers that he and Ronnie could smoke pot without getting hassled, and we all agreed it looked good, and we headed over there. Just as we were getting ready to lay down our towels and set up our area for the day, I heard the sounds of Skynyrd's "Gimmee Three Steps," and I turned around to see Christina off in the distance, holding her portable radio high above her head and smiling at me. "Hey, Douglas!

How are you?" She began to walk toward us.

"I'm good," I answered, surprised to see her, and feeling a little sick to my stomach. I wasn't sure if it was from the Egg McMuffin or if the sight of Christina was reminding me of Natalia. "How you doing?"

"Hey," Ronnie said in sotto voce, "is that that chick from the party? The one who made the beer run?"

"Yeah, man," I answered. "Be cool."

"Hey, guys," Christina said as she and her friend—not Alexandra from the party but someone else—reached us.

"What's up, Christina?" Ronnie, Hank, and Weddy said in perfect unison.

"Whoa!" Christina joked. "Did you guys practice that or what?" They all laughed sheepishly, and then Christina, who looked especially hot in her skimpy bikini and omni-present cowboy hat, asked, "Any of you boys holding?"

"Of course!" Ronnie said, whipping out a fat one.

"Cool!" Christina's friend shouted out. "I'm Samantha. Nice to meet you. Now why don't you fire up that puppy?" Geez, these girls wasted no time.

"Douglas," Christina turned and flashed her eyes at me, causing me to momentarily melt into the sand. "What happened to you the other night? One minute we were hanging out, and the next minute I couldn't even find you. Why did you leave without saying goodbye?"

"Well, uh, I looked all over for you when we were ready to go, but I couldn't find you," I lied. Then again, she had actually been the one who ditched me, but she was probably too fucked up to remember that.

"Yeah, right, cowboy," she said. "I know when I've been dumped."

"What? No, really, I—"

"I'm just joking, silly boy," she laughed. "God, you're a serious kid."

"That's what I'm always telling him!" Ronnie yelled, passing the joint to Christina.

"Yeah, well, this serious boy is going to go have some fun in the water. Anyone want to join me?" I looked around for takers, but only Hank grabbed his board.

"Sure. Let's go," my buddy said. I could always count on Hank for backing me up.

As cute as Christina was, she also now represented the reason why Natalia wasn't speaking to me, so I just felt like I should keep my distance from her. And it turns out that as the day wore on, Christina and Samantha stayed close to Ronnie and Weddy since they had the weed. Hank and I spent a good chunk of the day out in the water, catching waves and just hanging out, lying on our boards while keeping cool and talking to other friends we knew from school who were also enjoying the ocean. At one point during the middle of the afternoon we took a break to grab some ice cream; they had a pretty decent soft serve machine at the snack bar.

"I still can't understand how you could possibly choose chocolate over vanilla," I said to Hank as we stood in the shade of the cement-block building. As usual, we had forgotten to put our flip-flops back on, and it was the only spot where our bare feet wouldn't burn. We had to run the last fifty yards or so because the sand was so damn hot.

Hank took an especially large, especially long lick of his dark cone and shrugged. "I'm actually an equal opportunist. Just as likely to order vanilla as chocolate."

"When it comes to soft serve, I'm vanilla all the way." My eyes drifted over to Ronnie and Weddy, who were still sitting with Christina and her friend. "Look at those guys, they've just sat there getting high for hours. Been at it all day long."

Hank looked over toward the group just as Ronnie let loose a huge cloud of smoke into the air, followed by one of his patented coughing attacks, which was followed in kind by all four of the stoners rolling around on their towels in hysterics. "How the hell does Ronnie get all that dope? Where does he get the money for it?"

"His dad gets it," I answered. "Ronnie told me the guys he works with down at the garage bring it back from Mexico. It's just cheap Colombian, nothing fancy, and certainly not anything from Northern California or Hawaii. It's not even Acapulco Gold. I think you actually have to smoke a bunch of it to get a decent high. My brother always told me it just gives him a headache, and he won't touch it. Weddy complains to Ronnie about it because he definitely prefers higher quality weed but, of course, when push comes to shove, Weddy will smoke anything."

"Well, at least they're having fun," Hank said, devouring the rest of his cone in just a couple of bites. "Let's get back in the water," he said, gesturing out to the ocean. "By the time we get out there this set will be over, and we can paddle out easily. You can even finish your cone out there," and then he held out his hand and we executed Soul Brother Handshake #7, in which we pantomimed all the moves from handshakes one through six, but without ever actually touching each other. It was our Soul Brother Handshake coup de grace and was meant to bring us good fortune.

I gobbled up the rest of the ice cream, and we turned and jogged back to the water's edge, where the sand would cool our fiery feet. Hank was right: Once we hit the water, the previous set had ended, and we paddled easily out to the break, where we had a few minutes to catch our breath. Then, for the next half-hour or so, we enjoyed killer ride after killer ride as the sets of three- to four-foot, nicely shaped waves kept rolling in, one set after another.

During one pause between waves, we sat on our boogie boards, straddling them with our legs, and looked back to the shore. "Hey," Hank said, sounding concerned. "What the fuck?"

I immediately looked toward Ronnie and Weddy and saw two guys who were obviously cops standing above the group. The cops would occasionally send a couple of young guys out to the beach to walk the sand and hassle anyone who was either drinking alcohol or smoking weed. They usually didn't arrest anyone, or even write them up a ticket; a verbal and the occasional written warning was all they'd really end up doing most of the time. And, of course, they'd confiscate whatever you were drinking or smoking and bring it back to the station for all the cops to enjoy. My guess was they saw Ronnie blowing one of his enormous clouds in the air, and it drew their attention. In fact, at the moment, all of the cops' attention seemed to be directed at Ronnie who, by the gestures he was making with his hands, seemed to be getting a little agitated.

Suddenly one of the cops took a couple of steps forward and pointed straight at Ronnie. At the same time, the other cop reached behind the waist of his dark shorts and removed the handcuffs hanging from his belt. "Oh, shit," I said. "Should we go over there?"

"Are you crazy?" Hank shot back. "No fucking way. I'm not getting involved in Ronnie's shit. Dude has a big mouth."

It was hard to argue with Hank on that point. Ronnie slowly got to his feet and stood facing the officer. I could see Weddy talking to the guy holding the handcuffs; he seemed to be pleading with him. Weddy, being as smart and well-spoken as he was, could be counted on in a situation like this to bring calm to the proceedings. I'd seen him break up countless fights at school and at parties. He just had that way about him and was smart enough to know how to use his people skills effectively.

Sure enough, things quickly de-escalated. The officer put the handcuffs away, and I watched as Weddy placed his hands in prayer in front of his chest and gave a slight bow to the cops. Like I said, Weddy was good at this sort of thing, always knew what to do. His dad was big into Eastern philosophy, meditation, yoga and that sort of thing, and he forced Weddy to learn about it, too, something Weddy would often complain about, but deep down I think he really enjoyed it and took it to heart.

Even Ronnie had calmed way the fuck down and appeared to be sharing a laugh with the cop who had ordered him to his feet. The girls, who had both sat quietly staring at the ground during the whole confrontation, were now working their charms on the officers, batting their eyelashes and being all flirty with them. After a few minutes, it was all over and the cops moved on, walking south along the beach toward Free Zuma.

Hank and I had sat out the previous set while we watched the shenanigans on the beach, and when the next set came we grabbed the first wave and rode it in all the way to the shoreline. We had had plenty of great rides that day, and while we still probably had enough time to catch another wave or two before we had to meet up with

Marilyn at the van, we wanted to find out what the hell had happened with the cops.

"Hey boys!" Ronnie said cheerfully as we approached. "You missed all the fun action!"

"We saw it from the water!" I said. "What the fuck happened?"

"We were having too much fun," Christina spoke up first, "and we didn't see the cops walking down the beach."

"Ronnie had just taken a *huge* hit right as they walked up behind us," Weddy said, laughing. "He practically blew the smoke directly in their faces."

"Figures," I said.

"No harm, no foul," Ronnie said. "They were cool."

"They didn't look so cool when they took out the handcuffs and ordered you to stand up," Hank said.

"It was no biggie," Christina responded. "Just a misunderstanding."

"And Weddy here has a golden tongue, don't you Weddy?" Christina's friend Samantha rubbed her hand down Weddy's leg.

"What'd you say to them, Weddy?" I asked.

"Just the usual bullshit. I noticed the one cop was Japanese, so I started talking to him about Zen meditation and even TM. Everything was cool after that."

"Sounds like you owe Weddy one, Ronnie," I said.

"Yeah, yeah," Ronnie said. "I already thanked him. Besides, what were they going to do? Arrest me? I'm a kid!"

Samantha suddenly spoke up. "My sister got busted on the beach for smoking pot, and they took her in and made my parents come down to the police station to pick her up."

"Good luck with that!" Ronnie said. "Maybe Marilyn

would come get me, but no way would my mom or dad come down. They're the ones who gave me the pot!" The girls found this to be incredibly funny and were once again laughing hysterically as they staggered to their feet.

"Well, it's been great hanging out with you guys, but we should probably be heading home. Give us a call some time," Christina said.

"Oh, don't worry," Ronnie replied. "We will!"

"Bye, Douglas," Christina said as she turned toward me. "Sorry we didn't get to hang out very much today. Maybe another time?"

"Yeah, sure, another time for sure," I said as sincerely as I could.

"See you, Weddy," Samantha smiled.

"See you," Weddy smiled back. "I'll give you a jingle."

"Bye, girls," Ronnie called out as they walked away.

"Damn, Sam!" Ronnie said loudly to Weddy before the girls were truly out of earshot, exchanging fist bumps in the process. "Older chicks dig us, dude!"

"Hey, Douglas," Weddy said, "I hope you don't mind that we hung out with Christina. I know you were sort of into her at the party and everything. But you and Hank took off and spent the day out there in the water, so I figured..."

"No need to explain," I answered. "I'm cool with it." It was true. Unfortunately, there was some bad karma circling around that girl. She was cute and could be a lot of fun and everything, but she had a certain sadness about her, and you got the sense that her life was going to be anything but easy.

"Did you know she lives on a farm?" Ronnie asked.

"Yeah," I said. "Yeah, she told me that."

"What was her friend like?" Hank asked.

"Really nice. She gave me her number."

"Cool!" I said, happy for Weddy.

"Yeah, her dad's a doctor like mine, so we had a lot in common."

Ronnie checked his watch and noticed it was nearing three o'clock. "Shit," he said, "we better boogie. My sister wasn't kidding about taking off without us. Last summer I had to hitch all the way home by myself. Can you believe that? A thirteen-year-old kid? And my parents didn't even bat an eye. 'You shouldn't have been late' my dad said. 'I bet you'll never be late again,' my mom added. Anyway, it was lucky a mom who lived in Encino drove by the corner of PCH and Kanan just a couple of minutes after I got there and stuck out my thumb. I had to sit with the family dog in the back of the station wagon 'cause she had a bunch of little kids packed into the car, but she took me right to my doorstep."

"Well," Weddy interjected, "with four of us it would take forever to get a ride, so let's hustle."

With that we all took off running across the wide swath of hot sand, the sun's reflection so bright our eyes hurt no matter how much we squinted. It took a while for us to figure out where we had parked, but thankfully Weddy had used a telephone pole that was clearly leaning a bit to one side as a landmark, and we arrived at the car just as Marilyn and her friends were packing the very back of the van with their stuff.

"You're cutting it awfully close," she said with a smirk.

"Yeah, well, we're here," Ronnie responded.

The car ride home was pretty quiet as everyone had had their fill of sea, sun, and sand for the day. *Cat Stevens'*

Greatest Hits had just come out, and Marilyn had bought a copy immediately upon its release. The eight-track proved to be a perfect soundtrack to the ride home, and as we wound our way through the canyon, Cat serenaded us with "Father and Son." It had been a long day out in the water, I had sand in my hair and my skin was hot to the touch. I was tired, but it was a good tired, the kind of tired that you could only get from a full day at the beach. I closed my eyes and rested my head against the wall of the van, my towel acting as a pillow, and inhaled the wild sage and onions wafting in from the canyon through the open windows. I silently sang along with Cat, my lips moving, but the only sound I created was the echo inside my head: "You're still young, that's your fault...There's so much you have to know."

Chapter Twelve

The dog days of summer slowly crept to an end, with ab-solutely no contact between me and Natalia. Not even a sighting. It was like she had turned into a ghost. Until one day, the Tuesday before Labor Day weekend, I was walking up to the newsstand when I saw her, unmistak-ably her, even from behind, reading a magazine at one of the racks. My heart practically leaped out of my chest, and I could feel all of my blood rush to my head; I practically floated the rest of the way over to her.

"Natalia?" I said as calmly as I could.

She turned and looked at me, expressionless, yet star-ing deep into my eyes which were locked with hers. It felt like hours went by in a matter of seconds as I waited for her to respond.

"Hi," was all she said. I took a breath.

"I—how—" I stammered. "Wait. Start over." I said, briefly closing my eyes and pausing to gather myself. "How have you been?"

"Douglas, I can't." She turned and looked back to her magazine, nervously flipping through the pages.

"Natalia, please, just give me another chance. I miss you."

She stopped and looked up. I could see a tear forming in her eye.

"Can't we just talk?" I pleaded.

She glanced nervously over my shoulder. "My dad's

coming back in a second. He shouldn't see us together."

"Why not?" I asked incredulously.

"Please. Just go away."

"How can you do this? How can you not even give me a chance to explain?" A customer had to reach around me to get a copy of *People* magazine; I simply ignored him, too focused on Natalia to even care about manners at this moment in time.

"Not now!" she implored.

"Then when?" I stood my ground. I didn't care if Mr. Guinzburg showed up.

"Okay, look. We're having a big family picnic on Sunday for Labor Day weekend in Balboa Park. How about if I meet you over on the other side of Balboa, across from the tennis courts under the cherry trees at one o'clock."

"Great! I'll be there."

"I won't be able to spend a whole lot of time," she said, once again looking deeply into my eyes with those green emeralds of hers. "Now go!" she demanded, glancing past me and expecting her father to come walking up any second.

I couldn't resist and kissed her on the lips. She stood there with a mixture of shock and awe, seemingly thrilled that I did it, yet angry at the thought of her father possibly having seen us. I slowly backed away, winked at her, and turned to grab a copy of *Basketball Digest*—training camps would be opening soon—before paying for it and heading home, all the while ignoring Natalia who had been joined by her father before I had even reached the cash register. He never noticed me, and I jammed out of there, skipping all the way home, joyful that I was going to get at least one more chance to win back Natalia's heart.

Sunday could not come soon enough, though everything almost fell apart when my mom and Art told me that we'd all been invited to a party on the beach in Malibu at a house in the Colony that some rich friends of Art's owned. For whatever reason, my mom had it in her head that this was going to be a great way for the three of us to bond, and she didn't take too kindly to the fact that I told her I couldn't go.

"Why can't you just go to the park with her on Monday or some other day?" she asked.

"Mom, you don't get it. She hasn't even been speaking to me."

"Son, trust me, this party is going to be incredible. Don't do this to yourself. I think you know it's over between the two of you."

"Mom, I can't go. I have to meet her at the park at one."

"Okay," my mom sighed. "Your loss. It's going to be a great party."

"I'm sure it will be," I said. "And I'm sure you'll have a wonderful time."

My mom looked at me and smiled. "Just don't get your heart broken," she said sweetly.

"Me?" I said doing my best Woody Allen impression. "I'm like a cat. I'll always end up on my feet."

She laughed. "I love you, Son."

"I love you, too, Mom." We shared a long hug.

By the time Sunday rolled around, I had everything prepared down to the tiniest detail. My mom and Art agreed to drop me off at the park before they headed out to their Malibu shindig, which was key because it was another in what seemed like a string of brutally hot Labor Day weekends, with temperatures in the high nineties, and I wasn't traveling lightly. When my mom went to Gelson's the day before, I had her pick up a couple of different pasta salads from the deli, along with some cheese and crackers, some grapes, a Tab for Natalia, and a Hawaiian Punch for me. Oh, and a beautiful bouquet of flowers. I was going the whole nine yards on this one.

Full picnic basket, blanket, and flowers in hand, I stepped away from my mom's car on Balboa boulevard. "Are you sure about this, Douglas?" my mom asked one more time. "It's not too late to change your mind and come with us."

"No, thanks, Mom. I know what I'm doing. Have a good time."

"Knock her dead," Art added. "Good luck."

"Thanks, Art," I responded, happy that he understood my decision.

I watched as they pulled away and even waited as they made a U-turn and came back down Balboa on the other side of the street so that they could hop on the 101. I waved, but I wasn't sure if they waved back to me, and as they crossed Burbank I turned and headed toward a shady spot under one of the numerous Cherry trees that lined that side of the park. It was only 12:30 P.M., but I wanted to give myself plenty of time to set up shop.

One thing about Natalia was that she was punctual, and sure enough, at one on the dot, I saw her running across the street toward me. From the direction she was coming from, I guessed that her family was having a picnic over on the other side of the tennis and basketball courts, far away from us.

She looked as gorgeous as ever, dressed in a lightweight cotton dress, bright blue with a pattern of small yellow flowers running throughout. A white bonnet she was wearing to protect her delicate skin from the sun completed the pretty picture.

"Hey there!" I said. "You look really beautiful."

"Thank you, Douglas," she said, blushing ever so slightly. "What's all this?" She gestured to my immaculate spread.

"I thought we'd have a little picnic."

"But, Douglas, I told you I was with my family and couldn't spend much time with you."

"That's okay. Sit down." I gestured to the red blanket. Natalia reluctantly took a seat, and I sat facing her. Looking at the flowers and the plates with the salads and the cheese and grapes, she said, "This is lovely, but—"

I cut her off, not wanting to hear her protestations, knowing I needed to get right down to business as my time with her was obviously going to be short. "Natalia, I understand why you're angry with me. But how can I make it right?"

"I don't know, Douglas. I just don't know if we can make this work." She glanced down and picked at a thread in the blanket.

"But why?" I said, placing my hand on her leg. "Why did it upset you so much that I was talking to that girl at that party?"

"Oh come on, Douglas, it was much more than that." She removed my hand from her leg.

"What do you mean?" I asked.

"Vicki said that the two of you left the party arm-in-arm and came back with a bunch of beer."

"Yeah, it's true, I took a ride with her to the liquor store, but what does that have to do with you and me?"

"Douglas, I just don't know if I can trust you anymore. And also, well, it's more than that." She went quiet.

"What do you mean? What else is there?"

Natalia looked back up at me lovingly. "It's just," she paused, "it's just that I think we're very different people. I think you might be a little too fast for me."

"Me?" I exclaimed. "But I'm the slowest of anyone I know."

"Exactly," Natalia said. "Look who you're hanging out with. Older girls who go get beer by doing who knows what. Guys like Ronnie and Weddy who are stoned out of their minds all the time. Or those kids I've seen you gambling with at school. It's just not a crowd I want to be around, but I know they're your friends, and I could never ask you to leave your friends for me."

Wow. I couldn't believe what I was hearing. "But Weddy's one of the smartest kids at school. Probably *the* smartest!"

"Yeah, and the biggest underachiever as well," she shot back.

"That's not fair," I said, trying to defend my friend.

"It is fair, Douglas. I'm sorry, I just don't think I can hang around you anymore."

My world was crashing down. "But-but Natalia. I—I love you!" I blurted out. And then, in the height of stupidity and awkwardness, I pulled out the ring and shoved it toward her. "I want to go steady with you. I want you to be my girlfriend."

Natalia took one look at the ring and recoiled as if in horror, as if I had just presented her with the biggest pile of Great Dane dogshit she'd ever seen. She quickly rose to her feet, saying, "I have to go, Douglas. I'm sorry."

And just like that she was gone, dashing across the street back to her family. I was left holding the turquoise ring in my hand, the makings of a beautiful lunch for two lying untouched all around me. It was going to be a long walk back home.

That night, I found out from my very drunk mother that, as expected, the party had been quite the event, and that Jodie Foster *and* Tatum O'Neal were there hanging out, looking like they wished they had more kids their age to talk to. I don't think the universe could have possibly provided any more salt to pour into my wounds.

Chapter Thirteen

Summer drifted to a close, the September heat reminding everyone of the Santa Anas and the fire season to come. People who visited California in June were universally disappointed by the "June Gloom" which resulted in overcast skies and relatively cool temperatures. If people really wanted to experience hot summer weather, with really warm ocean water, September was the month to come to SoCal.

The weekend before school started, my mom took me to The Surprise Store up the street, where we bought a few new outfits for school. Mostly jeans and pocket T-shirts, but a couple of nicer shirts as well.

"Thanks, Mom," I said, giving her a hug and a kiss on the cheek as we walked out of the store toward the car.

"You're welcome, honey," she replied, kissing me in kind. "Are you excited about the new school year? You're going to be the big man on campus!"

"Yeah, I guess so. I just don't know what I'm going to do when I see Natalia."

"Well, if it were me," my mom advised, reaching for the car keys in her purse, "I'd just be cordial, say 'hello,' and move on. She made her feelings clear, Douglas, and I don't think there's anything you can do to change her mind. Unless, of course, you're prepared to get rid of all of your friends."

"I can't do that!" I insisted.

"I agree," my mom, always wise, said. She stopped before opening the door to the Buick, placed her hands on my shoulders, and looked me in the eye. "If you're going to get involved in a romantic relationship with a girl, she has to love you for who you are. And that means loving and accepting your family, your friends, everything about you. If she doesn't, it'll never work. And the same holds true for you, too, mister. Don't try to make substantial changes to someone you think you love just to try and make a relationship work. Small changes, maybe. But telling someone to get rid of their friends? Or their family? *Red flag!!*" she suddenly yelled, throwing her hands up high in the air.

We shared a laugh and climbed into the Riviera. My mom immediately started the car and cranked up the AC, rolling down the windows briefly to let the intense heat escape from the car. "Douglas," she said, once again turning serious, "there are a lot of girls out there in the world. If you play your cards right, you'll have many wonderful experiences, many fantastic relationships, and eventually you'll find that person who you not only can love, but can make a life with, can share a life with. It's not about finding 'the love of your life,'" she continued, making quote marks with her fingers and then rolling up the windows and shifting the car into reverse. "It's about finding a partner for life, someone with whom you can raise kids and lean on during hard times. That person isn't necessarily going to be 'the love of your life,'" she said, taking her hands off the wheel before shifting into Drive and once again making quote marks with her fingers.

"Never forget that," she continued. "Too many people marry the person they are head over heels in love with, and it blinds them to faults and realities that will eventually doom the relationship. How does the person respond to stress? Are they supportive during difficult situations? Are they trustworthy?"

I knew that my mom was talking about herself . . . and my dad. They were high school sweethearts who were really too young to get married and have kids. Hell, by the time my mom was only twenty-one, both my brother and sister were already born. Once I came around, I think they were already beginning to realize that they were very different people than they were when they were teenagers. And even though they were each other's "love of their life," they weren't very well matched to survive a long-term marriage and the raising of a family. So after nearly twenty years, they called it quits.

"I'm going to give you one more piece of advice that my father said to me and which I ignored: When you're in a relationship with someone, look at their mother and father, but for you, especially the mother. That's who you are marrying. If there are major problems with the mother, or the father, or between the parents and the girl you're dating, *red flag!*" and once again she shouted directly up into the air, and we both laughed, the air conditioning vents aimed directly at us, blowing our long hair back with its cool air, like we were rock stars.

As it turned out, seeing Natalia at school wasn't at all weird. First of all, I didn't have one class with her, so that made things a lot less awkward. And when I did see her in passing, either between classes in the corridors or during lunch or nutrition, we were, as my mom would say, "cordial" to each other. We'd wave or say "hi," and that would be it. Of course, the pain in my heart was still there, but it had gone from a stabbing, piercing pain to just a dull, occasionally throbbing type of hurt.

The year had started well, and while it was fun to be able to walk across the senior quad without penalty and to simultaneously be able to reprimand the new seventh graders who didn't yet know the rules, there wasn't a whole lot different about being in ninth grade instead of eighth grade. My friends and I still gathered in the mornings to pitch coins and bet on sports, arguing all the while about which team was going to win the championship or what player was the best in his sport.

One significant thing that was different about this school year was that the celebration of the United States Bicentennial next July was going to be a major theme running throughout every class, with all kinds of special projects, assemblies, and celebrations planned for almost every month of the school year, getting especially heavy next spring as we got closer to the two-hundredth anniversary of the country.

One day, in mid-October, I caught up to Hank on our way into English. "Hey, Hank," I said, "how's it going?"

"Hey, buddy," he replied, rather unenthusiastically.

"What's up?" I asked. "Something wrong?"

"I gotta go to the doctor after school today."

"How come?"

"I don't know, man. Something weird is going on. You've seen me out on the court. I'm just not myself."

It was true. All summer long Hank had been complaining about little aches and pains, and he had definitely grown a lot taller. It was even noticeable to those of us who were around him almost every day. And when we got back to school and started playing ball at lunch and after-school, Hank's game had taken a nosedive. He was turning the ball over way more than he ever had, and just didn't seem as fluid on the court as he had been in the past.

"Well, I'm sure it's nothing," I tried to reassure him. "The last time you went, the doctor just said you were going through a growth spurt, and the pains were normal, right?"

"Yeah, but now it seems like I can't even walk and chew gum at the same time," he complained as we strode into class. "I feel like a total dufus."

It turned out that Hank's growth spurt had also cost him a good deal of coordination. "You're going to have to get used to your new body," the doctor told him later that day. "And it could take a while. In fact," he continued, in what Hank later described to me as a dagger to his heart, "you might be a different type of player than you were before. Maybe more of a power forward than a point guard." The doctor was trying to be encouraging, but he didn't realize how much of Hank's identity was tied into being a point guard. All of his heroes—Jerry West, The Big O, Walt Frazier, Earl the Pearl, Tiny Archibald, Pete Maravich—every single one of them was a point guard.

It was sad to see Hank stumbling around the court, but Hank always had an amazing attitude about everything, and as the weeks went by, slowly but surely he started letting other guys bring the ball up while he set up down in the block with his back to the basket. He was still getting comfortable figuring out what moves he could make from down low, and it was hard for him to *not* try and take the ball from one end of the court to the other, but he just wasn't as effective doing it as he used to be, and as the days passed he slowly got better and better playing down low against the bigger players. He still had another month or so before try outs for Pop Warner, and he was determined to make a good showing, whether it was as a dominant forward or, if he were to somehow regain his old coordination by then, as the great point guard he had always been. But the chances of that happening so soon were slim to none, and all Hank really wanted to be able to do right now was to run up and down the court without tripping over his own two feet.

By the time Halloween rolled around, L.A. was suffering through Santa Ana conditions that drove the temperature up into the high nineties. Fortunately, Hank, Weddy, Ronnie, and I had agreed not to get dressed up in any costumes this year—as ninth graders, we felt we were too old for that stuff—so we wouldn't have to suffer under a rubber mask or beneath some sort of heavy costume. We would just wear our regular clothes, but in a brilliant suggestion by Weddy, we decided we'd each carry a pirate's eye patch, so that when we did go up to a door to grab some free candy, we could claim to be "modern-day pirates." We knew we'd get some questioning looks, but in the end, who's going to really deny a kid candy on Halloween just because they didn't like their costume?

We didn't have any specific plans for the night, and just figured we'd roam the neighborhood streets, maybe come across a party or two where one or more of us knew some of the kids. We met outside of Ronnie's apartment building at 5:30 P.M., just after it got dark. Daylight Savings Time had kicked in the weekend before, and we were all still adjusting to the shorter days, such a huge difference from those seemingly endless summer afternoons, which now seemed like a lifetime ago. When Hank and I arrived, Weddy and Ronnie were already waiting out front. I immediately noticed that Ronnie's pillowcase seemed to be sagging.

"Did you guys already do some trick-or-treating?" I asked, gesturing to Ronnie's bag.

Ronnie looked down and smiled, and as he reached deep into the pillowcase he said, "Nah, but I do have a dozen eggs at the ready!" He pulled out an egg carton filled with twelve extra-large eggs, raw and ready to explode.

"No way!" Hank said. "Who we going to go after?"

"I don't know," Ronnie said. "Let's see where the evening takes us. Maybe a couple of seventh or eighth graders. A passing car or two. And at least if someone comes after us, we'll have some ammunition of our own."

Leave it to Ronnie. It's true that Halloween was a popular night for egging. Cars, houses, trick-or-treaters—anything and anyone was fair game in the Valley. It was almost like every kid got a free pass on Halloween when eggings were just sort of accepted as an occupational hazard for that evening. "We should probably save a few for Vineland's house," I suggested. Everyone knew where Mr. Vineland lived, and his house had been subjected to numerous eggings and teepeeing over the years, and not just on Halloween. Rumor had it that he had taken to hiding in the bushes on Halloween, just waiting to spring out and attack anyone who dared to threaten his property, but we figured that was more rumor than fact.

We decided to walk over to the neighborhood where we had gone to the party where I had met Christina and which had effectively ended my relationship with Natalia. The houses were much bigger and nicer over there, which always translated into more generous candy. Some of the owners of the homes even gave out regular-sized candy bars! But it was crucial to get over there in the early part of the evening, because the neighborhood was so popular with trick-or-treaters that by seven or eight o'clock the people who lived there would be all out of candy and their lights would be dark.

As expected, the streets on the other side of White Oak—Weddington, Margate, Shoshone, Andasol, etc.—were packed with kids. It was a fun, celebratory atmosphere, and everyone seemed to be in a good mood. There were tons of kids dressed as the shark from *Jaws*—all of them struggling to walk in the full-length body costume—and I saw everything from Inspector Clouseau to Billy Jack to Grizzly Adams . . . one kid was even dressed as Igor from *Young Frankenstein*, complete with a hump on his back. Fortunately, we didn't even elicit so much as a raised eyebrow with our "modern-day pirate" costumes, and we managed to collect a nice load of candy in our pillowcases.

As we were walking down Weddington toward Louise, we stumbled across a party with a bunch of high school kids out front. "Hey, I know this house!" Weddy said. "My brother was friends with a kid who lived here, and he had a younger brother not much older than us. What the hell were their names?" Weddy was racking his brain, trying to remember.

"Here," Ronnie said, handing Weddy yet another joint. "Maybe this will help." I had lost track of how many they had already smoked tonight.

"I know!" Weddy said, exhaling a cloud of smoke. "Jack and Jared—no, Johnny and Jared Martell. That's it. Johnny is my brother's age, and I think Jared is in tenth, maybe eleventh grade. Let's head in."

"You sure?" I asked. "You really know these guys?"

"Yeah, yeah. No problem. Johnny and my brother were pretty good friends. I've even been in the house a couple of times when we picked up Johnny to go to a Dodgers game."

As we approached the house, a large, traditionally styled home with plenty of used brick, multi-paned windows with white trim, and a wood shingled roof, I could hear the Stones' version of the Temptations "Ain't Too Proud to Beg," blasting from every open window in the house. Even the upstairs bedrooms were alive with the sound of Mick making the song his own. I experienced a moment of déjà vu, but then quickly remembered that at the party where I met Christina, they had been playing the Stones as well.

We headed through the front door of the rather palatial house and made our way to the backyard where we figured the keg would be. We were right; in fact, there was a whole line-up of kegs, all sitting on ice in trash cans, about six different beers to choose from. Even though the Santa Anas had calmed down as the night progressed, it was still pretty warm outside and all of us were dying of thirst. As we stood there downing our beers, I looked around the yard.

"Nice place," I said, intentionally understated, checking out the gorgeous pool with a fully lit tennis court lying beyond. Kids were dancing and running around on the court, scuffing the surface with their various types of non-tennis-court friendly footwear.

I turned around and was suddenly face to face with Natalia and Vicki, who were both dressed in long, flowing dresses with a corset-like top.

"Hi—hi, Natalia," I stumbled. "Wow. You look beautiful."

"Thanks," she smiled, at first seeming equally as shocked to have run into me, but then recovering and explaining, "We're dressed as the Raquel Welch character from *The Three Musketeers*."

Like Raquel Welch, Natalia filled out her corset beautifully, her large breasts pushed together until they were almost popping out of the top. Her cleavage was incredible, but of course, Natalia kept it tasteful at the same time, though I did wonder if her dad had seen her leave the house looking like this. As for Vicki, well, let's just say she didn't pull it off quite as well.

"Aren't you hot?" Hank asked.

"Boiling!" Vicki blurted out. "We were actually about to leave so we can go home and get these things off!"

"What are you dressed as?" Natalia asked, giving me, Hank, Weddy, and Ronnie the full once over.

On command, as we had been doing all evening, we pulled out our eyepatches and said in unison, "Modern-day pirates!"

"Uh, yeah, right," Vicki said skeptically. "And people actually still gave you candy?"

"Natalia, can I talk to you alone?" I wasn't sure what I was going to say, but this was literally the first time I had been this close to her since that day in the park when she broke up with me, and I knew I had to take advantage of it.

"I'm sorry," she said. "I don't think that'd be a good idea. Besides, like Vicki just told you, we were just leaving."

"But—"

"Goodbye, Douglas. It was nice seeing you." And with

that, Natalia took Vicki's hand and turned and walked away.

"Bye, Hank!" Vicki said over her shoulder.

"Well, that was awkward," I said to Hank.

"Don't worry about it, buddy. There are plenty of other fish in the ocean," he reassured me.

"Have another beer, my friend," Ronnie said, taking my empty cup, and filling it to the brim with Heineken. Like I said, the people who owned this house were definitely rich, so they had only the finest of beers on tap: Heineken, Anchor Steam, Sierra Nevada, Foster's ... "I've always found that there's nothing like alcohol to mend a broken heart," Ronnie continued, handing me the cup.

"Yeah, I'm not so sure about that," I responded, taking the drink without much enthusiasm.

"Hey, you hear the latest about BJ Turner?"

"No, what?" Ronnie asked Hank.

"My sister said she's been hanging out with Zeppelin down at the Riot House and is thinking about dropping out of school and joining the tour as one of the roadie's groupies."

"Damn, sounds like fun," Weddy said.

"Can you imagine?" I added.

"Fuckin' a," Ronnie said, caught up in his own images of what it'd be like to tour with Zeppelin. "I'd love to hang with Bonzo," he said wistfully.

After a few more minutes of small talk, we started to grow bored. We never did see Johnny or Jared and we didn't really recognize most of the kids at the party, so we eventually decided to head out. As we reached the sidewalk in the front of the house, Hank said, "Now what do you guys want to do?"

"Well," Ronnie replied, "I still have these eggs. Want to go over to Vineland's place?"

"Yeah!" Weddy said enthusiastically. "Let's go egg that fucker!"

So we walked over to Louise and then up Louise under the Ventura Freeway to Burbank, where we walked for a bit before cutting up Andasol to Martha Street. The houses on Martha were much more modest than the neighborhood we had just been in, more in keeping with a teacher's salary. We walked along Martha trying to find Vineland's house among the mostly nondescript, small homes that lined the street.

"I think he lives closer to Balboa," Hank said.

"Nah, I'm sure he's up ahead near White Oak," Ronnie insisted. Luckily, everyone knew what his car looked like—it was a cherry red Mustang Fastback—and since most of the people on the street left their cars in their driveways—their garages were mostly used for storing their stuff—we figured we'd eventually find it.

Sure enough, just as Ronnie had said, as we got closer to White Oak we saw Vineland's car, gleaming in the glow of the streetlight in front of his house. Weddy was the first one to spot it. "There it is," he whispered. We immediately stopped and froze.

The street was quiet; this neighborhood wasn't nearly as popular on Halloween as the streets on the South side of the Ventura Freeway and Ventura Boulevard, where the bigger homes were more generous with their candy offerings and, as such, drew much larger crowds of trick-or-treaters. "Remember," Ronnie whispered. "He could be lying in wait. Let's walk on the other side of the street."

We crossed over as quietly as possible, practically

tiptoeing, and I noticed the leaves on the Ficus trees lining the street begin to rustle as a Santa Ana suddenly picked up a bit. I could feel the warm air blowing a few strands of my hair askew. We crept along the sidewalk in silence until we found ourselves directly across from Vineland's house. Ronnie reached into his bag and handed each of us three eggs. I placed two of them in my left hand and the other in my right, cocked and ready to throw.

"Let's get his car, too," Ronnie said.

"Fuck. You sure about that? He'll kill us if he ever finds out," Hank pointed out.

"Fuck that asshole," Weddy said almost too loudly. "Let's do this shit!" He was obviously feeling the effects of all the pot he'd smoked that night as well as the beers he'd downed at the party.

"Shhhhh!" Ronnie cautioned him. "Shut the fuck up, Weddy. You want to give us away?"

"Sorry, man."

"Ready?" Ronnie looked at us. "Let's each throw two eggs at his car and one egg at his front door. One, two, three, GO!"

With that we ran toward Vineland's house and launched our assault, creaming his car with bright yellow egg yolk and littering his front door and porch with eggs and broken eggshells. And all it took was a matter of seconds. Instantly, the lights in the house came to life. We took off toward White Oak, and about halfway down the block, I thought I could hear a door open. Just before we reached the corner, Hank tripped and fell.

"Fuck!" he cried. I turned to look behind us, and I could just barely make out Mr. Vineland, standing at the back of his car, his hands pulling at the hair on each side of his head. Now, I can't say that this next bit is one hundred percent accurate, because we were all the way to the corner by this point, but my eyesight is pretty good, and I could swear that Mr. Vineland was wearing nothing but a white jockstrap, and that this is why he didn't give chase.

"Come on, Hank!" I said, stopping, offering him my hand, and quickly helping him up to his feet

We didn't stop running until we had crossed back under the freeway, even racing right through the red light at Burbank, where a couple of cars honked at us and gave us the finger.

"You think he saw us?" Hank asked. We were all breathless, our hearts pounding from both the run and the thrill of sticking it to Vineland.

"No way," Ronnie said. "We were out of there before he even knew what hit him."

"I'm not sure. I could just barely make him out. I swear the only thing he had on was a white jockstrap!" I laughed.

"Seriously?" Hank laughed even harder.

"That was awesome!" Weddy added with a huge grin.

"I thought you two were dead meat there for a second," Ronnie said, looking at me and Hank. "What the hell happened?"

"I fucking tripped and fell," Hank replied, shaking his head in disbelief at his own awkwardness. "Thanks for helping me, buddy." We immediately exchanged a Soul Brother #1 handshake, the first and original of our creations, and the one we saved for truly special occasions.

"Any time, my friend," I smiled. "Hey, we better get off of White Oak in case Vineland decides to get in his car and drive around."

"No way is he driving that thing until he washes it!" I

laughed. The others joined in; we were all feeling pretty cocky and extremely pleased with ourselves and our little bout of retribution after suffering years of abuse at the hands of Vineland.

White Oak was mostly lined with large apartment buildings and condos, so it was the last place you wanted to be on Halloween anyway. It was pushing 9:00 P.M., and we knew we only had a little bit of time left if we wanted to get any more candy, so we hustled across Ventura and over to the streets off of Valley Vista heading toward Lindley. The last time I had been in this neighborhood was when I had had my little confrontation with Mr. Detention, but since that time Ronnie told me the idiot had gotten busted for driving with an open container, not to mention no license, and had been sent to Juvenile Hall, so we wouldn't be seeing him for months, if ever again.

Suddenly, from out of nowhere, a group of younger kids came running toward us down Valley Vista, screaming in terror as eggs came raining down on them from behind with a tremendous amount of accuracy, covering them in yellow yolks and broken eggshells.

"Shit!" Hank suddenly called out. "That's Moose and Clark behind them."

"Oh fuck!" I said, spotting the unmistakable duo, costume-less. "You're right! And we don't have any more ammunition!"

"Into the bushes!" Weddy ordered in a sort of whisper-scream. The four of us dove behind a small row of very fortunately placed Oleanders. We hid in silence as the terrified kids raced by, followed closely behind by Moose and Clark, who were having the time of their lives pulling eggs out of their bags and nailing the kids on their heads, arms, shoulders, and backs in a relentless barrage.

"Fuck," Ronnie whispered, "I wish we still had some eggs left. We could nail those guys right now with a surprise attack from behind!" he said with a bit too much enthusiasm.

"Shhhh," I cautioned. "If they find us, they'll slaughter us."

We sat there for several more minutes in silence, bummed that we couldn't go after those guys, but knowing our only choice was to wait until they had hopefully left the neighborhood. After several *more* minutes passed, Ronnie had had enough. "Fuck this. I'm tired of hiding in the bushes like a pussy." With that Ronnie emerged, and we all slowly followed his lead.

"You think they're gone?" Hank asked, quietly.

"Yeah, they're probably on the other side of Ventura by now," Weddy surmised, his voice rising to a normal level.

"I hope so," I added, looking up and down the street and seeing and hearing absolutely nothing.

"Come on," Ronnie said. "Let's go get some more candy before everyone shuts down for the night."

We hit the houses that still had their porch lights on, but the people weren't always thrilled to see us—"What are you guys dressed as, anyway?" had by this late point in the evening become the typical response to our own admittedly lackadaisical "Trick or Treat?" greeting, which was beginning to sound more like a whine. We tried to explain away our mish-mash assortment of daily clothes and our eyepatches with our by-now tired routine about being "modern-day pirates," but it was a tough sell to the sleepy and often drunk homeowners.

"Yeah, I don't know if I'm buying into that one," was the usual reaction. But it was most often said with a knowing smile, as they were typically a thirty-something parent with two kids, who remembered what it was like to be too old for costumes, but too young to stop relishing the free candy and, just as everyone seems to continue to do throughout life, recognizing that our wanting to hold on to the vestiges of our youth for as long as we possibly could was just normal human behavior.

We were actually doing pretty well, and our bags were starting to have a little heft to them. In addition to Weddy and Ronnie being stoned out of their minds, the four of us were also on sugar highs from all of the sampling from our bags that we'd done throughout the night, laughing and giggling and just in general being silly, especially when Ronnie and Weddy broke into their Three Stooges patter.

Weddy (as Curly): "I grow on people."

Ronnie (as Moe): "So do warts!" Ronnie fake smacked Weddy across the face.

Ronnie (as Moe): "Tell me your name so I can tell your mother."

Weddy (as Curly): "My mother knows my name."

Ronnie (as Moe): "I got an idea: We'll make a mummy out of you."

Weddy (as Curly): "But I can't be a mummy, I'm a daddy."

Smack!

Hank and I just roared. Weddy had obviously spent a lot of time over at Ronnie's this past summer watching the Stooges on channel 52 in the afternoon and learning a couple of these routines. Even though he looked nothing like him, Weddy did a perfect Curly imitation, right down to the shuffling of his feet and the running of his hands up and down his face. And Ronnie already had Moe's demeanor. He'd simply brush his bangs down across his forehead and put on his normal Ronnie "fuck you" attitude and the whole thing worked. They were even considering auditioning for this year's Holiday Performance at school.

We rounded the corner from Alonzo to Tarzana, a short street with just a few houses still in the Halloween business. After saying our thank yous at the third and last open house on the street, we all mutually agreed to call it a night. We'd head back down Zelzah to Ventura and over to Lindley to my house where we'd hang out in my bedroom and trade candy. I hated anything with coconut, so Mounds and Almond Joys were always high on my trading list, and because they were popular with the other guys, I could command a pretty decent price for them—at the very least a bag of M&Ms or a Butterfinger or Snickers bar.

Walking down Zelzah we heard some commotion behind us, and when we turned around all of us at once experienced one of those times in life when fate decides to throw you an "Oh fuck" moment.

Mr. Detention and his gang were all frighteningly dressed as the Droogs from *A Clockwork Orange*. With their white pants, long-sleeved white button-down shirts, black top hats, suspenders, black boots, and—the coup de grace—the oversized jock strap/weight belt worn on the *outside* of the pants, making it look like they each had the most enormous prick and biggest balls in the world. They were all carrying some form of a nightstick or club and made for a pretty menacing group.

They were also carrying cloth sacks, and as they moved toward us with a combination of military-like precision mixed with badass, street-gang machismo, we knew we were in trouble.

"Hey, moron!" Ronnie yelled from out of nowhere, obviously recognizing his foe. "You guys got a problem?"

Nice going, schmuck.

Hank and I looked at each other and Hank mouthed, "What the fuck?" to me while stretching his arms out, palms open. I just shook my head knowingly.

Mr. Detention didn't take too kindly to Ronnie's mouth either. "What the fuck did you say?"

"What's the matter? Are you fucking deaf?" Ronnie yelled back.

"Let's get 'em, boys" was the last thing I heard—and I'm not even sure which Droog said it—before we were caught in a hail of raw eggs, which they were lobbing at us with great accuracy, landing on our heads and our backs, pulling from a seemingly endless supply in their cloth bags.

We took off running toward Ventura, Mr. Detention and his Droogs in hot pursuit, continuing to fire eggs which were now thankfully mostly missing us, maybe occasionally catching us on our arms or legs, as we were definitely moving targets by this point. Still, every one of us had some amount of egg yolk dripping from our hair and down our back; I don't think anyone had gotten hit in the face, but all of us had already been nailed on the head several times over.

As we ran, I noticed my candy leaping out of my bag a couple of pieces at a time, so I tightened my grip and closed the top of the bag. At the moment I did that, I saw

Hank simply toss his bag into the bushes. Normally, Hank would be way out in front, followed by Weddy and Ronnie, and I'd be bringing up the rear, but I was scared shitless and the pounds I had dropped over the summer were serving me well as I kept up with all of them step by step. The surprising thing was that Hank wasn't turning on the afterburners. Once again, his sudden growth spurt and the corresponding demise of his coordination were being unkind.

While most of the Droogs had stopped running after a short distance, probably too drunk to chase us any further and satisfied with the amount of damage they'd already inflicted, several Droogs were still in hot pursuit, including Mr. Detention, and a couple of them even seemed to be gaining on us. Ronnie, who always did seem to have the most adrenalin of any of us, gradually pulled impressively ahead of everyone. As we approached Ventura the light was yellow, and we had no chance of making it. Traffic was light, but still . . . racing across Ventura Boulevard against a light was never a good idea, no matter what time it was. Especially on Halloween.

"I'm going for it!" I heard Ronnie yell back over his shoulder as he approached the intersection.

"Don't do it!" Weddy shouted. But I doubted Ronnie could hear him.

As Ronnie flew across the boulevard, I glanced back only to see Hank trip and fall once again. The closest Droog caught up to him and raised his baton, about to strike.

"Hank!" I called out.

Hank stumbled to his feet, and the Droog swung at him, catching Hank on the side of his face. Hank spun around, the whole horrible episode seeming to play out in slow motion, and I saw blood pouring from a cut that ran straight across his cheek. The Droog seemed stunned by what he had just done, and he and a dazed Hank, his hand pressed against his cheek and now dripping with blood, just stood there frozen in a stand-off, not knowing what to do next. The other two Droogs paused for a moment as well before continuing on past them in pursuit of the rest of us.

I made a quick assessment, and Ventura looked clear so I followed Ronnie's lead and not only crossed the street against the light but followed him toward the Encino Spirits liquor store, which could provide refuge from Mr. Detention and his pack of Droogs.

For some reason—maybe he was scared to cross against the still-red light—Weddy decided to hang a left up Ventura and was now racing toward Newcastle. Mr. Detention, with no chance of catching Ronnie, had focused his pursuit on Weddy, and Weddy, who had ingested a large amount of pot, alcohol, and sugar throughout the evening, was starting to fade. I checked behind me; thankfully, nobody seemed to be following me any longer, and I crossed Newcastle, the liquor store only a handful of steps away. While in the crosswalk I turned and saw Mr. Detention catch up to Weddy as they reached Pizza Peddler and the corner of Newcastle and Ventura opposite the liquor store, whereupon Mr. Detention leaped into the air, Bruce Lee-style, and delivered a flying karate kick to the back of an unsuspecting Weddy that sent my friend flying toward the center of the intersection. Weddy never knew what hit him.

At that very moment a station wagon came tearing

up Newcastle, just missing me as I had yet to leave the crosswalk, hurrying to beat the yellow light and get across Ventura. The driver either didn't see Weddy in the intersection or was distracted by her kids—we never did find out for sure, and it might have been a combination of both—and Weddy, still staggering from the silent death kick to his back, never saw the car, never had a chance.

"Weddy!" I screamed.

His body was thrown high in the air, "thirty feet at least" I would hear Ronnie tell the cops later. I didn't know if it was true, but that's how I remember it as well. Within seconds, the clerk in the liquor store, who had seen the whole tragedy unfold through the front window, called for an ambulance. Ronnie, who was standing in the doorway and watched the whole horrific accident go down, tore out of the liquor store, running toward Weddy, who was lying in the middle of Ventura and Newcastle, his body twisted and turned in so many unnatural positions, motionless, with blood pooling out of several different locations—his head, his leg, his shoulder. It was so red, redder than anything I'd ever seen in my life. The brake lights of the Chevy wagon, stopped just ten or so feet from Weddy's body, added an eerie glow to the whole scene, and only further enhanced the saturation of red all around Weddy.

"Weddy! Weddy!" I heard Ronnie crying. He was bent down, trying to find a heartbeat or a pulse. Ironically, it was Weddy, with his family's medical background, who had taught us all how to do this correctly when we were just hanging out at the park one day between basketball games.

"Oh my God! Oh my God!" I remember hearing the driver screaming after she had gotten out of her car.

Just then a bloodied Hank came around the corner from Zelzah, along with a few of the Droogs. As Hank got closer to the intersection where Weddy lay, the realization of what had just happened hit him, and he began to run toward Weddy and Ronnie; the other Droogs, however, turned and hurried back down Zelzah away from Ventura, wanting no part of whatever was about to go down, and leaving Mr. Detention alone to fend for himself against what were likely going to be some serious criminal charges, even if all he intended to do, as he repeatedly claimed to anyone who would listen, was to give Weddy a little kick that would simply knock him down on the sidewalk, just a playful Halloween "trick."

When I saw Ronnie's shoulders slump, and heard Hank crying, I wasn't surprised. There was no way anyone could survive a blow like that. Weddy was surely dead upon impact. The driver, who was by now in tears, sobbing, stood in a daze, her eyes fixed on Weddy.

"Oh my God! Oh my God! Oh my God!" she kept repeating over and over again, her body shaking violently from head to toe. She was a normal-looking woman, probably in her late thirties or early forties, and she had several young kids in the back seat of the car. They had by now climbed over into the rear of the wagon and were looking through the window at Weddy, lying dead in the street. I could see their faces in the glowing taillights, confused and not quite understanding what was happening or why their mommy was crying. They still had bits and pieces of their costumes on, and I remember thinking that it was sort of late for kids that age to still be out on Halloween.

I was sitting on the curb outside the liquor store. I wasn't sure how I had ended up there. Everything was hazy and nothing seemed real. Some time passed. An ambulance showed up, followed by the police, who quickly cordoned off the intersection and rerouted traffic. After a while, the coroner arrived.

I remember Hank and Ronnie coming over to sit and talk to me. I couldn't really hear them, couldn't really speak much. Hank's cheek looked like shit. One of the paramedics worked on him for a few minutes, had given him some ointment and a cotton pad, so the bleeding was under control, but it was still a pretty bad cut, and his cheek had swelled and was already turning black and blue.

The police questioned all of us, but I think Hank and Ronnie gave them most of the information as I just couldn't seem to get the words out. They told them about Mr. Detention and the rest of the Droogs and the chase and the egg throwing and how Weddy went flying into the intersection just as the station wagon blew through the yellow light. Well, the last part only Ronnie saw, but Hank knew all the stuff that had happened earlier, and he was better able to identify some of the other Droogs who were involved and then ditched the scene of the crime because of his basketball connection to them. It turned out that the guy who hit Hank knew him from Pop Warner, had actually played against him several times, as had a couple of the other Droogs. They had all apologized to Hank before they had even reached Ventura.

A bit later in the evening—time had just ceased to exist for me so I honestly don't know how long it had been— one of the cops brought the guy who had treated Hank's cut over to see me. He took my blood pressure and shined a flashlight into my eyes.

"You okay?" he asked.

"Yeah, I'm okay," I said.

"Did you get hit by the car?"

"No," I said. "It missed me."

"What day is it today?"

That one I could handle. "Halloween," I answered.

"I think he's okay," the paramedic said to the cop.

I turned, and for the first time I noticed Weddy's sky-blue-striped Superstars, the same color as mine, lying in the middle of the intersection. A chalk circle had been drawn around them. I looked up at the cop, pointed toward the Adidas, and said, "Can I have my friend's shoes?"

"I'm afraid not, son. They'll have to be booked as evidence."

"Oh, yeah, I guess you're right."

"You want me to call your parents to come and get you?" the cop asked me.

"No," I answered. "I can walk home."

"We live a couple of blocks over on Lindley," Hank said. I hadn't even noticed him standing there. I looked around and didn't see Ronnie.

"Where's Ronnie?" I asked Hank.

"He decided to go home. He said goodbye to you a while ago."

"Oh," I said. "How is he?"

"You know . . ." Hank shrugged. For the first time I noticed bits and pieces of egg in his hair and on his shirt. I looked down to see the same splats of yellow on my shirt and reached up to touch my head, which felt like a mishmash of dried scraps of wood, as chunks of my hair and egg had congealed together all over the place.

"Did they tell Weddy's parents?" I asked.

"Not yet," Hank replied. "They haven't been able to

reach them."

The shock from everything that had happened was beginning to lift a bit. I was seeing and hearing more clearly than I had for what must have been close to a couple of hours. The last thing I really remembered was when they were loading Weddy's body into a white station wagon, the coroner's hearse I guess, and I saw his two feet, clad only in white socks since his Superstars had been torn off at impact, disappear into the back of the car, and the door swing to a close, the darkened window preventing me from seeing any more of Weddy, from ever seeing him again.

I looked up past Hank and was immediately struck by the neon sign above the Encino Spirits liquor store. The green neon of Time to Buy with the red neon shooting stars was a constant in my life, reliably there night after night, spilling its colorful light on the corner of Newcastle and Ventura. But tonight, for the first time that I could ever recall, it was on the fritz, and the shooting stars were out, their red lights dimmed, the outline of the stars and the streaks of light behind them formed by the darkened neon bulbs barely visible in the green haze of the Time to Buy light from above.

"That's weird," I said to Hank, pointing up at the sign behind him. He turned around to see what I was seeing.

"Yeah . . . strange," he replied.

The blur of activity around me continued to come into focus, policemen diverting traffic, coroners taking photographs and calculating distances in the street with long tape measures, and I sat there for a few moments longer, somehow finding the green light cast about me from above soothing, healing almost. I glanced back up again at the sign, and suddenly one single red star, the last star of the group of four, the falling star, flashed back on and then off and then on and then off. Again and again, over and over, in an odd, but somehow recognizable pattern.

"Hank," I said, quietly. "Check it out." I pointed up to the sign, and Hank took another look.

"O-K," Hank said after a few moments.

"What?" I asked.

"O-K," he repeated.

Then it hit me. "Holy shit," I whispered, awestruck.

You see, Weddy, who was so brilliant, a kid of so many talents, had also been a Morse Code freak when he was in fourth grade. He and his dad used to message other enthusiasts, spending hours together on one of the few—and maybe only—hobbies or interests they ever shared. Every now and then, Weddy would teach us some code, and both Hank and I knew enough to make out some basic words and phrases: "Hi," and "Bye," and "SOS," of course. "OK" was also a part of our Morse vocabulary.

We continued to stare at the sign in amazement, knowing we were experiencing something that would somehow change both of us, altering how we would each view the world for the rest of our lives.

The falling star continued flashing, but it was soon joined by the other three stars. One by one, they each began to flash, until all four stars on the sign were communicating "O-K" in unison.

Hank turned and looked at me in disbelief. "Incredible," he said in quiet reverence. And just like that the flashing stopped, and all four stars were lit up together in unison once again, as if what we had just witnessed had never happened.

"Maybe it's time to go home," I said.

"I think so," Hank replied, helping me up to my feet. As we walked down Ventura to Lindley, we turned around every so often to glance back at the neon stars, but by the time we got near the corner and turned around for one final look, the stars had all dimmed and gone completely dark once again.

Coda

The days in November flowed by in a blur. Nothing seemed real, and it was difficult to concentrate in school. There had been Weddy's funeral, a somber affair as one would expect, with lots of tears and outpourings of grief. Cabrillo had brought in special counselors to work with anyone who had been affected by Weddy's death, especially Ronnie, Hank, and me. But none of us felt like talking about it to anyone else besides one another and maybe our parents or siblings.

Natalia had written me a nice note, but she didn't even come to the funeral, and when I tried to call her to thank her for her sentiments, she wasn't home. I left a message with her dad, but she didn't ever call me back, and I couldn't be sure that her dad had even given her the message. She remained cold and distant at school, so I simply gave up any hope that we could ever be together again.

Everyone in my family had been super supportive, and they all came to the funeral with the exception of Julie, who was still in San Diego and couldn't get away, but she called me a few times, and we had some nice conversations. And David came by one day to see how I was doing. We sat in my bedroom for a while, listening to Springsteen's *Born to Run*, which I had been digging for a month or two, but which David was still resisting a bit, though he finally came around that day. "Okay, you've convinced me," he admitted. "Bruce is pretty damn good.

And his band is fantastic. Who plays the sax?"

"Clarence Clemons," I answered. "The Big Man."

"Speaking of big men," David said, "Dad called me this morning. Guess who's going to the Lakers–Bucks game tonight?

"Dad's taking you?" I said, disappointed. This was going to be a huge game. The two teams had pulled off a mammoth trade in the off-season, with the Bucks sending Kareem to the Lakers in exchange for a bunch of players, including former UCLA star Dave Meyers, one of my personal favorites Brian Winters, and shot-blocking machine Elmore Smith. But Kareem was Kareem, one of the greatest players in the history of the game, and a former Bruin to boot, so we would've gladly given up our whole team for him.

While the Bucks and the Lakers had played early in the season in Milwaukee, this would be their first matchup at The Forum, and everyone wanted to be there to give our former players a warm welcome and then watch as Kareem would surely dismantle them.

"No, he gave the tickets to us. I'm taking you," David said, smiling.

"Really? Why isn't Dad going?"

"Some business thing he has to do," David answered.

"Of course," I replied.

That night at The Forum, the game was a bit tighter than we thought it'd be—it was tied at the half, but the Lakers pulled away in the third and fourth quarters, eventually winning by a cool dozen. Kareem absolutely dominated his former team, scoring thirty on twelve of fifteen from the field, with nineteen boards, six assists, three steals, and three blocks. Just another day at the office for the center with the gorgeous skyhook.

As we drove home after the game on a high, David was in such a good mood that he suddenly said, "Hey, Douglas, I've been thinking: I started to learn how to drive when I was about your age."

"You did?" I said, surprised. "I didn't know Dad let you do that."

"Not Dad, you dope," David laughed. "Sam and I would take his grandfather's car out when he was sleeping."

"Jesus," I said.

"It was no big deal. At first we'd just go over to the parking lot at Sav-On early in the morning when nobody was there. As we got better, we got a little bolder."

"Okay, but what does this have to do with me?"

"I was thinking that maybe me and you could go out to Chatsworth or Simi or somewhere sorta empty and I'd teach you to drive." David looked over at me to see how I was going to react.

"Really?" I was intrigued. "Whose car would we use?"

"Mine, of course. You could learn in the Capri." Now, you have to understand that David's yellow Capri was his pride and joy. He never liked the Dodge Duster that my dad had picked out for him, but he loved the clean, sporty lines of the Capri. He had really wanted a red one, but this yellow job was such a good deal he couldn't pass it up. Plus, he figured he could always take it to Earl Scheib once he had saved up the $49.95 for a new, cherry-red paint job.

"That'd be awesome!" I said, awestruck at David's generosity. Maybe Mom's kicking him out of the house had changed him for the better.

"Cool. Maybe we'll do it next weekend."

I stared out the window, imagining myself behind the

wheel of David's Capri, the windows rolled down, my hair blowing in the wind, sunglasses on, my right hand on the wheel while my left hand rested on the windowsill, my palm spread out and feeling the air roar by as we cruised at top speed. We'd take the Santa Susanna Pass Road instead of the recently built Simi Freeway, and I'd navigate the old, windy stagecoach route with the panache and skill of Mario Andretti or Jackie Stewart.

By the end of the month, the Mill Fire had exploded in the Northeastern part of the Valley, up in the foothills near Tujunga and back into the Angeles National Forest. The Santa Anas had been particularly awful, with temperatures soaring into the eighties and winds as high as sixty miles per hour. The sky was filled with smoke, practically blocking out the sun over the entire Valley, and ash rained down onto the streets like snow. I found myself standing at the corner of Newcastle and Ventura after school one day; I hadn't gone anywhere near that intersection since that awful Halloween night.

Everything seemed so normal. Cars traveled back and forth across the exact spot where my friend had lain, motionless, his body contorted. People came in and out of Encino Spirits as well as Pizza Peddler on the opposite corner, as if nothing out of the ordinary had ever happened at that spot. And I guess that's just the way life goes. People move on. Even friends move on. While Hank and I had remained close through everything, Ronnie didn't really seem to be around much anymore. He hadn't even shown up at school the last week or two. When Hank and I tried to call his house, there was never an answer. Art eventually found out that Ronnie's dad had sold his garage and had moved the family to Texas where he had taken a job as the lead mechanic for a large Chevy dealership. If they had really moved, Ronnie never even picked up the phone to say goodbye. I know he felt guilty about Weddy's death; hell, we all did. We were all complicit in one way or another, and I guess it was just something we were all going to have to carry with us for the rest of our lives.

I looked up the boulevard to the corner of Ventura and Zelzah where Weddy had made his fateful decision to not cross Ventura and to instead hang a left and run over toward Newcastle on the south side of the street. How can one instant, one simple choice, have such a huge impact on not only your own life, but on the lives of others?

If only Weddy had followed us across Ventura.

I returned my gaze to the spot in the intersection where Weddy went down. The falling ash was starting to cover my Superstars. I don't know what came over me, but on a whim I sat down on the curb, and took my shoes and socks off. When the light for Newcastle turned green, I got up and began walking across Ventura. While there were plenty of cars lined up at the red light, there wasn't one car traveling along Newcastle, so when I was halfway through the crosswalk, I veered off toward the middle of the intersection and headed straight for the faint red stain on the pavement where Weddy had landed. I placed my Superstars, the same color as Weddy had on that night, directly on top of the sacred patch of my friend's spilled blood and turned and walked back toward the sidewalk in front of the liquor store where I had taken off the shoes. The light had turned green for the cars on Ventura long before I had finished crossing back, but nobody honked, nobody screamed or flipped me the finger. The drivers all just watched in stunned silence, somehow realizing that whatever I was doing was important, had weight, was necessary, even mandated somehow, by someone, or something. I didn't know what had come over me, but it had just felt like the right thing to do. Besides, it was time for a new pair of Superstars, maybe even a pair with different-colored stripes.

I reached the curb and stood for a moment, looking up at the Time to Buy sign, which was not nearly as cool in the daylight as it was when it was lit up at night. But the odd light in the smoke-filled sky cast an unnatural glow of its own on the unlit sign, and I couldn't help but just stand there and look up at it for a bit. I could feel the ash landing on my head, but I didn't even care, didn't even shake my hair out, but instead just let it pile up, like snow on a cool, winter's day somewhere far, far away.

When I got back home, my mom made me take L for a walk. The routine hadn't changed: Grab her leash from the hook hanging behind the closet door on the second floor landing; call her several times because she's starting to go deaf, or is just plain old and stubborn and won't always come when she's called anymore; then head out the door and weave our way through the complex using the same well-worn path on the brick walkway that we had used a thousand times before, with L stopping to smell the exact seven places on the way out where she *always* stopped and smelled; and finally going through the front gate and out onto the street.

Only this time, as I approached Mr. Asshole's building, I noticed that the signs on the lawn that had warned about the use of pesticide were suddenly gone. "What the . . . ?" I muttered to myself.

Just at that moment, Mr. A came out of his building,

happily bounding down the stairs with Prince at his side. He was wearing a green Oregon Ducks cap, and walked Prince over to the parkway to let Prince do his business. I approached cautiously, unsure of what I was seeing and why it was happening.

Mr. A turned and saw me and L approaching. He smiled in a way I had never seen before. Even Prince seemed calm and happy, totally ignoring L as he went about his business.

"What happened to the signs?" I asked. "To the chemicals on the lawn?"

"The city shut us down. Apparently, you're not allowed to put chemicals on the parkway, you can only do it on your own lawn. Anyway, it doesn't matter. Prince and I are moving to Oregon. Feel free to let your dog crap wherever she wants." He smiled again and looked down at Prince to see if he had finished.

"Come on, Prince," he said, tugging on the leash and heading back toward the stairs leading to his apartment building. And with that, Mr. Asshole and Prince were gone forever from our lives.

"Well, L," I said, looking down at my trusted friend, "I guess you've regained some valuable real estate." L looked up at me, seeming to understand, the falling ash, which had lightened up a bit, occasionally dotting her fur but fortunately missing her tongue which was sticking out of her mouth as she panted lightly. L quickly adapted to the new parameters and was sniffing and peeing upon seemingly every square inch of parkway that was now back as part of her domain.

I looked up to see the sun peeking through the smoke, hazy but there, letting us know that days filled with blue skies and sunshine would soon return to Southern California, as would clear, clean, crisp fall evenings when a thousand stars would light up the Valley from a moonless sky, the smell of sage and jasmine mixing with the dreams of everyone who is lucky enough to grow up in this corner of the world, creating an intoxicating potion that would flow through my airways directly into my soul, injecting my whole being with a sense of hope and optimism, for a future filled with friends and girlfriends and experiences that would always be sweet and true.